Afte.

Christine Mustchin

Sormazzana Press

A catalogue record of this book is available from the British Library

First published in 2022 by Sormazzana Press

ISBN 978-1-7398684-1-3

Cover design by Sarah Hosken

Contents

'You're such a friend, I know I can count on you.'

Prologue

She wasn't expecting him. She thought it would be Charlie but then it's not her thing to apologise even after the big row they had.

He looks like a thunder cloud against the deep blue evening sky. She pushes the front door in his face but it's not enough, he has his foot in the door. It slams against his toes. Why the hell did the management never put an intercom system in each flat? She used to laugh that it kept her fit to run down each time the doorbell rang to see who was there. She's not laughing now.

He follows her upstairs and into her flat. She ignores him and goes back into the kitchen. She's got nothing to say to him after their phone call but he has plenty to say to her. He controls himself at first, though she can tell it's an effort.

'This is not part of our agreement. You can't just walk away.'

He gives his reasons, each one more selfish and more evil than the one before. His voice is getting louder and angrier as he enumerates them. He goes on and on until she reaches her limit.

'Just get out.'

She pushes him into the hallway. She knows it's not going to end well but she's not going to give in. What he's doing is unforgiveable and has to be stopped.

Chapter One

Saturday 2 May

The taxi accelerates away into the night. I'm left alone on the pavement to take in the unaccustomed smell of ozone and sound of waves crashing on the nearby beach. I turn away from the sea and cross the road. A chill breeze ruffles my hair as I approach the front door of a large, detached Victorian house. There are no signs of any lights inside the building but from the nearby streetlamp, I can just make out her name by the top buzzer. There's no need to press it as I have a key. I push the door open and drag my case through. The door swings back heavily and slams shut. I'm plunged into complete darkness and overwhelmed by a sudden, unexpected sense of foreboding.

I grope around for the light switch in the hall and then climb the two flights of stairs to her flat. The key turns easily enough in the lock but the door only opens a couple of inches and I can't get in. It feels as if something is wedged behind it. I can just reach the light switch inside the flat. I press it and a slit of light appears as the stairwell behind me goes black. I lean my weight against the door and push hard again and again, determined to get in. At last it opens enough for me to squeeze through the gap. I wonder what on earth Jaq has put behind the door and why. And then the smell hits me, a smell I can't mistake, sickly and unpleasant, a smell I can taste, a smell I want to spit out.

A figure is crumpled at the foot of the stairs. There's only one person it can be. She's lying in a face-down position except that her head is skewed towards me. I stare at her face with its waxy mask of death. Shivers sweep over my skin like icy waves. I feel sick and want to vomit. Blood has seeped all around her body. I take a deep breath and force myself not to think of her as my long-lost friend, Jaq. I can't see a wound or any sign of what could have caused the bleeding. My instinct is to reach for her carotid pulse, even though there's no need, but I don't. I know enough not to contaminate a crime scene. As it is, my prints will be all over the door. I have to get out but I can't manage to wriggle back through the gap. I've no choice so I step over Jaq and climb the stairs. I go into her living room and make the call.

I pace up and down until I hear clattering footsteps on the fire escape at the back of the building. A short time later and I'm sitting opposite a weary detective while the blue light from an ambulance outside flashes across his face. He's perched on a dining chair, tapping his pen on a notepad, waiting for an answer. The minutes tick by. I'm slumped on the sofa so he moves his chair closer and stares down at me. I smell cigarette smoke on his clothes. I glare back at him, knowing his patience has limits. I force myself to sit up straight, then I spit out the words he's waiting for.

'I could see it was a body and it had to be Jaq.'

'Why's that?'

'Well, who else would it be?' I resent his questions and I resent even more his insistence that I've got something to hide. I feel like telling him I know exactly what he's up to, it was once part of my training.

'And she was dead when you found her?'

'Yes, I've already told you. And, before you ask, I didn't kill her. She was my friend.'

Not the best response. I've heard enough angry protests of innocence at crime scenes to know exactly what he's thinking. He scribbles in his notepad while I force myself to calm down. It'll do me no good to show him I'm angry.

'So, let's go through it again.'

I know the score. He's trying to catch me out, find inconsistencies in my account that he can pounce on and pull apart.

'Well, Doctor, shall we begin?'

The sarcasm in his voice is unmistakeable. It's a technique I once used myself. I'm glad to be free of it now. I think of refusing to say any more until I've called a solicitor but suddenly I feel too tired to argue: tired like I've been on hospital duty for thirty-six hours without sleep. I can still remember the feeling. You get a buzzing in your head, every nerve in your body tingles and all you want is to blank out the world in a deep sleep.

I start again and he stabs his notepad as I speak, following the bullet points of my account.

'I came by train from London, the 22.46 from Victoria. I took a taxi from the station and must have arrived a few minutes after midnight. As I told you, the flat belongs to my friend Jacqueline Grey. I was going to stay with her while doing a GP locum job here. She was supposed to be going to Italy on business today so she met me in London last week to give me a set of keys.'

'And when exactly was that?'

'Last Monday.' Only five days ago and the first time we'd met up in a very long-time.

'And you've not seen her since?'

'Not until just now.' I'm surprised I can be so blunt.

'So, let's go back to what happened when you got to the flat.'

I plough through it all again. My words sound like a monotonous drone, a far cry from what I'm feeling. I just want to forget, forget that Jaq's dead. She can't be, but she is. The forensic circus has already begun. Even through the closed door of the sitting room I can hear them in the hallway. I want to go and ask what they've found, what ideas they've got about the cause of Jaq's death. It's impossible to imagine anyone would want to kill her. I want answers and not only that; I want to be the one asking the questions. Instead I'm the one expected to reply to interminable and repetitive queries that bring no understanding at all of what has happened.

At last the questions stop and the detective closes his notepad. He gestures to his colleague to take charge of me. Looking young enough to be moonlighting from secondary school, she's trying to appear genuinely sympathetic. I find that even harder to deal with. She's doing her best to help me sort out a solution to my sudden lack of accommodation by making what appear to be interminable phone calls. The flat will be off limits for a while. It's a long time since I was last here. It was supposed to be my home for the next six months. I stare at the wall opposite me. A striking painting stares back at me: swirling shades of blue and mauve, enough to distract me until the interminable phone calls have ended. I'm escorted out of the flat by the front door. The only sign of Jaq's body now is an outline on the floor. I'm relieved when I'm free of it all and sitting in the back of a taxi, staring out of the window as the city lights flash past. I lean my face against the glass, barely registering its coldness. I'm so numb it's as if all my senses are frozen.

'Watch your head, love.'

I turn slowly towards the taxi driver who's offered this advice. I'd rather be left alone.

'You all right?' he says, glancing over his shoulder at me. I guess he's used to checking on all his late-night fares.

'I'm okay. Just need to get my head down. Thanks for asking.'

Good manners - the first refuge of the emotionally embarrassed.

The journey doesn't take long and there's no further attempt at conversation. My relief at being allowed to wallow in my own thoughts comes to an abrupt end when I see my destination. I'm faced with a type of hotel familiar to me from years when money was tight and the services of a concierge and twenty-four-hour comfort were distant priorities. Ubiquitous, anonymous and functional but the very opposite of what I need right now. Not that I want five-star fuss but I certainly don't want impersonal corridors, a plain chilly room with its institutionalised fittings and no one to give you more than a cursory welcome. I want the care and attention of a homely country B&B where a welcome smile and a few kind words are followed by a hearty breakfast the following morning. What I find instead is a bathroom that's cold, the heated towel rail disconnected for "safety reasons" and a damp room, which gives off a musty smell when the heater begins to work. I sit on the bed shaking with fatigue and emotion. Through my shock and grief, one thing is clear, I cannot just sit back and wait for a police investigation to unfold. After that thought, I have no recollection of anything else before I fall into a deep sleep disturbed by dreams of a porcelain doll that shatters into a thousand pieces, its face the very image of Jaq.

Chapter Two

Sunday 3 May

I wake with a start late the next morning as a door slams across the corridor. It takes several expletives before I sit up and realise where I am. As I look around at the unimaginative corporate furnishings of the hotel room, the nightmare hours before I collapsed into bed come crashing back to me. I slump back down onto the bed and stare at the blank ceiling. It's not enough to stop the churning in my stomach. I haul myself into the tiny en-suite and lean over the hand-basin where my efforts at vomiting produce very little. At least it makes me feel better. I gulp down some water from the tap and splash more over my face. I wonder what the time is. There's no clock in the room and I haven't worn a watch for years. I reach for my mobile and see that it's off. I put it on charge. I remember noticing the battery was nearly flat when I finished packing but I'd put my charger at the bottom of my case. I'd spent the train journey to Hove plugged into my earphones, listening to music. While I wait for the phone to charge up enough to be used, I plug in the kettle. I make an unpalatable drink with the complimentary packet of coffee powder and gulp it down, disguising the awful taste with a couple of sickly custard cream biscuits.

Against the odds, my nausea disappears just as the screen on my phone lights up with a message alert. I grab the phone and stare at the few words in front of me. I'm taken aback to see it's from Jaq. *Look out for Chiara. Trouble in the shop. Letter following. J xx*. It must have been sent while I was travelling, and stayed in cyberspace until now. I grip the phone until my fingers go white as if that will dispel my anger at missing her message. I grapple with an utter sense of disbelief as I realise there's no point in tapping out a reply now. I'm simply left with a stampede of questions about Jaq's death. From the predictable sequence of how, why, what, who, it's the last that strikes me most. Jaq may have had her faults but she had a personal magnetism that drew people to her. She was not one to generate animosity. Not only is it appalling to think that someone could kill Jaq, but to think that I'm under suspicion is upsetting. I was the one to report her death to the police after all, even if I well know that marks me down as the first suspect. I run through last night's interrogation, but I can recall the questions more clearly than my answers. I need to see my statement and gauge just where I stand.

Several sharp knocks on the door goad me into action. The cleaners are waiting. I ask the front desk for a reliable taxi service. Reliable it may be but prompt it isn't and I wander over to a leaflet display as a five-minute wait becomes ten then fifteen. I pick out the brochures at random paying them little attention until one makes me take a closer look. It features the reproduction of a painting in the same style as the one I saw hanging in Jaq's flat. Above the image are the details of a Brighton Festival event: *Artists' Open House Exhibition 2009*, with the address. I stuff the leaflet in my handbag together with a map of Brighton and Hove just as the taxi beeps from outside the main door of the hotel.

When I enter the police station, there's a sense of familiarity, even after all these years: the reception area reeking of dirty boots and stale dusty bureaucracy and the faces of the reception staff primed for boredom and aggravation. For a moment I feel reassured; it doesn't last long. Seeing the glass screen in the reception area reminds me I'm the opposition now. I'm surprised to see the place is empty. Police stations are like provincial airports. There are slots when people crowd in and waiting feels endless, and slots when no one comes in and you can be seen straight away. Early morning is a good time but it's past midday. Nevertheless, I'm the only one waiting so I approach the desk. I start to explain the reason for my visit when I'm interrupted by someone calling out my name. An unmistakeable voice and completely unexpected.

I turn around to see a familiar figure who's just come through the main entrance. Even from behind, his eagle eye has spotted me. I remember his reputation from our time working together. I haven't seen him for years.

'Mike. I didn't know you were in Brighton.'

'Kate, good to see you again.' He ushers me through to the other side.

I ignore the look of reproof from the on-duty reception staff, no doubt wondering which rulebook allows for such instant familiarity.

'I guess you want to see your statement?'

'You know all about it, then?'

'Sure, I'm the Senior Investigating Officer on the case. Did Tony, Inspector White, give you a hard time last night?'

I shrug my shoulders, not wanting to say the wrong thing.

'Don't worry. I'm sure we'll clear things up soon.'

I feel a friendly slap on the back. It was a trademark of his when I was on his team and investigations were getting tough, a mark of encouragement but also a warning not to slack. I'm not sure how to interpret it in these circumstances.

He tells me to follow him and we end up in a dismal interview room. There's a smell of sweat mixed with cheap air freshener. I don't register much else. Mike goes off to fetch my statement and I sit up straight as though about to face my first viva voce medical exam. When he returns, he places the typed sheets of paper on the desk and sits opposite me, lounging back in his chair. He gestures to the statement which I fumble with as I pick it up. I hadn't expected to be dealing with someone I know. He smiles.

'Your hair's longer. It suits you.'

I shift my eyes away from his, unsettled by the personal statement. Not the most appropriate comment to make to a possible murder suspect. I feel my cheeks flush. I'm annoyed when I want to stay calm. I should just ignore the remark but Jaq's death has affected my emotional threshold.

'Not a fair comment in the circumstances, is it?'

He merely smiles again. I notice he's going grey. The tinges to his dark hair make him seem rugged rather than distinguished, a personal observation I keep to myself. I shift back a little on my chair and concentrate on reading over the transcript of my interview. I'm reassured. There's nothing I want to correct and nothing to throw suspicion on me.

'Anything to add?'

'No, I don't think so.'

'You're sure?' I'm immediately on the alert to the subtext.

'You don't seriously suspect me of killing Jaq, do you?'

The pause is revealing.

'So, I am a suspect?'

'Let's say you're helping the police with their enquiries.'

'Like I don't know what that means.' I haven't meant to sound aggressive.

'I thought it would amuse you.'

I'm not impressed by his attempts to lighten my situation, even when I know I've nothing to hide.

He stands up, again the slap on the back.

'I've got to get back to work. Why don't you take yourself off to the seafront: mingle with the masses, take your mind off things? Hordes of day-trippers arrive from London on Sundays like this. The weather's great, quite a plus for the first May bank holiday. The Brighton end gets packed very early but it's better towards Hove, at least until the families pitch up.'

'You think that will help me forget all this?' I look down at the statement in my hand.

'Just an idea.'

'I've got too many questions.'

'You're not the detective now, Kate.'

'Even so you can't expect me to just to hand over my statement and leave it at that. I know the procedure.'

'Okay. Okay. Look, I've got your mobile number. I should be through here soon. I'll give you a call.'

I follow his recommendation, better than a lonely hotel room, anyway. He's right. The seafront is awash with people, acting out in the typical manner of seaside crowds. I join them and walk past the main pier towards Hove with the sea on my left and the Regency terraces across the road on my right. I reach the Meeting Place café and join the takeaway queue. The taste of a strong, sweet espresso coffee brings back thoughts of Jaq. She was always in search of the perfect caffeine shot. I hurl the empty cup into the rubbish bin. Who could have thrown away Jaq's life just like that? And why? I gaze out at the featureless seascape impatient for Mike to make contact. I don't have to wait long before he rings me.

'I'll meet you in front of the West Pier in a quarter of an hour. You can't miss it. It's that ruin in the sea. Wait on the upper promenade at the bottom of Regency Square.'

He rings off, then immediately sends me a text. *Make that half an hour.*

I send him an okay, then return to my message list and call up Jaq's text. Just like her to be so cryptic. She used to leave similar scribbled messages around the place when we were living together at uni but in those days she could follow them up with an explanation in person. No chance of that ever again. Just the promise of a letter. I look at her final text. The few words on the tiny screen become blurred as I struggle with the finality of her death. I blink back my tears and stifle a sob. I force myself to concentrate on trying to figure out who Chiara could be and why Jaq didn't mention her when we met up in London.

That only leads to more questions. Is Chiara someone to worry about or be wary of? How did Jaq come to know her? What did Jaq mean by *trouble*? Had Chiara been working in Jaq's bookshop and causing problems? Is she Italian? She could be from the name. Jaq went off to Italy after she graduated and taught English as a foreign language for a couple of years. Perhaps Chiara is one of the friends she made during that time or one of her students. Or maybe she's come over here to attend one of the language schools in Hove.

I give up speculating and turn back towards Brighton. The tide is in and the West Pier stands out as a minimalist tangle of metal against an unblemished blue sky. It's a view Jaq would have known well. I reach the pier and stand gazing far out to sea, as though willing her back on the tide. I shift my focus back onto the West Pier, curious that it has not been dismantled.

'Something of an icon, you know. Strange really for a pile of old iron.' Mike's voice breaks into my reverie. 'You know it was made a listed building after it was burnt down.'

'How odd.'

'Quite. Anyway, do you fancy something to eat?'

I'm not hungry.

'I'd rather just walk.'

We turn towards Brighton Pier.

'You're looking good, Kate. You used to look like one of the boys.'

Again, the personal remark. Why? He never made any when we worked together. How does he see me now, as an old friend, a former colleague or suspected murderer? Or perhaps all three?

I try not to take offence and attempt to shift the conversation away from myself.

'I didn't expect to bump into you here.'

He ignores the cue, preferring to focus on me.

'That's not really what's on your mind, eh?'

Without waiting for a response, he continues speaking.

'Let's get something straight before we go one step further.'

He stops and leans over the promenade rail towards the sea. We both stare out at the thin horizon line.

'I've been checking you out.'

I turn to look at him but he keeps his gaze firmly out to sea and carries on talking.

'Nothing on your mobile phone log after a text from Miss Grey and you made a call from the landline of your London flat round about the estimated time of death.'

I take a deep breath in.

'You've not wasted any time.'

He ignores the remark. 'You phoned for a cab, right?'

'I was supposed to drive down but my car was still being repaired. Some idiot scraped the side while it was parked. No idea who.'

'Hence the train.'

'Hence the train. Anyway, the taxi firm in Hove found the driver who picked you up from the station. He remembered it was about quarter past midnight.'

I stop and look him straight in the eye. 'Is all this part of your investigation?'

'Not exactly.'

'So, what then?'

'Just trying to get my bearings?'

'I'm not a murderer.' The very words make me feel sick.

'You know the form. There are still some questions outstanding.'

'And I'd better be prepared to answer them.'

'Don't worry. It'll be okay. I shouldn't have said anything really but well, you were one of us once. You're bound to have questions, I know, but best not talk about it anymore.'

'So why are we here?'

He doesn't answer.

'You're not the Good Samaritan by nature, Mike.'

'Let's say I'm curious. What are you doing in this fine city by the sea? Last I heard on the police tom-tom was that you'd got yourself into a good GP practice in south London.'

'The tom-tom was right for once.'

'So how come you're down here?'

'I needed a change.'

That admission only makes him more curious.

'You're not leaving General Practice?'

'No, no. I've got a locum job in Hove for six months, after that, I'll decide what I want to do.'

'You know you could've had a good career in the police service, especially with five years' medical school under your belt. You had all the makings of a good detective.'

I'm afraid he'll move on to ask me why I left the police and went back to medicine and I don't want to go into that.

'Perhaps. Anyway, what about you? You must be a Chief Inspector now.'

He shrugs as if dismissing his steps up the career ladder since I worked with him.

'How come you're working in Brighton?'

'Like you, I needed a change.'

Now I'm curious. I never thought Mike would leave his London patch.

'How does Carole feel about moving here?'

'She's stayed in London. Didn't want the boys to move school. GCSEs coming up in a couple of years.'

'They okay?'

'Fine when they take their eyes away from the computer screen and their feet from a football.'

A helicopter passes overhead. Mike looks up. He seems glad of the distraction.

'One of yours?'

'No, just a coastguard patrol. You'll not be surprised how stupid people can be. Some silly bugger'll jump off the end of the pier for a laugh and then remember they can't swim. Usually blokes, of course.'

'Men in the sexist firing line, that makes a change.'

He laughs. 'Trust you to pick up on something like that.'

I join in the laughter and I realise that he's made me forget, just for a moment, the reason we've met up again. Immediately the questions about Jaq's death resurface.

'Mike?'

He's sees the implication at once.

'What are you after, Kate?'

Perhaps it's the gentle way he says my name or simply his directness but I find myself choking back what I want to ask, torn between the effort of seeming to be objective and my barely controlled emotions. Mike's not to know how a perfect friendship slipped into years of estrangement that hurt more than I ever admitted. Jaq had always been a bit wild, up for a challenge, a free spirit who hated authority. She loved to party, she'd never say *no* to a glass of wine, always full of enthusiasm and a hard worker too. She got a good degree. But when her mother died, she had difficulty accepting what happened. She changed and started drinking heavily and smoking pot. One night she ended up unconscious in the Emergency department when I was on duty. I hadn't seen her for a while and she was a mess. Her blood alcohol was at a dangerous level and she had been snorting cocaine. After that she refused to see me and I heard later from a mutual friend that she'd gone off to Italy to teach English. I tried to keep in touch through her parents but she never responded. Now the chance to recover our friendship is gone for ever.

Well?' He's waiting for my reply.

The thought of what I've lost threatens to overwhelm me but I can't afford to break down. I take a deep breath and face Mike.

'Well?' He's waiting for my reply.

'I want to find out how Jaq died, why she died, who did this to her.'

'That's what *we're* here for, remember.'

'But you'll keep me in the loop, won't you? Like you said, I was one of yours once.'

He makes a vague gesture which I choose to interpret as an affirmative and then says he has to get back to work. I watch him stride away across the road with an acute awareness that he's the only person I know in this sprawling seaside city. It accentuates my sense of Jaq's loss. Having him in charge of her case has to be a bonus but no police evidence is ever going to provide a true understanding of Jaq's death or its import on those left behind. After Jaq's final text to me, instinct tells me that Chiara is the key and I'm not going to wait for the results of a police enquiry. As far as I'm concerned, that text gives me the right to go looking for Chiara myself. I have no idea who she is or where she could be and I'll need more than a first name if I'm to track her down. A photo would be a help. I kick at a few pebbles washed up on the promenade by a high tide, then turn back towards Hove and break into a sprint in an effort to allay my frustration. I come to an abrupt halt just past the Meeting Place Café as the answer comes to me. I pull out my phone. The number I'm after is not in my contact list and it also proves to be ex-directory. I've no alternative but to head back to my dismal hotel room with the hope that I've packed my old dog-eared address book.

Chapter Three

Monday 4 May

A restless night comes to an end when I open my eyes to excruciating sunlight. I've forgotten to close the curtains. My tongue tastes of grit, my lips are dry as ash. I blast a four-letter word across the room and fight my way out from the tangled duvet, annoyed to have wasted the previous evening in self-pity. That won't bring Jaq back or help me understand why she died. I step on several deflated crisp packets and two empty wine bottles. I've dispatched a week's alcohol limit in one night. I take some consolation in the fact that doctors are usually the first to ignore their own advice and then I see the half-consumed packet of cigarettes. What am I hoping to do? Burn away my grief in tobacco smoke? Then everything concertinas: disbelief, anger, sadness, hopelessness. Acceptance of Jaq's death is never going to come quickly or easily. I look at the fag packet in disgust. What am I thinking of? After all that struggle to give up. I open the window and throw it out, immediately regretting my action, then lauding my self-will. I remind myself that yesterday evening was not totally wasted. I managed to contact Jaq's parents, achieved thanks to my inability to cancel even the oldest of addresses and telephone numbers from my battered address book. I've arranged to call in later. Jaq must have sent them photos from Italy. I'm hoping there's one of her with Chiara.

I stand under the shower for a good twenty minutes hoping that the pummelling water will wash away the effects of my excesses. It has some effect but it's no caffeine fix. I avoid the ghastly hotel coffee and go in search of a cola from the machine in reception. I retreat to my room and wrestle with the metal pull tag until it comes away abruptly and I spill at least a quarter of it onto the carpet. I almost throw the can at the wall but gulp down the rest to clear my brain. I take another look at Jaq's final message to me. Mike must have had time to go through Jaq's mobile phone data by now so I call him. I might get some clues about Chiara from him.

'You do sound rough,' is the first thing he says. Some sympathy!

'Never mind that, my brain still works.'

He laughs. 'And what does your brain want this morning, doctor?'

'It wants to know if you've finished looking at all the data on Jaq's mobile.'

'Why's that? I'll not be able to tell you.'

'Have you got to the final text Jaq sent me?'

'Remind me.'

'It mentions someone called Chiara.'

'Yes, I remember. That's one of things we'll be asking you about.'

'I won't have any answers as I don't know who she is or what trouble Jaq was referring to either.'

'Something between you girls I expect. I wouldn't worry about it.'

I could strangle him for the sexist remark.

'Aren't you going to try and trace her?'

'One thing at a time, Kate. We're still sifting data and doing interviews, you know how it is. Better get on now.'

He hangs up and I'm left convinced of the importance of my own enquiries. A photo of Chiara might just push her up his priority list. I've got to wait until later to see if I have any success in getting hold of one. In the meantime, I decide to check out Jaq's bookshop. I'm curious to see it. I catch a bus to the main pier where I join the throngs of people who are milling around in Bank Holiday mode. There's a festival going on, after all.

'Happens every May: lots to see. Good time for you to arrive.' That's what Jaq had said.

As I walk along the promenade, I try to spot Italian-looking girls that might be Chiara. It's pointless and I soon give up. The sun is strong and my head is aching. The unremitting traffic noise and loud voices of the people around me just make it worse. I take a deep breath but instead of the salty tang of the sea or the fumes from passing cars, all I can smell is Jaq's stale blood as if I'm fixated on it like a dog on a scent trail. I crouch down, breathing rapidly and when I look up, a young couple with pierced faces and tattoos are bending over me. From my squatting position they look like giants silhouetted against the blue sky.

'You all right?'

I stand up slowly.

'I'm okay now, thanks.'

They head away from the beach, crossing the road, impatient, dodging the cars, not waiting for the green light. I keep going in the direction of the bookshop. Jaq told me she bought the lease when she returned from Italy. I know it's somewhere on Church Road and not far from Hove library. I pull out the map and find the library. I carry on along the promenade to Brunswick Square then turn right and walk past the creamy yellow Regency facades. The Square still retains something of the splendour of a bygone era, even if the buildings have morphed into multi-occupancy buildings and parked cars have blighted the area.

When I reach Church Road, I turn left and walk past rows of diverse small shops and restaurants until I reach the bookshop.

I find a flimsy police cordon in front of it. I lift the tape and slide under it so I can peer into the window. No sign of anyone inside. No surprises there. The shelves of books look back at me, inviting me to run my fingers along their spines as Jaq would have done. I ache to get inside the shop and root around for clues to Chiara's whereabouts but that will have to wait. I take one last look through the glass and it's then that I see the poster. It's advertising *Open House* and the painting that it features is the same as the one on the leaflet I'd picked up in the hotel. I pull out the map from the hotel and look up the road. It's not far away.

I walk along Church Road, past St Marks' Church, incongruously sitting next to a Tesco supermarket, then cross over Hove Street until I reach a large crescent on the left with impressive detached houses in various styles, all fronted by immaculate gardens and sweeping driveways. I stop in front of the address on the leaflet, a large rambling house with traditional hanging tiles.

It feels odd to be invited into a strangers' home without a prior appointment or a ring on a doorbell, but the sign outside confirms that's what I'm expected to do: *Open House: all welcome.* Curious, I go in. I'm greeted by a high-pitched voice. A girl with bright orange hair is talking excitedly about one of the paintings that hang on the wall. As I look around I see paintings everywhere, on every wall, in every room. Different painters, different styles, being scrutinised by people as eclectic as the paintings. I drift into what looks like the main sitting room. I find myself alone with a variety of watercolours, abstract and representational, in shades that vary from fiery reds to softer more pastel hues. I'm not alone for long. The orange-haired girl has followed me in.

'Hi. I'm Charlie.'

She takes my arm and guides me across to a vivid seascape of fluid blues and yellow, wild skies and wanton seas – impressionistic and compelling and in the same style as the one in Jaq's living room.

'What do you think?'

'Is it yours?'

She points to the bottom right hand corner of the painting. I lean forward and squint at the letter C followed by a few squiggles.

'It's very dramatic.'

She shows me some more of her paintings.

'Do you like them?'

'Actually, I do, especially this one of cliffs.'

'They're the Seven Sisters.'

'I remember: the seven cliffs near Eastbourne and Beachy Head, right?'

I've never seen them but Jaq used to talk about them, the chalky cliffs with their hidden fossils crumbling daily into the sea. It was her favourite place.

'I've seen a painting very similar to this one in a friend's house, Jacqueline Grey. Did you ever meet her?'

'What's it to you?'

I'm surprised by the sharpness of her reply.

'She was a friend of mine.'

'She never mentioned knowing a Kate to me.'

I ignore her put-down as my heart beats faster.

'So you're.. were friends?'

'What if we were. I don't want to talk about it.'

I wasn't expecting such a brusque reply. She must know Jaq is dead from her use of the past tense. Perhaps she's just upset. She turns her back on me as someone shouts out her name.

Charlie goes over to the girl who's just entered the room and gives her a hug. There's nothing I can do but leave them to it. I walk out of the room, wondering how to find out more from Charlie. I follow the signs to the kitchen which has been turned into a mini café with a farmhouse table covered in cakes and biscuits for sale. I help myself to a cup of tea and a cookie and put my coins in the honesty box. I sit down and browse through some of the pamphlets that the artists have left scattered around. I don't hear the back door open and only look up when I hear a voice call my name.

'Kate. Kate Green. Well, well. Here we are again.'

Standing in front of me, I see my first and best, anatomy demonstrator from medical school. It only takes a moment for her to size me up.

'You look good. You've certainly smartened up since your student days. Mind, you always could carry your clothes well with that figure of yours. Even those terrible jeans you used to wear.'

'You haven't changed at all.'

Not the most original reply. She laughs.

'I certainly hope not. I hate to think of time passing.'

But it has. It's been quite a while since we last saw each other. For one academic year, we were friends. She made one or two futile attempts at something more between us but had to settle for being a part of our Friday night pub group and the occasional coffee *à deux*. We lost touch when she left to take up a new post.

'So, what brings you to Hove?'

'I'm doing a GP locum.'

She wants to know which practice, for how long and why. I give short answers to all three questions, factual, unemotional and at odds with the maelstrom of my feelings. It's uncanny but I'm relieved at the banality of the exchange, as if I'm back in a world before Jaq died.

I point to the pamphlets on the table. 'Don't tell me you've become a painter.'

'Good grief, no. I'll stick to anatomy drawings, thank you. My partner's the painter. You must have met her. You can't miss her. She doesn't let anyone get away without seeing her work.'

'Not Charlie, the girl with the orange hair?'

'Absolutely.'

I have difficulty in seeing them as a couple.

'I like her paintings.'

'I think she's quite gifted. But don't tell her I said so.'

'Is this her house?'

She laughs. 'Charlie hardly makes enough to pay the rent on her flat. No, this is my house.'

'It's beautiful. But how come you've got all these paintings on view and people wandering around looking at them?'

'It was Charlie's idea and I thought it would be quite fun for once. It's a part of the Brighton Festival. Lots of artists have this sort of *Open House*. It's a chance to show off their work and hopefully get some sales. Charlie's flat is much too small and then she suggested inviting some other artists along and the thing just grew. Still, it's only at weekends and I quite like the people watching. When I want a break, I just take myself off into the garden.'

I glance out of the window and then turn back to Chris.

'And what about you? What are you up to these days?'

'Forensic pathologist.'

'Really! What happened to that surgical career, then?'

'This work is more intriguing.'

I'm surprised. I've obviously got a lot to catch up on.

The kitchen is filling up with people enjoying the home-made goodies and conversation is becoming difficult. We exchange mobile numbers and Chris goes off to pile up more cakes and chat to the visitors. I wander back keen to corner Charlie about Jaq. She's surrounded by what look like fellow artists and is thick in conversation with them. She glances over to me a couple of times but makes no attempt to acknowledge me. When I make a move to interrupt her, she speeds out of the room. I console myself with the fact that she's Chris's partner. I'll find a way to contact her through Chris.

I make my way along the hallway, reluctant to take myself back to a bleak hotel room, and stop in front of a painting I haven't noticed before. As I look at it, I wish I'd passed it by. I stare at the swirls of crimson and black paint so like the ominous shifting background of the Norwegian painting known as *The Scream*. In the foreground, a figure crouches, his face cast upwards in despair. It speaks to me of death and a hellish afterlife. I'm taken straight back to the image of Jaq's body surrounded in blood. I feel sick and close my eyes to fight off the feeling. It's definitely time to go.

Outside the house I take a few deep breaths of sea air to steady myself and then stroll back to Church Road. I rein in my natural instinct to rush. I've arranged to see Jaq's parents a little later and I don't want to arrive early. I try and imagine how it will be meeting Jaq's parents after such a long time and in such sad circumstances. I wonder what it feels like to lose a daughter. How do they deal with their pain? Parents should die before their children, that's the natural order of life. I guess their grief must be greater than mine unless age confers a hidden strength.

I remember their large detached house as one of many similar from the nineteen thirties, overlooking Hove Park. I recognise its round bay windows jutting out at the top of a long sloping drive, the epitome of suburbia. Jaq disliked the area. She preferred urban living, never happier than when surrounded by the clatter and chatter of a city, just like me. I find it hard to imagine her childhood there. Mrs Grey answers my ring on the door bell with such alacrity that I suspect she's been standing by the door waiting for me. She shows me into their front sitting room where I offer my condolences to her and her husband. Their eyes are dull as they each thank me in turn. They both look older than I expected. Mrs Grey goes off into the kitchen leaving me with Jaq's father. I take my place on the sofa in front of a heavy oak coffee table.

The conversation is surreal, small talk in place of what is at the centre of our thoughts. I'm glad when June comes in with the tea and some home-made cake, which crumbles into a wonderful almond flavour in my mouth.

'This is really good,' I say, accepting a second piece and hoping for an end to the stilted formalities.

'It was a favourite of Jacqueline's. I used to make it when she came to stay the night.'

This revelation takes me by surprise. I never considered Jaq sleeping over at her parent's house.

'Did Jaq often stay with you?'

'At least once a week. We always kept her room ready. She called it her oasis. Funny, if I think about it. When she lived with us, she was always complaining about how bourgeois we were.'

I smile at the word, Jaq liked to think of herself as anything but.

'It'll take a while to get used to her not coming.'

A film of tears makes June's eyes glisten but she recovers herself quickly.

'Do you find looking at her photos a help?' I ask.

'June's tried going through our albums but it's too soon for her,' John says. 'They'll give us good memories later on, I expect.'

'All my photos are in my London flat. I was wondering if it would be possible to take a quick look at some of yours. If that doesn't upset you, of course.'

'Not at all.' John replies.

June goes over to the bookcase and selects an album which she hands to me. The photos begin with those of Jaq as a baby. I begin to leaf through them, a record of a whole tranche of experiences before Jaq came into my life: parental memories that form no part of my own recollections.

'Kate might prefer to see this one.' John hands me another album. 'These are more recent photos starting with her university years.'

I hand back the first album and begin working through the photos noting a number where I feature too. I don't linger over them, I'm interested in the ones that follow, taken during the time she spent in Italy. I find there are very few from this period of her life and mostly of Jaq alone in front of various recognisable sights, the Duomo in Milan, Lake Como, the Ponte Vecchio in Florence, the Coliseum and St Peter's in Rome. When these come to an end, Jaq seems to have given up sending her parents any photographic record of her life, no doubt because she had returned to London and then Hove. I flick though the blank pages at the end of the album, and am getting ready to hand it back when I find a loose photo tucked into the back page. It's a photo of Jaq in front of an Italian school with a group of teenage girls who must be pupils. I turn the photo over and read the few words scrawled on the back.

Milan May 2007. Chiara's English conversation class.

As I recognize Jaq's handwriting, the room swirls around me.

'Are you all right, dear?' June asks. 'You've gone quite pale.'

I swallow a mouthful of tea and then take several deeps breaths.

'I'm okay now, thanks. Just looking at all these photos of Jaq, I guess.'

I show June the one in my hand and ask if I can borrow it. That's not a problem so I put the photo in my bag.

'Did Jaq ever mention a girl called Chiara?'

They both shake their head.

'But then she never much talked about her friends,' John notes. 'When she stayed with us, we mostly talked about the bookshop or chit chatted about books and films, you know, she's still got quite a collection of books in her room upstairs.'

I'm surprised that Jaq had such close contact with her parents. I wonder how that came about. When she was at university she was dismissive of their lifestyle and values and never enjoyed returning to Hove for the holidays. It makes me curious to see her old room and I ask if I can take a look.

'If you wouldn't mind, of course.'

'Not at all but perhaps you could come back another day. We've got to leave shortly. We've an appointment with the vicar about arrangements for Jaqueline's memorial service.'

'Memorial service?'

'It's next Monday 11th May in St George's Church, Church Road at 1.30 pm. We're just sorting out the details at the moment; please do come, if you can.'

I tell them that I'll be there and leave wondering what a confirmed atheist like Jaq would make of a church memorial service in her name. Perhaps she had become more sympathetic to their views, though I can't see it, knowing Jaq.

But then, how much do I really know about Jaq's life here in Hove?

Chapter Four

Tuesday 5 May

Any thoughts about Jaq take second place the next morning as I face an unfamiliar GP practice, something I've not done for quite some time. For the past five years I've had a permanent post in a well-established GP consortium in London. Steve thought I was mad to give it up for the precariousness of a locum job, but then he couldn't see he was one of the reasons I wanted to leave London. Steve's attractive enough, and as an academic sociologist, intelligent conversation was never in short supply but he's never had to grapple with the practical consequences of his theories. He's never had to deal with the grey areas of a job on the front line, whether medical or in the police. Add to that his vision of a life mapped out by work, marriage, kids, and retirement and it was inevitable that we would drift apart.

As I open the front door of the surgery, I wonder if Steve was right after all. I stare at the new faces behind the reception desk and realise what importance I'd placed on the anchor of Jaq's friendship. In the event, I'm greeted by smiling faces and an eagerness to show me round. With that reassurance, I sit down in front of the computer in my room, confident as I begin the familiar GP routine of a day's appointments.

I've left my door open and he barges straight in and up to my desk.

'Settling in okay?'

I'm irritated by the condescending tone of his voice and the reminder that I'm the new guy.

'Yes, thanks.' I look up at the suntanned face peering over my shoulder. He introduces himself as Dr Andrew Gull.

'I hope they've not overloaded your first session. I'm the duty doctor today so if you've got any problems, just give me a shout.'

Again the patronising manner.

'Thanks, but I'm sure I'll be fine.'

He shows no sign of moving. He leans closer and peers down at the screen as I scroll through the appointment list. I shift forward to avoid contact. He notices and steps back.

'Nothing there to cause problems. None of our heart-sinks or druggies.'

I wince at his use of such pejorative terms, especially to someone he's only just met. Better not take issue on my first day. No point in creating bad feeling before I've even started work. I'm relieved when he turns and leaves.

During the morning I'm faced with an uncanny number of straightforward problems. No autoimmune disorder to sort out, no new diagnosis of a Type 1 diabetic to spot, no pneumonia for emergency hospital admission. No complex disorders, just the routine troubles that disrupt people's lives on a daily basis. Not what I was hoping for. I want medical challenges to keep me focused and free from thoughts about Jaq.

At the doctors' meeting later that morning, I discover everyone has had a straightforward morning. But that's not the only surprise. As the meeting is about to close, the senior partner, Clare, has an announcement to make.

'Some of you may already have heard the sad news about one of our younger patients, Jacqueline Grey.' She pauses to ensure she has everyone's attention. 'I'm sorry to report that she was found dead in her flat late on Saturday night. The police are currently investigating the cause of death and the autopsy result will be available in due course. I've spoken to her parents and they are, of course, devastated by the news.'

There's a general murmuring among the doctors, as they register expressions of surprise, sympathy and disbelief. I had no idea that Jaq was registered at the practice. I take a few deep breaths and stare down at the floor to control my emotions as Clare continues to speak.

'We all know that Jacqueline had her problems over the years but she always managed to pull herself together. She was a determined young lady and more often optimistic than not. You couldn't help but like her.'

When I look up, I notice Andrew Gull is staring out of the window. He's the only one not to have made a comment. His face is cold and expressionless and he's the first to leave without saying a word. My dislike of him doubles in an instant.

I catch Clare before she leaves for her home visits. I've not been allocated any which is a relief with my car being in London. I mention this to Clare and then explain my involvement with Jaq and the circumstances of her death. Clare is very sympathetic when she hears my story and suggests I be excused visits for the moment.

'It will give you more time to adjust to our GP practice and allow you a bit of space to come to terms with the terrible loss of your friend. I'll just put you down for routine surgeries too. I'm sure we can rearrange the duty doctor rota.'

That's an unexpected bonus.

'How about the Young People's Clinic on Monday evenings?'
I'd forgotten about that.

'I can get Andrew to step up from his once a month commitment, if you like.'

'No, that's all right. It's the least I can do.'

I hate to think of Andrew as the only doctor at a clinic largely attended by teenage girls, even if I've never found it easy dealing with adolescents who see mobile phones as an essential part of their identity . But I've another reason not to renege on my commitment to the clinic. I want to check if Chiara has attended, even if this is a remote possibility. If she has, I'll be able to get hold of her contact details. The records are not computerised and only accessible to clinic staff.

With nothing to do until my afternoon surgery, I log onto my computer to see what I can find out about Jaq's problems from her medical notes. I'm hoping they haven't been archived and I'm in luck. Her medical record is still active and accessible. I scroll through it and see that over the last two years mild anxiety evolved into a moderate depression and a prescription for anti-depressants. A hiatus of six months without any consultations or prescriptions is followed by an overdose of paracetamol, caught in time to be treated successfully in hospital. Another hiatus of three months and then insomnia initially managed with amitriptyline which was stopped because of unacceptable side effects. A short course of a benzodiazepine follows and then no further appointments over the last two months. Jaq's excessive drinking and abuse of drugs when she returned from Italy had taken their toll and a move to Hove hadn't improved matters. Could I have helped her? By the time she arrived that night to the Emergency unit where I was working, I'd lost my chance. Realising that only adds to my pain at losing her.

I print out a copy of her records and look at the doctors she'd consulted. Clare's name features a lot but also that of Andrew Gull. I can't imagine Jaq seeing him by choice. Perhaps he was the only doctor available at the time. As I exit Jaq's records, it occurs to me that Chiara could have been registered as a temporary patient at the practice. I can't do a computer search as I don't have a surname or date of birth. I check with one of the girls on Reception and they confirm that details of temporary patients are held on a card index. I take a look through but can see no one called Chiara. Back in my room I munch on a cereal bar which acts as lunch and pull out the photo of Jaq with the students in Milan. I look at the inscription on the back. If Jaq entitled the photo *Chiara's conversation class* then Chiara must have been a favourite of hers. I look at the girl standing next to Jaq; I've a hunch she is Chiara but how to be sure?

After work, I take a walk along the nearby esplanade towards Brighton. I reach the West Pier. Apart from a tangled iron wreck, there's nothing to see but an expanse of water. The remains of the pier fascinate me. I'm not sure what to make of them. A light sea breeze flutters across my cheeks and brings a tang of salt to my lips: what a contrast from my previous London patch. I watch the ebb and flow of the waves, listening to the swish of its rise and fall across the pebbles. Years ago, Jaq told me she found the sound of the water soothing. I imagine her sitting alone at dusk contemplating the horizon, forgetting the stresses of her life, whatever they were. It's for me to discover those stresses if I'm to get any idea of why she died.

Back in my dismal hotel room, I perch on the bed with a stodgy take-away pizza while I power up my laptop. Social media is just taking off but I can find no trace of Jaq on any of the popular platforms. The only site where she features outlines details of her school, university and employment history but nothing more. It gives me some idea of the time-line of her movements but no clue as to why she was murdered or how to find Chiara. Until I can find out more about the photo from Milan, my only other resource is Charlie and the only way to contact her is through Chris. I'd like to see her anyway. She's someone I trust and as a forensic pathologist, the perfect contact for information about Jaq's post mortem. I call her and ask if she's free to meet up this evening.

Chris arrives by taxi to pick me up at seven. With a sideways look and a wry smile, she shows me exactly what she thinks of the hotel. Ten seconds in reception are enough for her to form an opinion. Outside she gives me a sympathetic hug then marches off towards the waiting cab. I hurry to catch up with her.

'So how long are you planning to put up with that?' she asks, pointing back to the hotel as I draw level with her.

'I'm not sure yet.'

'Whatever made you choose this place?'

I stop walking and she turns to look at me. I tell her it's a long story and she doesn't insist.

Our destination proves to be in the style of a good old British pub. I like the Victorian building: scruffy round the edges with a faded carpet, old photos on the walls and stuffed full of people who appear to run the gamut of the wise, the wonderful, the weird and the wild. Jaq told me Brighton was an inclusive city. We push past a crush of bodies to get served and then weave our way between the tables to find the only one free in a tiny indoor courtyard area of the former coach house.

'Here's to old times.' Chris lifts her glass and chinks it against mine.

We're soon getting through a second glass, and plunging into reminiscences of medical school and our junior doctor days.

'You know, I still have dreams about my on-call,' I say. 'Those awful weekends when there was only you on the wards to hold back a tsunami of medical disasters. At least that's what it felt like when your SHO went off to bed and the consultant went home.'

'No help from the internet either in those days,' Chris adds.

'But a lot of off-duty help from this.' I raise my glass.

'Absolutely.'

Chris picks up our empty glasses and goes to the bar for another round. When she returns she brings with her the question I've been expecting.

'So, what are you doing in that awful hotel?'

Suddenly my bravura ebbs away and my head begins to thump. The light-heartedness of the evening segues into a bleak reality. All I can see is Jaq's body, an inert bundle that will never come to life again. I've never thought of either of us dying. Death doesn't belong to today. It's for a tomorrow in the distant future. I realise Chris is staring at me.

'Hey, have I said something? You look awful.' She gets me a glass of water, which I drink without stopping for breath.

'Sorry about that, Chris.'

'So, what is going on, Kate?'

What indeed is going on? Here I am, in a city I don't know, starting an unfamiliar job, a good friend dead, her flat off-limits, stuck in a dull hotel room, facing a conundrum called Chiara and the only people I know here a former police colleague and an old medical friend. As I explain my situation, I feel I'm talking about a stranger.

'I only arrived in Hove last Saturday evening. I'd arranged to stay with an old friend Jaq while doing this locum job in Hove. She was going off to Italy on the day I arrived but, when I got into the flat, I found she hadn't gone to Italy at all.'

By the time I've finished telling Chris all the details, I feel sick. The memory of finding Jaq is so vivid. Add to that a few glasses of wine on an empty stomach and the stuffy atmosphere of the pub and I have to rush off to the Ladies where I throw up. Afterwards, I gulp down some water from the tap, not caring if it's fit to drink and open the window to let out the smell of vomit. I take some deep breaths before returning to face Chris.

'You okay?'

I nod and take a sip of water from the glass she has refilled.

Chris takes out a cigarette. 'I was on duty Saturday night.' She flicks open her lighter only to replace it, unused, in her handbag with a frustrated sigh.

'Damn Parliament. Trying to stop me smoking myself to death.'

I look enviously at the cigarette packet as it vanishes into her bag. She can't know how much I sympathise with her. I say nothing about my own urge to smoke, a pathetic attempt to maintain some sort of moral high ground.

'Jacqueline Grey,' she continues. 'I've just done her autopsy.'

I lean forward in anticipation.

'What did it show?'

'I've only made a preliminary report but just between fellow medics, there's no doubt that Jaq died as a result of a penetrating chest injury.' She lowers her voice so I can hardly hear over all the chatter around me. 'I'm putting it down as a homicide.'

'Can you give me any more details?'

'Best not, eh?'

'Jaq was registered as a patient at our GP practice so I'll get to see the final report.'

Chris ignores my prompt and takes a swig of wine.

'Were you close friends?'

'We were very close during our uni days. We were both at University College London. She was reading English and Italian Literature while I was doing my pre-clinical medical studies. We hit it off straight away. It was good to have a friend outside Medicine. In fact, we shared a flat for a couple of years but began to drift apart after she graduated. I kept trying to make contact, but she never replied, at least not until a few weeks ago. I last saw her in London just over a week ago.'

I'd been thrilled when Jaq had contacted me but shocked when we met up. She'd lost weight to the point of looking anorexic, her skin was sallow and the sparkle had gone from her eyes. She had all the signs of chronic drug abuse. She told me she was making a big effort to stay clean and was keen for me to come to Hove.

'I remember she had a wonderful smile,' Chris says.

I feel as if an electric shock has passed through me.

'You knew Jaq?'

'No, no. I just saw her when I popped into her book shop. That's where I met Charlie. She worked there part-time.'

I think back to my first encounter with Charlie and her reaction to my enquiry about Jaq. Had working in the bookshop created tensions between them?

Chris finishes her wine.

'Come on, you need something to eat. There's a good Italian restaurant just down the street. You don't have to book.'

'I'm happy to stay here.'

Chris goes and fetches a couple of menus and I choose a smoked haloumi and corn burger without giving it much thought.

'This is on me,' she says, and reaches for a large designer bag.

As she rummages in it to find her purse, I get a glimpse of an official-looking file. I'm betting it's the preliminary autopsy report on Jaq. I watch as Chris heads over to the bar and gets buried in the crowd of other people waiting to order food. I calculate she'll be busy for quite a few minutes. I've got time. I reach into her bag and pull out the file. Inside I find what I'd been hoping for. I skip through the post mortem details picking out the essentials.

1 stab wound - depth of thrust 10 cm through 6th intercostal space: trajectory – pericardium to right heart ventricle, 1 stab wound - depth 11cm through 3rd intercostal space to mediastinum. Cause of death exsanguination. Manner of death: Homicide.

I'm used to reading and writing clinical reports, but this one is about Jaq and it's impossible to be objective. I'm upset to see her death reduced to a few lines of forensic analysis: a few typed words that convey the brutality of her end more than any purple prose. As I scan the rest of the report, my eye lands on a detail that disturbs me. Chris has found traces of a white powdery substance in Jaq's nostrils. Toxicology analysis will take weeks but forensic chemistry should provide a quicker answer. Knowing Jaq, it has to be cocaine unless proved otherwise. With shaking hands, I shove the file back in Chris's bag and compose myself before she returns.

Jaq's efforts to stay clean had clearly slid backwards. I'm not surprised, it's a difficult path to follow. But it would be a mistake to think that Jaq was keen for me to come to Hove just to help her quit drugs. The way she was killed leaves no room for doubt that what was at stake was so much more than that. With Chiara untraceable, I have to talk to Charlie and find out what she knows.

Chapter Five

Wednesday 6 May

It proves to be easy to get Chris to arrange a dinner party at her house, Charlie included. Unfortunately, it won't be until Friday evening. Meantime, I spend my first free afternoon attending an interview at Brighton Police Station. I know it's normal procedure, but I resent having to go now that Mike has all but confirmed I'm no longer a suspect.

He's there to meet me. As a formality he asks me if I've got a contact number for legal assistance. I'm not anticipating I'll need one as I'm not under arrest and I know what to expect. In any case, I'm reassured by his presence. I soon realise my mistake. He hands me over to a detective sergeant who could double for many a suave screen actor and a pony-tailed DC who carries herself with the grace of a ballerina. The sergeant goes through the preliminaries as if he's been briefed about my previous experience but, nevertheless, I'm still alert to any hidden agenda behind the interview. I've seen too many people give themselves away by clever questioning and I'm only too aware how words can be manipulated.

I'm surprised by the effort it takes to keep my composure. Vivid memories of the evening I discovered Jaq's body make concentrating difficult. The sergeant picks through the details of my first statement. It's unnerving to think anyone could doubt my account of events. At the end of the interview, I'm advised to remain available in case of further need.

It's not until I exit the police station that I notice I'm trembling from the effort of keeping my emotions in check. It's raining and the air is steamy from the May warmth. Despite the heat, I feel cold as the rain soaks through my clothes. It reminds me to get my car back soon and not just to avoid the effects of a Brighton downpour. I'll have to start doing home visits sometime but more than that, I feel like a part of me is missing. I dive into a café on the opposite side of the road and warm myself over a cappuccino. I'm betting Mike will be listening to the interview. I give him enough time to skip through it, then ring his number. I want to find out why I was made to feel so uncomfortable. There's no reply so I head off towards the station to find out if I can get hold of him. I get soaked as soon as I leave the café. I'm just debating whether to give up and take a bus back to the hotel, when an umbrella is hoisted over my head.

'You look like someone's emptied a bucket of water over you.

'Thanks very much.'

He laughs.

'I called you just now.'

Mike pulls out his phone. 'It's still on silent mode.'

'I wanted to know why I was given such a hard time. You must've listened to the recording my now.'

'Let's talk about it in the car. I'm off duty now, I'll drive you back to the hotel.'

The rain is easing as we drive off.

'So why all those questions about my arguing with Jaq and her being high on cocaine when I arrived in Hove? What was all that about?'

'Look, it's not gone unnoticed that we were once colleagues. I don't want anyone getting the idea you've had a soft ride.'

'Well, thanks very much.'

'Don't worry, when the exact time of death comes through, you'll be in the clear.'

'I'd like confirmation of that, please.'

'Fair enough.'

As we pull into the hotel car park, the rain starts up again. It hits the windscreen like machine gun fire. We sit in the car waiting for it to end. The force of the water jets reminds me of the day in London when Jaq and I got caught under torrents of rain as we ran across Regent's Park. Her laughter comes back to me and I feel an ache inside me. I turn to Mike to take my mind off painful memories and ask him about the investigation.

'Actually, we're having trouble finding a lead. She kept herself to herself, that friend of yours. Nothing much on her phone and apart from a couple of contacts in her address book, nothing, nada, zilch.'

I'm not surprised. Jaq would scribble numbers and addresses on scraps of paper and then stuff them in a drawer which she'd clear out periodically without checking what was there. But that didn't matter. She had a phenomenal memory and once she'd made a mental note of something, she could recall it anytime.

'What about Jaq's computer?''

'We're working on it.

'Perhaps you'll come up with something in her bookshop.'

'Who's in charge of this case, Dr Green?'

There's a light-hearted note to his voice but a steely look in his eyes.

'No clues about Chiara, then.'

'Nothing so far.'

'I've got a photo of Jaq with some Italian students in Milan. I think one of the girls is Chiara.'

'Bit of a long shot, don't you think?'

I open the car door ready to make a run for it but I slip as soon as my feet touch the greasy tarmac. Such are the rewards of impatience. I lie on the ground, becoming completely sodden, unable to get up. Mike hasn't noticed and reaches over to close the door, only to discover an ungainly heap, half-hidden under the car.

'Kate. What on earth are you doing?'

'Actually, I've fallen awkwardly, Mike. I could do with a bit of help here.'

By the time he gets me back to my room, we both look as if we've taken a fully-clothed dip in the sea. There's a spare towel in the bathroom and I toss it over to Mike. We take turns to have a hot shower. Afterwards, I have the luxury of a snug dressing gown. Mike has to sit wrapped in his towel while I attempt to dry his clothes with the hairdryer. He's smiling at the ridiculousness of my efforts but it's not his smile that catches my attention. He may be more than a decade older than me but he's clearly in good shape and knows it. Cheesy phrases like, *swarthy good looks* pop into my head. I push some other inappropriate thoughts to the back of my mind and concentrate on drying his clothes.

'I don't think you're achieving very much there,' he says. 'I can't stay here all night.'

Our eyes meet.

'Unfortunately,' he adds.

There's an awkward pause and I look down. I'm aware of being naked underneath my dressing gown. I hand him the hair dryer.

'Here, you do this. I'm going to get dressed.'

I go into the bathroom and pull on jeans and a tee shirt. When I return Mike has given up drying his clothes even if they're still damp. His trousers are in place but he's bare chested and about to put on his shirt.

'Not bad for an old man,' he jokes, feeling his biceps.

I wave a hand vaguely as if dismissing his comment. I watch him as he buttons up his shirt, rather more slowly than is necessary, I think. All the time he keeps looking directly at me. It's time to take a stand.

'Mike! Stop it.'

'What?'

'You know what I mean. It's bad enough being together like this. And what's more,' I pause for effect, 'you're married.'

'Not for much longer. Carole and I are getting a divorce.'

The implications of that are all too clear. If I'm going to find out anything more about Jaq's death from Mike, I'm going to have to navigate around his advances and deal with my own feelings of attraction, a complication I hadn't foreseen.

Chapter Six

Thursday 7 May

After I pushed Mike out of my hotel room yesterday, I returned to the idea of Chiara being an English language student. I use a variety of search engines to find the names of schools in Brighton and Hove. I'm dismayed to see such a long list with no guarantee of it being complete either. I look at it again after a perfunctory breakfast of a croissant and black tea and realise I'll not get through the list in a morning, or in fact any time in the near future. As I clean my teeth, another idea occurs to me and I go back to my laptop and do another search. Chiara will have arranged somewhere to stay as none of the language schools are residential. Impossible to track down families or apartments that may have accommodated her but I find the address of one hostel for language students in St Aubyn's.

A taxi drops me at the bottom of a wide street that forms part of Hove's grid system of roads. From the curved sweep of the elegant Regency buildings on the corner, I follow the row of Victorian terraced houses until I reach a large double fronted property. I walk up the few steps to the porticoed entrance and approach the reception office. I find it staffed by a young girl with purple nails and lips, who gives the impression of being more interested in the fashion magazine she's reading than in looking after the needs of the resident students.

'You'll have to talk to Mrs Bun,' she says, when I eventually get her attention and introduce myself as Dr Green. 'She's out. I'm just minding the office till she gets back. She's gone for a Dentist appointment. You'll have to come back later.'

She returns to her reading, disinclined to make any effort to help and not interested in why I'm there. I'm about to take her advice when I notice the wall behind her is covered with photos of young faces.

'Excuse me, are those photos of the residents staying in the hostel?'

'I guess. What's that to you?'

I pull out my photo and force her to look at it.

'That girl there,' I say, with my finger indicating the one I think is Chiara, 'can you look and see if she's one of your students? Her mother is ill and I'm trying to contact her.'

I'm sure Mrs Bun would find my explanation quite implausible but the girl just shrugs her shoulders.

'You can check yourself if you like.'

She goes back to her reading.

It doesn't take long to scan the photo gallery. There's no one that resembles the girl in my photo even allowing for the passage of a couple of years since it was taken. I thank the girl who grunts a reply and resign myself to tackling the language schools. I take a bus along Church Road to an area of Brighton with a high concentration of such academies.

The first one I approach makes it clear that the privacy laws are a barrier to getting any information. I'll have to invent a convincing story if I'm to surmount that obstacle. I wish I had a police badge to flash, there would be no problem then. I have some success with the sob story about needing to make contact because her mother is desperately ill, but not a single Chiara can be found on the registers I manage to access. I show the photo to some of the students who come and go, again with no success. My doubt about which girl in the photo is Chiara adds to my frustration. Perhaps she isn't even in the photo, but taking it instead. I give up at lunchtime and buy a roasted veg ciabatta to eat in the Royal Pavilion Gardens. The sun is approaching its highest point and very hot. The grass is strewn with people sunbathing and picnicking. I grab one end of a bench as an over-tanned blond girl in shorts finishes her ice cream and vacates her spot.

I tuck into my food while I watch a group of motley figures congregating around a giant circular mirror. When I've finished eating, I go over to join them and discover that it is concave on one side and convex on the other. Each side of the sphere produces a distorted reflection of the garden and people approaching the mirror, but in different ways. I study the distortion of my body in the concave surface as I walk towards it. It reminds me of those mirrors in funfairs. Walking around to the convex side is more surprising. Everything reflected by the mirror is turned upside down. I put out a hand to touch the surface, with the feeling that I'm not just facing an inverted image of my body but also confronting the way my perception of the world has been turned upside down by Jaq's death.

As I stare into the mirror, I catch sight of Mike striding across the gardens behind me. I turn around to put him in the right perspective. He hasn't spotted me so I hurry after him intending to exchange a few words before setting off for the GP surgery. I come to a halt when I see him approaching a young girl, dressed like a punk, all in black with heavy bovver boots, garish make-up and spikey green hair. He slots in beside her as they walk across the gardens together. From their body language, it's difficult to decide the purpose of their encounter. Could it be to do with Jaq's investigation? It's odd for a Senior Investigating Office not to send one of his team. I watch as they set off together towards the backstreets.

With my curiosity piqued, I follow them, digging into my police memory bank for what I must do to avoid detection. I'm surprised how easily it comes back to me. After several minutes in their footsteps, I discover their destination is a dilapidated terraced house in Regent Street. The paint is flaking off the window frames and the plaster is peeling from the façade. There's an old mattress propped up under the front window and the rubbish bin next to it is overflowing and giving off a foul smell. I watch as the girl enters the house while Mike waits outside at a discrete distance, looking at the screen of his smart phone.

I'm aware that time is ticking away towards the beginning of my afternoon surgery. Unless I leave now, I risk being late back for the beginning of it. I stay put, becoming more anxious as I wait. After a few minutes, the girl reappears and goes over to Mike. I'm too far away to get any clear idea of what's going on between them but the exchange only takes a few seconds and then the girl vanishes inside the house. Mike turns away from the house. He appears to be stuffing something into the inside pocket of his jacket and I pull back into a doorway to avoid being seen. I can just see Mike move off in the direction of the police station. I check my phone for the time and, in a panic, set off at a sprint towards the bus stop on North Street with fingers crossed that Brighton's public transport system will live up to its reputation for frequent services.

It does, but progress along Western Road and Church Road is slow. I phone the GP practice with a good excuse at the ready to explain my late arrival. The number is engaged. I keep trying but can't get through. I lean forward in my seat as though this will help speed up the traffic. After what feels like eternity, I reach my stop and sprint along the road to the surgery. I burst into Reception and apologise to the staff. I'm preparing to do the same to my waiting patients when Andrew barges up to me.

'You're late.'

'I got held up. I was just explaining to the staff.'

'And what about all those people who are waiting to see you.'

'They'll all get a full apology.'

'Being part-time doesn't mean you can start your sessions when you like.'

I flush and push past him, anxious about the reaction of my patients. I'm torn between embarrassment and anger. My cheeks are still glowing hot as I call for my first patient. I'm on the point of hyperventilation and so out of breath that the old lady who enters the room asks if I suffer from the same chronic respiratory problem as her. As I offer my apologies for my late start she surprises me with her response.

'Don't pay any notice of that doctor, just now. None of his business I should say. He thinks he's better than anyone else too. I went to him once, never again. I asked if I could wash my hands after he examined me and he made such a fuss about not using his special towel. Made me feel awful.'

I feel like bursting into tears at her kindness but limit myself to a smile and a thank you. She produces a number of medicine packets from her handbag and hands them to me.

'Now, about these new tablets,' she says.

The rest of the afternoon passes without further dramas either from patients or from interruptions by Andrew. I manage to slip out of the surgery at the end of the day without bumping into him. Andrew's words are plaguing me. I've always prided myself on my professional approach to medicine and it hurts to acknowledge that he had a valid point, even if made with an unacceptable vindictiveness.

I head for the Churchill Road shopping centre in Brighton to take advantage of the late opening hours for some retail therapy. The indoor mall could be anywhere in the UK. Rows of predictable brand names glare out at me from the shop fronts. I saunter into the entrance of the only department store. The rows of perfumes and make-up that greet me prompt an immediate about-turn for the exit. I try one or two clothes outlets but the bustle of eager shoppers rifling among the racks of summer dresses is off-putting. The whole experience does nothing to lift my spirits. My only purchase is a bottle of wine from the chain store across the road. After that, I wander through the narrow Lanes, one of Brighton's attractions, and home to a multitude of jewellers, boutiques and places to eat. I ignore the Italian chains and opt for a veggie restaurant which manages to squeeze me in thanks to a last-minute cancellation. I remember Jaq praising its food and promising to bring me here.

It's late by the time I leave to return to my hotel. I trudge uphill along Queen's Road to the station to pick up a bus. Rough-sleepers are huddled in doorways. The night breeze carries the smell of their unwashed bodies my way. They are all men, settling down for the night in dirty sleeping bags and gathering their few possessions close to them to prevent theft. A stench of stale sweat mixed tobacco and alcohol makes me hurry past. Not like Jaq. She would stop and speak to the down-and-outs that she came across in London. She had a knack of establishing a genuine rapport with them. I ease my conscience by going back and handing a couple of fivers to two of guys. As I'm getting my purse out of my handbag, I see the photo of Jaq and the girls. I find it hard to picture Chiara sleeping on the streets but it's worth a try. I show the photo to the guys but by then they're more interested in the money than scrutinising a line-up of girls. I'll have to see what I can get out of Charlie tomorrow.

Chapter Seven

Friday 8 May

I wake the next morning to unwelcome flashbacks of finding Jaq. My body feels tied into one giant knot. I try and displace the upsetting images by thinking about how to find Chiara, but that only makes things worse. I'm frustrated by my lack of progress and this turns even the simplest of tasks into a battle of wills. I fiddle with the shower control until scalding hot water threatens to give me first-degree burns. I then manage to rip the trousers I'm in the process of putting on. When I overfill the kettle in the room and water pours onto the carpet, I know I've had enough of hotel living.

I take myself off to a café on the promenade where coffee, a croissant and the sea air clear my head. I come up with an idea to solve my hotel dilemma. I then have a second idea about Mike. I'm curious to know what progress he's made and keen to tease out of him anything that can help my own search. I send Chris a message asking if I can bring someone to the dinner party. She replies at once confirming that it's okay. A quick call to Mike and it's all in place. After a few glasses of wine, he might drop his guard and say more than he should. Encouraged by the chance to tackle both Mike and Charlie, I'm irritated to have my positive mood dented by Andrew who is hovering around the door to my room when I turn up for work. He follows me in without asking. He exudes the sort of confidence that I always associate with a public-school education. He dresses with an impeccable casual chic and not one of his blond hairs is out of place. I notice the label on his polo shirt and his expensive loafers. Brands well above my budget. I sit down at my desk and place my handbag in one of the drawers.

'I'd lock that away if I were you,' he says. 'For anything of value, you can't be too careful.'

I hate being given superfluous advice but I bite back a retort. I'm learning to ignore his patronising manner. Instead I ask if there's anything I can do for him.

'No, no. Just let me know if you run into any problems. I'm only next door.'

I turn towards my computer and he has no alternative but to take his neatly dressed figure off to his own room. He's the only one of the doctors to bother me and I remind myself there's bound to be one annoying person to deal with in any GP practice.

I work my way through my appointments efficiently but with a feeling of detachment, as if someone else is sitting in my chair and listening, advising and prescribing. At the end of the afternoon, I shut down my computer and stare at the blank screen. With nothing left to distract me, a shadowy image of Jaq's face appears for a second on the screen as if she's been pixelated back from the dead. It's an unexpected and dark recollection. I brush it away and pick up a bundle of personal mail which has been redirected from my London flat. I hadn't wanted to use Jaq's address in case my staying with her didn't work out. One look at the envelopes tells me Jaq's letter is not among them. As it hadn't arrived before I left London, she must have forgotten about it. Another frustration. I must make progress this evening.

Chris welcomes me with a friendly hug and examines the label as I take out a bottle of prosecco from a plastic carrier bag.

'It's just something I picked up at by the Churchill Centre.'

Chris knows her wines and won't drink anything that sniffs of the mediocre.

'Actually, it's surprisingly good. Charlie bought some last week.'

'Well, that's a relief, I've not yet tracked down a decent wine shop.'

She laughs. 'You certainly won't find one near that hotel of yours.'

I seize the opportunity.

'I've been thinking it's time to do something about that.'

Chris gives me a quizzical look.

'It might sound a bit cheeky but I do need to find somewhere a bit more permanent and convenient than that hotel room.'

'And more comfortable, I should add.'

'True. I was thinking....'

'..whether you could move in here with me.'

Chris is as sharp as ever. I'm relieved when she says she won't charge me but I'm worried about Charlie's reaction.

'She doesn't seem keen one me.'

'She can be moody sometimes. I'll sort her out. It'd be quite good to have another medic around. Charlie's fun but no intellectual.'

'And I am?'

'You know what I mean. We speak the same language. Now come on, I need to keep an eye on the food.'

We go into the kitchen and she opens the prosecco with a characteristically extravagant gesture that makes the cork hit the far wall. She pours out two glasses and hands one to me.

'So, who's the mystery guest?'

'Mike Black. Detective Chief Inspector in Brighton. You must know him.'

Chris almost chokes on her drink.

'Isn't he in charge of Jaq's investigation?'

'That's right.'

'How come....?'

'He's a former colleague of mine. After medical school I went into the police force. I got as far as junior detective. We worked together for a short time.'

Chris raises her eyebrows.

'Well, that's something I didn't know, but you've come back to Medicine, obviously?'

There's no time to take the conversation further as the doorbell rings. Chris goes to answer it and Mike steps inside. He looks good. He's changed into smart jeans and a polo shirt. No sign of his grey work suit. He's clearly comfortable in Chris's company. When he takes the glass of bubbly on offer, he puts an arm round her, suggesting they've known each other for a while. Chris excuses herself and goes into the kitchen. Mike smiles at me.

'You look great, Kate.'

I've not put on anything special, just a cerise coloured linen shirt and black trousers. His comment unsettles me. I'm not much good with compliments and coming from Mike, it feels awkward. I envy Chris's easy aplomb. I manage a *thank you*.

'How come you're friends with Chris?'

I finish explaining just as Chris comes back in with Charlie. Charlie gives me a frosty stare. I smile back nevertheless. Chris draws Mike and I together like a couple as if to reassure Charlie. I have to say we match up better than Chris and Charlie. Charlie is the very antithesis of Chris. You only have to look at her clothes. This evening she's wearing a flimsy short dress, thick orange leggings and pink boots, a style that clashes both with itself and with Chris who is elegant in black palazzo pants and a grey silk blouse. I'm glad Charlie's not in charge of the food, I'd be anxious about the result. Fortunately, the meal is firmly under Chris's control. It's cooked to perfection, vichyssoise followed by whole baked salmon and French patisserie for dessert, accompanied by an appropriate wine. I haven't eaten so well for days.

Mike is animated and talkative and has plenty of anecdotes about police work. Inevitably the Brighton festival is a key topic of conversation. Charlie hardly says a word but when we've exhausted the festival chat, I turn to her and ask her if she enjoyed working in Jaq's bookshop.'

'Why wouldn't I? If you were a real friend of hers, you must know what a great person she was.'

'We'd not seen each other for quite a while but I was going to stay in her flat for a few months while working in Hove.'

'Really!'

At this point Chris takes charge.

'You probably don't know this, Charlie, but Kate was the one who found her. She's very upset about that.'

Charlie is not deterred.

'Well, I'm upset too. I saw Jaq most days, not like Kate. She meant a lot to me.'

I keep my feelings under control by folding my paper table napkin into a smaller and smaller square. Mike concentrates on stirring his coffee slowly over and over again as though conducting a scientific experiment. Finally, I look up and fix Charlie in the eye.

'Jaq was special to me too. It's true we hadn't seen a lot of each other lately but that's not all that matters in a friendship.'

'You haven't got a clue, have you. What do you really know about her feelings?'

Charlie sits staring at her glass, then snatches it up and gulps down what's left of her wine. I notice her hands are trembling. She puts down the empty glass and rushes out of the room.

Charlie's exit signals a change in Mike's mood. He frowns and empties his glass then turns to Chris and asks if he could have a word in private, if I don't mind.

I tell them it's no problem. They leave the room and I take the chance to go after Charlie. I bump into her coming out of the sitting room. She rushes off in the direction of the kitchen. I catch a glimpse of Chris and Mike on the sofa, locked in an intense conversation. They're keeping their voices low and are too engrossed to notice me. Chris is taking a piece of paper out of a file and showing it to Mike. I see Chris light a cigarette as Mike raises his voice but I still can't hear what he's saying.

I head off to the kitchen in search of Charlie where I find her at the table, stirring a hideous pink cocktail. Her hostility is palpable. I sit down opposite her.

'What do you want?' She looks at me like a bored adolescent.

'I'm sorry, I didn't want to imply that Jaq wasn't a special friend to you.'

She rolls her eyes to the ceiling. I ignore it. I refuse to be put off by her show of petulance.

'What do you know?'

I can see resentment spilling out of her eyes. She stands up and paces the room.

'For God's sake sit down, Charlie.'

I watch her patiently until she sits down again and looks at me with eyes that would kill me if they could. Chis appears but, with her back to the door, Charlie doesn't see her. I shake my head at Chris to suggest she leave us alone and she turns back along the corridor.

'Look, Charlie, we're both upset because of Jaq and you're right, I know nothing about her life in Hove. The one thing that's going to help us both is understanding why she died like she did. I've got no idea. What about you?'

'Isn't that up to the police?'

'Of course, but Jaq sent me a message to look out for someone called Chiara and mentioned trouble in the bookshop. Chiara's the only person who can tell me what Jaq meant. That's why I have to find her. She might have some idea as to who murdered Jaq.'

Charlie starts to tremble and focuses on her cocktail. She's become even more pale than usual and the freckles on her face seem to be burning bright.

'Jaq..... no, you'll only tell that policeman friend of yours and I don't want to answer any more of their questions. It was horrible.'

'I won't say a word, not if you don't want me to. Honestly, you can trust me. As a doctor, I'm used to keeping the secrets that people tell me.'

I hold my breath.

'Jaq was hiding Chiara in the basement of the shop.'

My heart thumps so much it's the only thing I'm aware of for a few seconds. I'm regretting that I can't show Charlie the photo from Milan. I left it behind in my work handbag.

'Have you any idea why?'

'No. Jaq said it was better for me not to know.'

'What about the police?'

'They never asked me about Chiara.'

'So where's Chiara now? She can't have been in the basement when the police came to search it.'

'I don't know. She ran off last Saturday after we closed.'

That was the evening Jaq died.

'How do you know that?'

'I went back to get my purse. I'd left it in the basement when I went down to make coffee in the afternoon. Chiara was nowhere to be seen and she'd taken her sleeping bag with her.'

'Why do you think she ran off?'

Before Charlie can reply, Chris returns.

'Come on, you two. Time for a nightcap.'

This time she insists and I'm left wondering how I can get an answer.

Chapter Eight

....Friday 8 May

We follow Chris back into the dining room, my head spinning with the information that Charlie has just told me. Mike is back to his earlier ebullient mood when we join him for a final brandy. As we leave, he suggests we share a taxi back. I tell him I fancy walking and would appreciate his company. My head is buzzing with questions I want to put to him and I'm still trying to process what Charlie has told me.

The evening is clear and, despite the light-pollution from the city, some stars manage to twinkle their way into the orange-tinged blackness of the sky. We make our way along the esplanade towards the pier passing the great sweep of steps up to Adelaide Crescent on our right. Its balustrade reminds me of the elegant ballroom entrance that Jaq and I waltzed down together one New Year's Eve when reluctantly participating in a luxury hotel celebration organised by our then current boyfriends.

We walk in silence for a while. In the distance the dazzling neon lights of the pier make the dark water beneath seem sinister. It's a striking contrast, that seems to me a metaphor for life and death. It reminds me that Jaq and I are now separated for ever. It also brings me back to the questions I still have for Mike. I'm limited by my promise to Charlie so I start by asking him if he went to Jaq's autopsy. He hesitates, then confirms that he did.

'At least I was there long enough for the essential findings.'

I have to smile. Mike's squeamishness was well known when I worked with him, an odd feature given the rest of his character.

'So, did you find out anything useful?'

Instead of answering the question, he adopts the annoying ploy of replying with his own query, asking me what I've found out from Chris.

'She said it was homicide from stab wounds to the chest.'

'There were two to the left anterior chest, 11 cm and 10 cm deep if I remember correctly, anyway enough for her to bleed to death.'

That matches up with what I read in Chris's report.

'Have you found the weapon?'

I hadn't noticed one near Jaq's body.

'There was a kitchen knife underneath her which fits the type and size of the wounds. We only found it when she was taken away.'

'Any fingerprints?'

'Forensics are still working on that.'

I'm surprised. It doesn't usually take what is almost a week to get a result.

'Anything else important?'

'Such as?'

'Any evidence of drugs, for example?'

'What makes you ask about that?'

He waits for an explanation but when none is forthcoming, he's quick to pick up on the implications of my question.

'You've seen the report?'

'I sneaked a look at it. Chris doesn't know.'

I give him the same justification I tried on Chris.

'A preview is not so very much out of order, considering.'

'I can see your detective training hasn't been wasted.'

His comment is not offered as a compliment. Mike's tone of voice shows he's annoyed that I've seen Chris's report.

'Don't get cross, Mike. I'm just trying to understand what happened?'

I change the subject, resolving to come back to the question of drugs another time.

'Have you found anything on Jaq's computer?'

'Nothing of use.'

'No mention of Chiara?'

It would be a good moment to tell him about Charlie's revelations but I keep my promise to her.

'None.'

'Pity, I'm sure she's key, given the text Jaq sent me.'

'What's that, a girl's intuition?'

I don't even deign to answer. I march on ahead, furious at his remark.

He catches up with me and holds up his hand in surrender. 'Okay, okay. Sorry.'

That's not much by way of an apology or an explanation but I let it drop. Once I've identified Chiara, it will be a very different matter. I'll want more than a throw-away sexist comment if he continues to insist that Chiara is not important,

'Look, we're doing all we can but you know we have to set priorities.' His voice is softer now. 'And don't forget, you're still our prime suspect.'

'That's not very funny.'

As a reply, he puts his arm round me. I find myself trembling at the contact. We walk along the esplanade towards Brighton until I break away from him and cross to a bench overlooking the beach. He follows and we sit staring into the blackness ahead of us.

'It must be pretty grim going back to that hotel room every night. Why don't you come over to my place sometime for a meal? How about Saturday evening? I've got to go to London in the day but I'll be back late afternoon.'

The invite is loaded, *a meal at my place* comes with the inevitable expectations. He has declared himself this time. I'm quick to reply.

'I'm not around on Saturday. I'm going to London too, to pick up my car.'

'How about I give you a lift?'

I hesitate, then decide to accept his offer. A couple of hours with him in a car will give me a good opportunity to see what else I can get out of him.

Chapter Nine

Saturday 9 May

Mike is half an hour late picking me up and doesn't bother to apologise. We drive in silence until we join the A23 to London. Grey clouds hang low above us in a claustrophobic formation and a light drizzle is falling. We both fix our eyes on the road, as though the car needs the concentration of two people to propel it forward. We're going at a dreary 70mph. I watch a small Kia overtake us. Mike reaches down and puts on the radio. We listen to the news: a catalogue of natural disasters, human violence, tragedy and stupidity that soon exceeds the limits of my tolerance.

'Can we have that off now?'

'How about some music?'

'No thanks. Not now.'

'Are you always this irritable?'

'Only when I'm not the driver.'

I settle back into my seat and watch the Sussex countryside flash past, dappled with the light rain. We chat about London and how it compares to Brighton and Hove. The traffic increases as we approach the Gatwick turnoff. It's time to move on from small talk.

'Do you think there's any mileage in the fact Jaq had a cocaine habit?'

'I doubt it, but it's early days yet.'

'Don't you think her cocaine use could be linked to her death, then?'

'We've not had the toxicology result yet.'

'I don't mean she died of an overdose. She bled to death, that much is clear. No, I was thinking about it as a motive for someone killing her.'

'Being killed in her own home, it doesn't suggest a settling of accounts, if that's what you mean?'

'Things don't always follow the expected pattern.'

'Finding a bit of coke at a post mortem is no big deal. You know the stuff is everywhere these days: big cities, small towns, villages.'

'That may well be the case but you can't ignore a person's drug habit in the middle of a murder investigation.'

'Look, Kate, recreational drugs are all part of the social scene nowadays. The fact that your friend used coke doesn't mean it's involved with her death or that a serious crime has been committed.'

I'm tempted to remind him of the people whose nasal septum rots away from overuse or the ones who've died from an adulterated dose.

'What about your street contacts? Wouldn't they know if the drugs angle was worth following up? You must have informers or undercover agents in the field.'

'What makes you bring up that idea?'

I turn my head towards Mike. I can see tension in his hands from the way he's gripping the steering wheel.

'I saw you with some punk girl in the Pavillion Gardens Thursday lunchtime.'

Mike turns his head and looks severely at me for several seconds while the car lurches onto the hard shoulder. He's quick to correct his lapse in concentration and focus on the road ahead.

'Not at work then?'

There's an edge to his voice.

'I don't have any consultations until the afternoon on Thursdays. I'd been looking at the sculpture in the gardens when I saw you. Just a coincidence.'

I hold back from telling him about my trawl around the language schools. There's an awkward silence. Mike's knuckles are white from gripping the steering wheel. His voice has an irritable edge when he next speaks.

'Look, Kate, you must just let us get on with our job.'

He turns to look at me again, this time with a smile on his face.

'Don't worry, we've got it all in hand.'

That does little to reassure me but I can think of nothing to add. A car flashes past and distracts me. I watch it disappear into the distance.

'Aren't you going after it?'

'No, I'm off duty and I'm not risking a ticket myself. This stretch of road often has unmarked police cars on patrol. I'd never catch him anyway.'

'You would in my Zuperga; it's a turbo charged sports car'

'Never heard of that.'

'It's an import. Looks like a saloon but goes like a rocket.'

He whistles. 'I remember you had an eye for fast cars. You'll have to give me a demo sometime.'

Mike switches on the sat nav as we approach the outskirts of London and its computerised voice is the only one to be heard for the rest of the journey. Mike drops me off at the garage. I'm slow to unfasten my seatbelt and he takes advantage, leaning over and planting a kiss on my cheek. I'm not sure how to respond so I get out and then pop my head back into the car to wish him goodbye. He's smiling when he drives away.

They've done a good job on my car. It looks like new. As I slip into the driver's seat and turn the ignition, the familiar throb of the flat-four boxer engine shudders through me. I smile in appreciation, even if a London street is not the place to exploit its potential. For me it's the best feeling. Steve never understood. 'What is it about a box of metal that gets you so excited?' He just didn't get it but I bet Jaq would have loved the car. I can see us spinning off together, one eye on the speedometer and one on the road.

I park the car in the garage I rent and walk the short distance to my flat. It's on the top floor overlooking the market in a short pedestrianised street. I love the sights and smells of the market stalls. The street is noisy and lively during the week but empties in the evenings and on Sundays to become a quiet oasis just a few metres from the buzz of Balham High Road. It suits me well, though Steve never understood my enthusiasm.

I buy some provisions from the market stalls and then let myself into the Edwardian terraced building, glad to close the door on the hum outside. I climb the stairs and open the inner door to my flat, stepping into its familiar space. Outside the chatter and bartering of the market continues, oblivious to how my world has changed. How strange that now seems. How can everything carry on as if nothing has happened, as if Jaq were still alive? I go into my bedroom with the empty suitcase I've brought with me from Hove. I open the wardrobe to pick out a selection of clothes to take back. This heatwave can surely not last and I need to be prepared for more usual British summer weather.

I fill the case and a sports bag with a variety of different outfits and then try listening to a CD of thirties big band arrangements. They are not the tonic I was hoping for. I eject the CD and go into the kitchen to make some lunch. I pick out a knife from the drawer then hastily put it back. It's triggered an image of Jaq's body. I was hoping some time in my own space would be good for my psyche but I'm wrong. Thoughts of Jaq lead me to concerns about where I go next in my search for Chiara. I can't delay a return to Hove but equally, I can't face another night in that hotel room. I phone Chris to ask if I can move in at once. She's her usual phlegmatic self and says she's already got a room ready for me. I give my flat a perfunctory clean as I don't know when I'll be back and force myself back into the kitchen to make a sandwich. I'm munching my way through it when I get a call on my mobile. I don't answer it at first but when it rings for a third time in succession, I check the call log. Mike's trying to contact me. He's also left a text saying *Urgent. Please call me.* He's not one for hyperbole so I ring back.

'Kate. Thank God.' He sounds out of breath. 'I'm on Clapham Common just behind the Windmill Pub. I've just been attacked. I'm in a bit of a state. Can you come. I can't move.'

'Where's your car?'

He struggles to answer. I can hear him breathing heavily. When he manages to speak, he tells me it's parked nearby but he can't get to it. I jump on the first of the frequent buses along Balham High Road. It doesn't take long for me to find him slumped on the ground with his back against a large chestnut tree. His head is bleeding from a cut above his right eye and he's clutching his abdomen. He raises his head when I call out his name but he's too beaten up to reply.

'What the hell has happened to you?'

'Later, Kate.' It's all he can manage to say.

'Where have you parked your car?'

He appears confused by the question then points back down the narrow road across the common and hands me the key. I leave him groaning on the ground and bring the car back as close to him as possible. I can't help blocking the road. I ignore the impatient car horns from the queue behind. It takes a superhuman effort on my part to help him off the ground and an even greater one from him, as he stumbles into to the car, leaning heavily on my shoulder. Mike collapses onto the back seat and I set off for Balham. I park on double yellow lines near my flat and manoeuvre him with difficulty, into the ground floor entrance hall. He crawls upstairs on all fours and flops onto the divan in the sitting room. I can smell the sweat from the effort he's made. I help him out of his cotton jacket and run off to find a more suitable parking place. It takes me half an hour, by which time Mike has fallen sleep. The dried blood against the pallor of his skin gives his face a grotesque look. I go to wake him and but he rouses of his own accord.

'I need to check you over. Can you make it to the spare room?'

He nods but only manages to get as far as the door to my bedroom when he turns green and retches. I help him into my room where he collapses onto the double bed. I undress him to get a proper look at his injuries. He moans in pain as I remove his polo shirt. Bruises are appearing over his ribs. I help him out of his chinos and see more bruising over his abdomen. He must have taken quite a beating. No evidence of broken bones but the cut above his eye is gaping and there's an egg sized swelling above it. I want to take him to A&E for a thorough check-up, but he becomes agitated when I suggest it. I resign myself to looking after him. I clean him up and apply a skin closure strip to the cut, then give him an analgesic intramuscular injection.

'So, what happened?'

'I was taken completely off-guard. I was just making my way to the pub on the common when they jumped me.'

'Who?'

'Two guys. They had south London accents, both Caucasian, one with dreadlocks, the other an albino. They were obviously after my wallet.'

His story sounds odd. He still has his wallet. It fell out of his pocket when I undressed him.

'So, they risked attacking you in the middle of the day near a busy pub?'

'You know druggies. They're desperate to get money for a fix.'

Again, I have my doubts. Mike's injuries are not typical of an opportunist grab-and-run, too vicious and too professional for a junkie.

He's soon asleep again. I watch his breathing take on the rhythm of deep sleep then take his wallet out of the back pocket of his chinos and go through it. Inside I find several ten-pound and five-pound notes, together with a credit and a debit card, his driving licence and a membership card for a London Rugby Club. I replace his wallet and go into the sitting room. His jacket is draped over the end of the sofa. I reach into the inside pocket and pull out his police identity badge and mobile phone. I check the other pockets which I find to be empty. I'm left with nothing that explains the real motive behind his assault.

I leave Mike to sleep while I try and distract myself by listening to some big band blues. The tracks follow one after the other but I'm not concentrating on them, they are no more than a background to my thoughts. I keep wondering what really happened to Mike and whether the reason for his London visit was, in fact, to see his wife. I wake him after a couple of hours. He complains that he just wants to sleep but I tell him it's necessary to keep checking him, standard head injury protocol in circumstances like his. I go off to make him a cup of tea and by the time it's ready, he's more alert and asking for a brandy. I just pass him the tea, with a couple of analgesic tablets. Later, I conjure up a ham and mushroom risotto which I insist he eats and refuse his request for a glass of wine. I perch on the end of the bed tucking into my own portion of risotto.

'So, what were you doing on Clapham Common. I thought you were seeing your wife.' I know they have a house in Earlsfield, to the west of Clapham.

'I was on my way to the Windmill pub. I was going to ring you to see if you'd join me for a drink.'

I don't know whether to believe him or not. He lies back down with a groan. Eating has exhausted him and sitting up has become too painful.

'You should get checked out at the hospital, Mike.'

'No way. You're doing a great job. I'll take the risk.'

I can't force him to go to A&E and he's in no state to drive so I resign myself to a night with an unexpected patient.

'Okay, but I'll be waking you every couple of hours. With your head injury, I'm not taking any risks.'

'Wouldn't it be better just to stay awake?'

'Well, *you* can if you like, but I need some sleep.'

I leave him to rest and pick out an original vinyl version of some progressive jazz. It cost a lot but it was worth it. I usually have no probem in losing myself in its idiosyncratic tempos but not on this occasion. Mike's presence in my bedroom is unsettling. I give up and make up the bed in the spare room for myself. When I check on Mike, he's staring at the ceiling, hollow eyed and pale, his face lined from the effort of dealing with his injuries.

'Can you get to the bathroom?' I hold out a jug. 'I need to check your urine for blood. Your kidneys may have taken a beating.'

He groans as I help him off the bed. I hand him the jug.

'Just leave it in the bathroom.'

He makes it back to bed on his own and I follow him into the room after checking the jug.

'All clear. How's the pain?'

He groans so I fetch a strong analgesic tablet which he swallows and then slumps back on the pillow. The lump on his forehead has increased in size and colour. He has dark shadows under his eyes and is still very pale. Not at all a macho-looking Mike. He suggests I sleep next to him. I undress in the spare room while I consider this. When I take a peek at him, I see he's fast asleep so I slip into bed beside him. I listen to his breathing as I lie awake thinking that Jaq and Chiara are not the only ones to have questions for me to answer.

Chapter Ten

Sunday 10 May

I wake to find myself snuggled up to Mike, though I've no recollection of shifting my position during the night. It's tempting to prolong the sensation of my body pressed close to his but I resist. I move back to my side of the bed and look at the swelling on Mike's face. Its shiny purple and green hues remind me of a psychedelic art work.

I slip out of bed to make some coffee. Mike joins me in the sitting room a short while later. He's recovered well, even if he occasionally lets out a groan when he twists or moves too quickly. Any further medical supervision is unnecessary and he's keen to get back to Brighton. I'm relieved that he doesn't want to hang around.

'Are you sure you're all right to drive?'

'No problem. You'll need to show me where you've parked the car, though.'

After he's gone, I wander along the High Road, stopping to buy a warm croissant and a steaming latte from one of the cafés nestling among the many of eating places that have sprung up in Balham over the past few years. Back at the flat, I mull over what happened to Mike. I'm sure he's lying about his mugging.

On the drive back to Hove, I run through a gamut of reasons why Mike would want to mislead me: gambling debts, broken promises to informers, bribes for useless information, drugs, failed black market dealings. None sit well with the responsibilities of his work or with the impression I formed of him as a colleague years ago. With nothing concrete to support any of my theories, I settle back to enjoy the drive, comforted by the sound of the flat-four engine as I take the car over the speed limit.

When I arrive, Charlie answers the door and tells me Chris has just popped out to get a take-away. I follow her into the sitting room where a music DVD is just ending. It reminds me of an old film that Jaq dragged me to see at uni, *The Cabinet of Dr Caligari,* expressionist and creepy.

'Do you want a drink or something?'

'That's okay, Charlie. I'll wait till Chris gets back.'

Charlie helps herself to a Campari and lemonade. She's no good at small talk and is about to watch another music DVD. I ask if she can hold off for a moment. I take out the photo of Jaq and the students in Milan and hand it to her.

'Do any of these girls look like Chiara?'

Charlie stares at the photo for a while.

'What do you think?'

'Well, she looks younger and her hair is shorter but I'm sure this is Chiara.'

She points to the girl next to Jaq. I'm elated, in the same way that I remember as a detective when I uncovered a promising lead in an investigation.

'Just one more thing and I'll let you get back to your music. You didn't have a chance to reply the other evening when I asked if you had any idea why Chiara left the bookshop basement.'

'I'm not sure but it was probably because of the men.'

Charlie seems to think she's said enough and is about to press the remote control and start the DVD. I seize the control and ignore the black look she gives me.

'What men?'

Charlie gives a sigh and takes a sip of her drink.

'They came into the shop one day while I was in the basement. I heard them shouting at Jaq and went up to see what was going on. Jaq was just telling them she had no idea where Chiara was. When they saw me, they left; Jaq was amazing, so calm. I was terrified.'

'When was that?

'Not exactly sure. Probably a couple of weeks before Jaq was k....' She can't manage to complete the word.

'Any idea why they were looking for Chiara?'

'None. Jaq wouldn't tell me but she did say she would never, ever tell them anything about Chiara.'

No wonder Jaq asked me to look out for her.

'Can you remember what these men look like?'

Charlie stares at the blank screen for a few moments.

'They were both very muscly, you know, like those bouncers you see outside clubs. One was very tall. The other had a black beard, sort of grey-black and they looked foreign to me.'

Charlie shudders.

'What sort of foreign?'

'You know, skin like with a deep tan and they smelt odd too, like stale curry. They were scary. I know Chiara was frightened of them, she kept asking me if they'd come back every time I went downstairs to make a coffee.'

'But despite that, she ran away.'

'She begged Jaq not to go to Italy. She said she didn't feel safe without her around.'

'Did you tell Jaq that Chiara had run off?'

'No. We'd had an argument earlier about her going away and leaving Chiara in the basement with just me in the shop. She even wanted to give Chiara my mobile number. I was furious and told her no way. Anyway, I didn't want to face her after that. I wasn't sure how she'd react if I told her Chiara had run off.'

Charlie restarts her DVD, just as the front door bangs shut and Chris arrives.

'Chinese take-away okay for everyone?'

We eat in the kitchen. I find it impossible to concentrate on conversation as I work out the implications of what Charlie has told me about Chiara. Until I know what they were up against, any confrontation with Mike will have to wait.

After the meal, Charlie makes an exit on the pretext of needing an evening's detox. I wisely keep to myself my medical opinion on its futility. It wouldn't change her misguided beliefs and I don't want to antagonise her. Chris and I clear the plates away after which she produces a bottle of champagne from the fridge. We take it into the sitting room and I sink into a soft leather armchair. Chris pours out the bubbly and then lounges on the sofa. We chink glasses in a toast.

'Thanks for this, Chris.'

'There's always a glass of something good in the house.' She winks at me and takes out a cigarette.

'You know what I'm getting at.'

'Well, if you're going to be my house guest for a while, first you've got to tell me about this interlude of yours in the police force.' She tilts her head back to exhale the cigarette smoke. 'How did that come about?'

'It was triggered by the death of Jaq's mother. She was killed in a car accident after Jaq graduated. Jaq was working in a London bookstore at the time and I was a junior doctor at University College Hospital. There was nothing the Emergency team could do to save her. The driver responsible was never found. Jaq became very angry. It changed her. She ended up going abroad and we lost contact. Seeing her reaction made me think about what I really wanted to do. By the time I'd finished my junior doctor training for General Practice, I'd applied and been accepted for graduate entry into the police force. There wasn't such a fast track system as now but I still made it to detective constable.'

'But you changed back to Medicine.'

'As a GP I'm more comfortable with the limits of what I can achieve. Detective work felt like an impossible task, trying to hold back an unstoppable tsunami of crime.'

'And you don't miss it?'

I think about Mike's comments. 'Perhaps, I can't help returning to old habits.'

I confess to sneaking a look at Jaq's autopsy report and I'm relieved to see Chris laugh.

'I should have seen that coming.'

'I wanted to see the detail.'

'So now you know about your friend's likely drug habit.'

'I knew she'd been a user for a long while but I thought she was trying to stay clean.'

'What's your view?'

'I just wonder if it has anything to do with her murder.'

'Shouldn't you leave that up to the investigating team?'

'Mike doesn't seem to think much of my theory.'

Chris tops up my glass and I change the subject by asking how Charlie is going to cope with my moving in.

'You were deep in conversation when I arrived. You looked as though you were getting on well.'

I tell Chris about Jaq's text and how Charlie had opened up about Jaq hiding Chiara.

'She's sworn me to secrecy.'

'Understandable. She wouldn't want to get involved with the police again. She found it bad enough being interviewed about Jaq's death.'

She stubs out her cigarette. 'What's your reaction?'

I tell her I've got no option but to chase down Chiara myself.

'Putting on your old detective shoes?'

'Not exactly, but Mike's not showing much interest in finding her.'

Chris gives me a sceptical smile.

'Charlie's said nothing of this to me but then she can be quite inscrutable at times.'

'Is that what attracted you to her?'

'You're wondering how on earth we've ended up together.'

'Well, she's not quite the type I would've expected you to go for.'

Chris picks up the cigarette packet but puts it down again.

'We're very different types, I grant you but I was on the rebound from someone I thought was *the one*. I thought I'd have a bit of fun with Charlie. She'll be off soon with someone more like herself. She's on the rebound too. She and Jaq were together for quite a few months before Jaq called it off.'

I stare at Chris.

'I had no idea Jaq was gay. When we were at uni in London, she only ever had boyfriends at least as far as I know. The last one I remember was a guy called Toby who played bass guitar in a small-time band and wrote poetry.'

I upend my glass of champagne. 'But that was a long time ago, of course.'

'Between you and me I think Charlie still carries torch for Jaq, even now.'

I spend my first night at Chris's house lying awake and thinking about what I've found out about Jaq. I would much rather she'd told me. She used to confide in me all the time when we were students together. I think back to those times when we were close, the sound of her laughter, the touch of her hand on my arm when she was surprised, the smell of the scent that she wore. She was always there for me. She always made me feel good. 'There's no one like you, Kate, never will be. What a pair we are.' I'm sure the Jaq I used to know was somewhere inside the person she'd become, waiting for our friendship to return to what it once was. I find that comforting but then the anger returns that someone has deprived us of that.

I toss around in an unfamiliar bed, wrestling with my feelings until sleep comes. It's short lived and I wake after two hours plagued with questions. If Chiara was in trouble, why hadn't Jaq got the police involved? And without Jaq's protection, where would Chiara go? I give up trying to come up with answers, pull on some clothes and leave the house.

As I hoped, walking has a calming effect. As I trudge along the empty promenade, there are no seagull cries and little traffic noise and the blackness of the sea has an eerie stillness. I imagine Chiara alone at night in a hostile city, exhausted, frightened, with nowhere to go. I think of the rough-sleepers. I hate to think of Chiara reduced to such extremes, it's worth showing the photo again to see if anyone recognises her. I head up to Church Road, where a sprint to the bus stop gets me onto the night service to Brighton station.

The scene is as depressing as that last time I was there. Unkempt men sheltering in doorways, trying to get comfortable in dirty sleeping bags, with all they possess stuffed in torn plastic bags. I can hear them mumbling to each other and the odd shout or curse. The smell is no better and I stifle a gag. Then I think again of Jaq and the compassion she would show, her words of more value than any odd coin tossed at them.

I recognize one of the guys from the previous night. I hold my breath and kneel next to him.

'Can I have a word?'

He pushes me away and I just avoid toppling over.

'You the Sally Army? I don't want none of your handouts.'

'No, I'm not from the Salvation Army. I'm here to ask your help.'

'Me? Help?' He gives a raucous laugh that ends in a coughing fit.

A succession of heads turns in our direction to see if the noise is worth more than a glance. I show him the photo.

'I just need to know if you've seen this girl.' I point to Chiara.

He looks at me as if I'm mad, then holds the photo up to get a better view from the street light.

'She's a bit young for this caper, eh.' He waves across to his companions.

'It's an old photo, taken a couple of years ago.'

He hands it back.

'Nice looker. Sorry, not seen her. Try the others.'

He indicates doorways further down the street. By the time I've finished showing the photo around, my cash is exhausted and no one has seen her. I'm about to go when one of the rough sleepers shouts out to me.

'Don't get women round here much, yer know. Try the promenade. There's a bit of a ladies' scene down there some nights.'

I thank him and trudge down to the seafront, aware that the night hours are ticking away, leaving me little time to sleep. I turn westwards towards Hove. In front of me, the wide stretch of asphalt extends into the night. I set off, searching for suitable sleeping refuges as I go. I can see none and wonder if my search should have been eastwards from the main pier instead. Keen to get at least a modicum of rest before work tomorrow, I quicken my pace only to stop shortly afterwards. I can hear someone moaning. The sound is coming from a stone shelter which I can just glimpse behind the rows of beach huts. I go over to investigate.

An unkempt woman is kneeling on top of her sleeping bag, rocking to-and-fro. She is pulling at her matted hair in despair. I kneel beside her, trying once again not to retch at the stench. She jumps up and makes to run off.

'It's all right. I only want to help.'

She crouches down beside me. I can smell alcohol on her breath.

'What's the matter.'

She gives me a wild stare. I root around in my bag to see if there's anything I can offer her. I find a cereal bar lurking in its depths and hand it over. She doesn't appear impressed but takes it nevertheless. I've nothing else to offer her. She takes a bite of the cereal bar then asks if I've got a cigarette.

'Sorry. I haven't but I was hoping you could help me.'

'Eh?' She swallows the last of the cereal bar, as incredulous as the guy at the railway station. I show her the photo and point to Chiara.

'Have you seen this girl, by any chance?'

She concentrates on the photo and then raises her eyes.

'You sure you not got a fag?'

I shake my head.

'She hated smokes, you know. Perhaps that's why she went off.'

'Who?'

'That one there.' She jabs her finger over the figure of Chiara. 'Clara, was it?'

'Chiara. You mean she was here?'

'She's gone off, she went tonight and said she ain't coming back. Left this behind too.' She holds out another rolled up sleeping bag. 'Now why she's gone off like that? We was friends. Didn't even say where she was going.'

She starts her moaning again, turned in on her own sad world of alcoholic desperation. There's nothing more I can say, so I leave her to her inner demons, with a feeling of guilt at my inadequacy in the face of her problems and angry that I've just missed out on finding Chiara.

Chapter Eleven

Monday 11 May

Monday morning brings the usual litany of post-weekend medical problems. A succession of people with summer sore throats, hay fever, tension headaches and the worried well. They force me to brush away my fatigue after last's nights efforts and push aside any thoughts about Jaq or Chiara. I have time enough for those as I make my way later to Jaq's memorial service at St Andrew's, a simple, traditional, stone and flint church, on the appropriately named Church Road. It's an anomaly set amongst a supermarket and the myriad small shops, restaurants and cafés that stretch along the road towards Brighton. Jaq once told me her parents were regulars at the church and shrugged in what I took to be an uncomprehending acceptance.

I arrive early and go through the lych-gate at the front of the church to the graveyard at the back passing along a narrow flagstone path flanked by small stone memorials. propped in front of flower vases, some full, most empty. As I glance down at the words of remembrance etched into them, I hate to think that this is all that will be left of Jaq. An overwhelming nausea makes my head spin. I take a deep breath and look up to see a dark-haired girl in a flowery dress at the far end of the graveyard. She's stooping to place something on the ground, then stands up slowly and bows her head as if in prayer. I start to walk over to her. The tap of my footsteps on the stone path alerts her. She looks over to me then darts off around the other side of the church. The similarity to the photo of Chiara is enough to make me run after her. She's too quick and by the time I reach the front of the church, she's nowhere to be seen. I make my way back to the spot she left behind, where a small posy of freesias is lying on the ground with a note balanced on top of it. I bend down to look at the handwritten words: *For Jaq, from Chiara.* I'm upset by the lost opportunity but at least I can be sure that Chiara is still here in Hove. I take a photo of the flowers and note on my phone, then switch it off ready for the service. As I walk back to the main door of the church, I see Mike coming down the path from the lych-gate.

'Hi. I didn't know you'd be here. I thought you'd be at work or is this part of your investigation?'

'You could say. Memorial services are not really my thing.'

Mike follows me into the church. There are a few people already inside. I sit towards the back and Mike sits next to me scrutinising everyone as they arrive. Charlie walks in with Chris, no doubt as her support. They sit near the front of the church, well in front of us. Mike continues to observe everyone as they come in. We're squeezed together as the number in our pew reaches its maximum. People are swelling the other pews too: middle-aged and older couples who look like relatives, friends of Jaq's parents or members of the regular congregation. Just as the service is about to begin, a solitary woman enters and takes a seat in one of the few places remaining on the opposite side of the church to us. She's heavily made-up, her black hair drawn into an old-fashioned chignon. Mike leans forward to get a better look at her. He stays on the edge of his seat throughout the service and casts intermittent glances in her direction as if keeping her under surveillance.

'Who's the women?' I whisper.

'Which women?'

'The one who just came in. The tall woman in the elegant suit. The one you keep looking at. I don't think she can be a relative or family friend; she looks more southern European.'

'I've no idea. She catches your eye, doesn't she?'

That doesn't explain why Mike's attention is more focused on her than anything else. As the organ strikes up, we all fall silent and the service begins. A large photo of Jaq has been placed below the pulpit and is surrounded by so many white lilies that the church is filled with an intense and slightly nauseous smell. The photo disturbs me. It reminds me that Jaq is no longer a warm and vibrant person but is lying in a mortuary, cold, stiff and lifeless, waiting for the coroner's verdict. The thought makes me shudder. I stare up at the stained-glass window behind the altar and blank out what follows, as hymns, prayers and eulogies echo around the church.

At the end of the service, we all file out in silence. The woman is one of the first to leave but is outside lighting a cigarette when Mike and I make our exit. As we approach her, she fixes Mike with an expression that would terrify anyone with a guilty secret, then walks off round the back of the church to the graveyard.

'Are you sure you don't know that woman? She seems to know you.'

'I could've bumped into her somewhere. You know how it is.'

Another unconvincing reply. Mike never forgets a face.

A traditional buffet lunch is waiting in the adjacent church hall but Mike doesn't stay long. He pays his condolences to Jaq's parents and then tells me he has to get back to work. I wait until he's left and then follow him out of the hall. He's heading for the graveyard and, keeping my distance, I see him deep in conversation with the woman. I return to the hall, curious to know just who she is.

The rest of the mourners have congregated in groups and I notice Chris has already left. With the exception of Charlie and myself, I can't see anyone young enough to be one of Jaq's friends. I make conversation with each group in turn, just in case I can learn something about Jaq but it's a fruitless effort. I come across no one who can tell me about Jaq's life in Hove. In the end, all I want is a stiff shot of alcohol to make it all bearable instead of the cup of tea on offer. Jaq's parents are constantly surrounded. I'm just working out how I can best squeeze through to them to say a few words, when Charlie approaches me.

'Do you think Jaq would've liked the service?'

'Not sure.' I reply, trying to gauge what Charlie thinks, though I'm certain Jaq would in no way want to be remembered as a conglomeration of hymns and prayers.

Charlie has the same idea as me. 'Not really her thing, is it?'

'No, but she would have liked that Chiara left her some flowers in the graveyard.'

Charlie looks startled by my mention of Chiara.

'I guess you didn't see them, they're round the back of the church. Shall I show you where they are?'

'No need.'

Charlie rushes out. I go to follow her but Jaq's parents approach me. They thank me for being there. I can see they're trying their best to hold back their grief. They seem to have aged since I last saw them only a few days ago.

'This must be very difficult for you.' I gesture to the people milling around and look across the room to see if Charlie has returned.

Mrs Grey gives me a hug, then excuses herself and her husband indicating the queue of people waiting to pass on their condolences. I just have time to arrange to see them later in the week before they return to their sad duties.

I walk back to the surgery in plenty of time for my first evening on duty at the Young People's Clinic. Rose explains how the clinic is organised. An informal approach is important so there's no receptionist. Rose shows me where the notes and supplies are kept and leaves me to get ready for the first teenagers to arrive. It's a busy evening as a succession of youngsters with predictable contraceptive and emotional problems comes and goes. It's not as bad as I expected and I soon tune in to the idioms and expectations of adolescents whose world is dependent on their mobile phones. At the end of the evening, I'm disappointed that Chiara hasn't shown up. I offer to lock up and, with Rose out of the way, go through the notes to see if Chiara is registered. She's not among the files, but may have given another name.

I hurry to shut up the surgery and set the alarms. As I switch off the last of the lights, I feel as if a light has gone out inside me too. I walk over to my car glad to feel the never changing touch of metal on my fingers as I open the door to get in; My car is a constant that never lets me down. It's just the therapy I need. As I settle in front of the steering wheel ready to take my car for a blast along an open road, an image of Mike talking to the unknown woman flashes into my head. I ring him on the pretext of wanting to show him what my car can do. He says he'll be free in about half an hour. I pick him up from the police station and head out of town.

'So, where are we going?'

'You'll see.'

'Are you abducting me?'

'Is that the best you can do for a joke?'

We reach the A27 dual carriageway, then turn off onto a much-used country road. He recognises the route.

'So, it's The Devil's Dyke, then.'

'Correct.'

Good luck presents me with an open road so I press down hard on the accelerator and show off the car at its best. He doesn't say a word as I exceed the speed limit and use the full torque of the car's engine to twist and turn my way to the Devil's Dyke.

We hit the top of a hill where the Sussex sky becomes a 360-degree circle around us. I crawl into the car park looking for a space. An elderly couple in walking gear are just returning to their car, no doubt anticipating a good supper. I wait until their Skoda pulls out and then slot into the empty space.

As we step onto the open land on top of the downs, the breeze blows my hair across my face. To the left, the sea stretches east and west, its shoreline throwing up landmarks that Mike points out: Brighton Marina, Brighton Pier, Shoreham Power Station. I turn my back on it all and look northwards across the Sussex Weald, with its rolling countryside, villages and tranquil forests. I remember Jaq talking of it as the epitome of rural beauty and then laughing. I hadn't asked her why she found it funny and now, when I want to, when I need to, I can't. I turn back to Mike, to avoid being swamped by the memory.

'I didn't scare you just now, did I?'

'What do you think?'

I don't tell him that it's my way of coping with stress.

'Are you going to arrest me for speeding?'

'Too much trouble.' He winks at me.

We cross the road to the Devil's Dyke itself. It's a misnomer to me. I find myself staring into a large grassy basin that sweeps steeply down from a circle of footpaths. We wander around the perimeter then walk back towards the pub which overlooks the South Downs.

'What made you come here tonight?'

'It's a place Jaq and I visited years ago. It just felt right to come back now; it's been quite a day.'

'You mean the memorial service? I must say it's been years since I spent any time in church.'

'So, why today?'

'Like you guessed, part of the investigation.'

'And did that include a discussion with that woman you don't know?'

'What do you mean?'

'I saw you together after you left the church hall.'

Mike's face darkens and, for a moment, I think he's going to explode but he composes his face into a smile and turns to me.

'She was a possible lead to Chiara but it came to nothing. I didn't want to get your hopes up.'

I look straight at him surprised that he's now showing more of an interest in tracing Chiara. He immediately shifts his eyes away from mine.

'Chiara was outside the church today. She left some flowers in the graveyard for Jaq.'

I pull out my phone and show him the photo.

He's dismissive. 'Anyone could have left them there.'

'I saw her myself and I've got more to tell, but not here.'

Mike persuades me to come back to his flat and spends the journey giving me directions. It turns out that he's renting a new-build apartment just opposite the back of Brighton Railway Station in an extensive modern conglomerate that reaches up into the sky like a series of giant filing cabinets. The flats are popular with London commuters. I have to leave my car at Brighton Station carpark, an ugly multi-story building a short distance from the flat.

Mike is fortunate in having accommodation on the opposite side to the station itself. It's on one of the higher floors and facing southeast towards the coastal expanse leading to Eastbourne. It's fitted out in a functional style but with evident good taste. I stand on the balcony looking towards the east of Brighton and beyond. High above the city, it feels like a place apart, free from the pressures and prying eyes of daily life. The sea is too distant to be seen but a light breeze drifts onto the balcony and folds itself around me. I feel relaxed in the night air. I enjoy its warmth for a few moments then step inside to join Mike.

My intention is to have one glass of wine, and then swap to coffee and get down to business. But when Mike produces a bottle of a chilled Sauvignon blanc, my intentions fade. I down the first glass all too quickly and Mike fills it up again straight away.

'I wonder why people turn to drugs when you've got such a wonderful panacea in alcohol.' I muse.

He goes back out onto the balcony and I follow him. Together we look at the night sky. It's difficult to see any stars even on such a cloudless night. All around us the lights of Brighton have stolen away their brilliance. I turn away from the view and step back inside to get the photo of Jaq and the girls in Milan. Mike closes the balcony doors and settles down on the sofa. I hand him the photo.

'Have a look at this. I found it in one of the photo albums that Jaq's parents showed me.'

He peers at it for a few moments. Then turns it over and reads the inscription on the back.

'So, what was Jaq doing at a school in Milan?'

'She spent a year there as an English Language Assistant and kept in touch with the school. She told me she used to go back every year for a visit.'

I point to the girl next to Jaq.

'That's Chiara and she was the girl I saw in the graveyard'

'Are you sure it was her? Did you get a good look?"

'Well, I wasn't that close if that's what you mean.'

'So, you could be mistaken?' He hands the photo back to me.

'Someone else has seen her recently. One of the rough sleepers.'

'And you believed him? They're so full of cheap booze, those guys, they'd say anything to get a hand-out.'

I recognize the cynical police assumptions.

'It was a woman, actually, and she was upset because Chiara had gone off and left her alone.'

Mike raises his eyebrows. 'Aren't you being rather naïve to believe that?'

I pull away from Mike in annoyance. One thing I've learnt from being a GP is to recognise genuine desperation from fake but I'm not about to point that out just to get another blast of his scepticism. I wonder how long I can keep my promise not to involve Charlie.

Mike doesn't wait for my reply but excuses himself to go off to the bathroom. I upend my glass of wine, ready to leave. He takes much longer than I expect, giving me pause to think I'm being over-sensitive. I don't want any sour notes this evening, not after the emotion of the memorial service. There's no point in sacrificing the rest of the evening for a moment's chauvinism. By the time he returns, I'm drinking the last of the bubbly and looking through the sliding glass doors at the orange flickers of the city lights. I'm ready to make some conciliatory remarks but there's no need. Mike bounds across the room in a burst of energy. His eyes are lit up as if charged with electricity and he takes me in his arms.

'No more detective work,' he whispers, while nibbling my ear.

I press myself against him. There's a sense of comfort in his embraces after a day of death and illness. His excitement is infectious and I'm soon kissing him with an urgency that takes me by surprise. He's not slow to respond and we undress each other in a frenzy of embraces and fall onto the sofa.

When I wake later in his bed, dawn is just peeping over the horizon. The open blinds are letting the city lights stream across the room. I slip out of bed and tip-toe into the sitting room to gather up my clothes from the floor. I dress in the bathroom and as I brush my hair in front of the mirror, I see a smiling face staring back at me. It's a smile that remembers the pleasure of Mike deep inside me, a comforting respite from the pain of losing Jaq. And then the reality of her death comes crashing over me and my thoughts return to the importance of finding Chiara.

Chapter Twelve

Tuesday 12 May

I'm relieved to find my car still in the station car park in the morning, with no sign of it being vandalised. Back at Chris's, I make myself a strong black coffee and take it into the garden. I'm hoping the early morning air will clear my head. One thing's certain, Mike's given no indication of Chiara being a priority for the investigating team. I summarise what I have to work on if I'm to find her: Chiara is Italian and got to know Jaq in Italy, she arrives in Hove, possibly as a language student and is hidden by Jaq in her bookshop basement. On the evening Jaq dies, Chiara runs off and ends up sleeping on the streets of Hove. But the girl I saw in the cemetery had a neat and clean appearance, not the slightest trace of being unkempt or unwashed. She must have found somewhere to shelter.

When I get to the GP surgery, I ask Rose if there are places in Hove where youngsters can go if they're homeless or in need of help. I use the pretext of getting up to speed on local facilities for my future sessions at the Young Peoples' Clinic. She tells me about a day centre for 16 to 21year olds in a converted church near the floral clock on Church Road. It's not far away and I'll have time to pop in over lunch time. Pleased with that piece of information, I get a further boost when I manage to avoid Andrew, at least until the end the morning. He strides into my room just as a mother with three toddlers stomps out of it, disgruntled at failing to get an antibiotic prescription for a sore throat. I'd struggled to explain the reason for withholding what she saw as her right. Andrew gives them a studied look as though he can smell a dysfunctional consultation.

I'm not about to share my difficulties with him. I see Andrew as one of those people who like to find someone's weak point and then exploit it. I'll not give him that chance with me. But it's not my consulting skills he has in mind.

'I hear you went to the Memorial Service for Jacqueline Grey?'

Everyone in the surgery knows about it. They also know that I attended and why. Clare made sure they were aware.

'Yes. She was a friend.'

'No funeral then?'

'That's up to the coroner. There's still a murder investigation going on, you know.'

I've no idea why he's taking an interest in Jaq now since he showed no emotion when her death was announced by Clare.

'She had psychological problems, you know.'

'Meaning exactly what?'

In response, his eyes bore into mine as if he's trying to read my thoughts. It's unnerving. I pick up my bag and leave.

There's no mistaking the day centre. It has a large sign outside the former Victorian church with bright lettering that calls out for attention. In a prominent position on a busy road and not far from Jaq's bookshop, I'm optimistic. I step inside the building to find stained-glass windows forming kaleidoscope patterns of light on an interior that bears no trace of its original function. Seemingly oblivious to a juxtaposition I find unsettling, a ginger haired woman approaches me with a friendly greeting as I enter the small reception area furnished with cheap looking orange and blue sofas. I introduce myself as Dr Green and ask if I could be shown round the facilities, explaining my involvement with the Young People's clinic. She's very obliging and as we wander around the converted church I'm impressed with what's on offer. There's a small library area with computer facilities, a café, a TV room and chill-out zone, as well as small rooms for counselling and a place to shower. My guide talks me through the various aspects of her work, as I keep a look-out to see if I can spot Chiara. There's no sign of her, so I show the woman my photo and ask if she's seen Chiara.

'She's in trouble and I'd like to help her.'

The smile disappears from the woman's face.

'Our youngsters come here expecting to be left in peace. They have various problems and we don't probe unless they open up of their own accord. We promise that they'll be safe here. For some, it's their only chance of privacy and freedom. For others, the only chance of a good meal and a shower. I can't just give out names.'

'I understand, but this girl could be in serious danger, that's why I'm trying to find her. I've discovered she's been sleeping on the streets but has disappeared.'

'You say you're a GP. Are you working with the police on this?'

'No, not at all. It's personal. I was asked to look out for her by a friend who was sheltering her. Look.' I show her Jaq's text. 'The person who sent this text has just died without being able to give me more details. I'm really concerned for Chiara.'

As I go to put my phone back in my bag, I see a couple of girls looking over at us. One of them, an overweight teenager with dyed blond hair, shifts a bit closer as if trying to overhear what we're saying. She catches my eye, as if she has something she wants to tell me. I raise my voice and repeat my concern that Chiara could be in danger but the woman is adamant in her refusal to disclose anything to me. I catch the girl's eye again before leaving and wait outside the entrance with my fingers crossed. She soon appears and comes straight up to me.

'About that girl Chiara, she was here, you know. Helen can't say anything, she's not allowed but it's not the same for me.

Chiara told me she was scared but would never say why. She said she was waiting for someone called Jaq to come back from abroad and help her, is that you?'

'No, she had an accident and can't help her. I'm a friend.'

'Oh.'

She seems reluctant to say any more. I get out my phone and find Jaq's text message about Chiara.

'Have a look at this.'

That seems to convince her so I show her the photo and ask if she recognises any of the girls. She points to Chiara.

'That's her. She was coming here every day but I've not seen her since Saturday. I hope she's okay. I really like her. Italian, isn't she? I hope you find her.'

We exchange mobile numbers in case Chiara shows up at the centre. I thank her for her help, then walk back to the surgery. At the end of my afternoon session, I phone Mike to tell him I've got another ID on Chiara. He asks me to bring over the photo and we arrange to meet after my visit to Jaq's parents' tomorrow afternoon.

Back at Chris's I bump into Charlie in the hallway on her way out. She pushes past me but only gets as far as the front door when her phone rings. She answers the call and I hear a few expletives as I reach the foot of the stairs. She turns away from the front door with a scowl on her face.

'Some people. No thought for anyone else. They just change their mind willy-nilly.'

I've no idea what she's talking about but I smile at her choice of words.

'It's not funny. I've got no one to go to this exhibition with, now.'

'I could join you,' I suggest.

Charlie frowns. 'Are you into contemporary sculpture?'

'Paintings are more my thing but I'm happy to tag along.'

I'm not going to let a chance to talk to Charlie slip away.

'It's on at the Warehouse in Brighton. Jaq used to rave about the sculptor.'

I had no idea Jaq was interested in the plastic arts. When she came to London, we'd concentrate on our favourite paintings: impressionist works or modernist masters.

We go by bus and sit upstairs. I watch other double-deckers pass in the opposite direction, amused to see they've all been named after someone more, or usually less, famous. I can't see any logic behind the choices. I guess they're all connected to the area one way or another. Charlie keeps up an incessant commentary, rather like a tour guide. I hide my embarrassment behind a studied silence. As we pass down Church Road, I see Jaq's bookshop, dark and shut up. I've avoided walking past it again. I notice the red and white police cordon is still in place. I turn to Charlie to make a comment but she doesn't hear or pretends not to. She's concentrating on tapping out a text.

The warehouse itself is a damp and uninviting shell of a building, but inside we're met with an explosion of vibrant colours, heart-stopping in their intensity. Geometric structures of vivid yellow and orange are spread around the place. Vibrant greens mix with startling bright blues. I wander about, gripped by the scale the exhibition. The last piece I look at stands in the centre of the space. Charlie and I walk around it staring at the undulating coils of blood red rope. The description on the stand next to the exhibit cites its eroticism but, for me, there's something disturbing, something macabre about it. I take a step back and realise that it evokes the image of Jaq's body circled in a red coil of her own congealing blood.

'I find that very unsettling.' I turn away. 'It reminds me of Jaq. What do you think, Charlie?'

'It's very powerful, but I can't see what it has to do with Jaq.'

I don't elaborate but shift the conversation towards Jaq's past.

'You know Jaq never told me she loved sculpture. Funny what you find out about someone after they've died. Like Jaq's cocaine habit. She told me she wanted to stay clean but she didn't appear to be getting anywhere. Did she talk to you about it?'

'Not about giving up. The odd bit of coke, it's no big deal, you know. I use it sometimes, mostly if I can get it for free.'

I wonder if I'm the only person in Brighton and Hove not to use the stuff.

'Any idea how deep she was into the drug scene?'

Charlie looks puzzled.

'Was it just the odd line or a lot more than that?'

'I can't say for sure. She always had plenty around. She was never short of it. She'd give some to me anytime I wanted, especially these last months.'

'Do you know where she got her supplies?'

'No idea but I never had to pay her for it.'

'Did she have any problems with money because of her habit?'

'I wouldn't know, she never talked about things like that.'

Charlie stares at me with a disgruntled expression on her face.

'What's this? Some sort of interrogation?'

'Sorry. I'm just trying to piece together Jaq's life in Hove.'

I decide we both need a drink. I ask her if there are any good bars nearby.

'There's one I like just across the road.'

She marches through the door without bothering to hold it open for me. The noise in the bar is at such a level that any conversation is going to be difficult but I like the place. The smell from the on-view kitchen area behind the counter is inviting.

'Can you grab a menu?' I shout at her.

We find a seat in a corner away from the main bustle of the bar area. They serve Thai food. We order some Pad Thai to share. There's a cocktail menu too. I settle on a martini and Charlie orders something blue and luminous with a rude sounding name. Drinking and eating together helps to overcome Charlie's fit of pique and she's soon chattering away again, though I can't hear the majority of what she's saying. After our third cocktail, I steer Charlie out of the bar and towards the promenade and a dose of sea air. She links her arm in mine in a confidential way that I accept, though it feels rather odd. We walk along from the pier towards Hove. After the Peace Statue we park ourselves on a bench overlooking the beach. The sky and sea seem to merge into one another and the sounds of the waves are like repeated sighs punctuated by the screams of the seagulls.

'Sometimes I can't believe she's gone.'

Charlie's words are slurred and emotional. She's on the brink of pouring out her grief. I seize the moment.

'What happened when you last saw Jaq, Charlie?'

'Why?'

'It might help me understand why she died like she did.'

I let my words hang in the air.

'I can't see how.'

'When *did* you last see her?' I ask gently.

She doesn't answer. I ramp up my question.

'Were you there when she died?'

I don't believe Charlie capable of the sort of violence that led to Jaq's death but I have to see how much she knows.

'No, I wasn't. Just what are you getting at?'

'Don't you have any idea, who could have killed her?'

'How would I know?' Her face has turned as white as the crests of the waves.

'I just thought.....'

'Will you just stop getting at me.' Her hands are trembling as she shouts at me. 'I've already been through it all with the police.'

I've gone too far. She stomps off along the promenade. I let her go. I'll get nothing more out of her now. I blame myself for antagonising Charlie. As a GP, I know only too well that it's a mistake to push too hard. I've left myself with the unenviable task of having to tackle her again.

Chapter Thirteen

Wednesday 13 May

I remind myself to be more tactful as I approach Jaq's parents in the afternoon. Again, June answers the bell as if she has been waiting behind the door for me. She shows me into the front sitting room and walks across the room, pointing out of the window to the expanse of Hove Park opposite.

'Those trees will outlive us all,' she comments. 'It's a comfort in a way.'

'They're splendid.' I make a vague gesture towards the park.

Jaq's mother smiles and asks if I'd prefer tea or coffee. I opt for the latter and she suggests I make myself comfortable while she prepares it. Her husband arrives a couple of minutes later.

'Excuse my clothes. I've been doing a spot of gardening and I lost track of time. It takes my mind off things.'

He sits down on the old-fashioned chesterfield opposite me. The smell of its faded leather fills the room.

'Jacqueline was always talking about you, you know. We made sure to pass on those birthday and Christmas cards that you sent to her.

At least now I know that she received them, even if she never replied.

June returns with the coffee and some sweet biscuits.

'We're glad you came to the memorial service,' says John. 'It's a pity we couldn't contact more of her friends.'

There's an awkward silence until I introduce the subject of the bookshop and whether they have any plans for it.

'We're not sure what to do about it.' June stares down at her cup.

John explains. 'We've had Jaq's mail redirected to us and one of the letters was from her accountant. We've discovered that until a couple of years ago, the shop was only just making ends meet. Then the debts began piling up until the last few of months when she'd been making an effort to pay back some of what she owed.'

'It will take a bit of sorting out,' June adds. 'We were wondering whether we should get someone else to take over the lease or just close it down.'

'It would be a pity if the bookshop shut. There aren't many independents left now.' I hate to think of Jaq's passion consigned to nothingness.

'I don't know. In a way I'd rather it was gone.' June is still staring into her cup as if it will give her the answer.

'Anyway, we'll have to sort something out soon. It's silly to keep on paying rent with no income coming in.' John clearly prefers to focus on more practical matters.

Another silence threatens so I ask the question that has been on my mind ever since I arrived.

'Would you mind if I went up to Jaq's room now?'

'Of course. You might like to choose one of Jacqueline's books, as a memento. Her room is the first left at the top of the stairs. It's the same one you used to share when you came to stay all those years ago.'

I feel like an intruder as I climb the stairs. I close the door behind me and can't help thinking of Miss Havisham from my GCSE studies of *Great Expectations*. But Jaq's bolthole is neither dusty nor frozen in a past era. It's more like visiting a ghost locked into the present. As I enter, I feel Jaq is there. The aroma of her favourite perfume still hangs in the air. I remember its characteristic smell from our uni days. Chanel No 5, an extravagance of hers. She always wore it despite my disliking the smell of any perfume but I tolerated it for her. I never allowed Steve the same liberty with aftershave.

I look around the room, hesitant about searching it. Rifling through Jaq's cupboards and drawers feels intrusive. I do it as quickly as possible and make sure to leave things as I find them. There's not much else to examine and I've not come across anything that could help lead me to Chiara. The only place left to look is under the bed so I kneel down and feel under the bed frame, aware that if Jaq's parents come in it will look extremely odd. This time, though, I get a result. As I run my hand along the underside of the bed, something falls on the floor. I pick it up, intrigued to see what I've discovered. It proves to be a clear plastic bag full of a white powder. I can guess what it is. I hurry to put it in my handbag with a guilty feeling that I'm betraying June and John's hospitality. I grab a book from one of the shelves and rush out of the room.

It's a relief to take my leave and cross the road to the park where I walk round and round its twisting paths, taking the time to think. I circle the green spaces and trees along the tarmac pathways. I pass wooden constructions for circuit training and gym work, a tiny children's railway, a playground and tennis courts. I pay only fleeting attention to them as I grapple with what I've just found. It's a lot of cocaine for personal use but the thought that Jaq could have been a dealer sends shivers through me.

I slump down on a bench, overwhelmed by a strange fatigue that clouds my brain. The sounds of the children playing reach me as a distant hum, like a background of white noise. I close my eyes and let my thoughts wander back to my uni days with Jaq: the noisy, smoke-filled bar where we would down a few glasses of wine together, the tatty, top floor flat under the eaves that we shared near Fitzroy Square, the clubbing in randomly selected nightclubs on a Saturday night, the parties in seedy basements reeking of pot. Why couldn't Jaq have stuck to a joint or two instead of getting involved with hard drugs? Or better still, been satisfied with a few glasses of wine. I force myself back to the present. I'm most likely in possession of a Class A drug and Class A drugs are a matter for the police.

I call Mike to see if he's free. No answer. I sign off as the voice message kicks in and I brace myself for another visit to the police station. I call a cab to save time.

The station is on the cusp of its usual busy evening.

'What'd'yer mean, yer ain't gonna do nuffinck?'

She's at the reception counter, a young girl in grubby cargo pants and a tight-fitting tee shirt, dropping cigarette ash onto the counter and jabbing a skinny finger onto the glass petition between her and the woman behind it. A stench of vomit adds to the scene. I decide to ring Mike later and turn to leave but a hand on my arm and a familiar voice holds me back.

'Kate. You're lucky to catch me. I've just finished here.'

'I tried ringing to see if you were free, but no reply.'

'I've been interviewing. Come on through.'

I sneak a sideways look at the girl who's now shouting out her complaint. Mike winks at me, then ushers me into the main office. I accept his offer of a coffee. While he goes off to get it, I wander around the room. In one sense it's like any open plan office but there's something about it, a familiarity that immediately connects with me. It's the end of the day and there's no one at the desks, just the odd computer flickering in the darkness, waiting for someone to return from a call-out. I have an urge to get my feet under one of the desks and log on to the police database and be part of it again. I'm just about to sit down to see what it would feel like when Mike comes back into the room.

He hands me a plastic cup. 'Here you are.'

I cover my awkwardness at almost being caught in front of a police computer by drinking half the coffee immediately and burning my tongue. We go into his office and sit facing each other across his desk. I start fidgeting with my bag as Mike leans towards me.

'So, have you got the photo?'

I hand it over and he puts the photo in his pocket instead of filing it away in Jaq's dossier. I'm glad I took a photocopy of it for myself.

'I've got something else for you too.'

I pull out the plastic bag and give it to him. He frowns and indicates for me to put it on the desk. He gets out some tweezers and uses them to hold the plastic bag up to the light.

'Where did you get this?' His tone is so accusatory that my instinct is to hit back at him.

'Well, I didn't get it off a supermarket shelf.'

'Kate, it's not a joke.'

'I know that. I found it in Jaq's room.'

His reaction is like a volcanic eruption.

'What the hell do you mean, in her room? The flat's totally off limits. How the hell did you get in. Who do you think you are, some sort of private Dick?'

I remember how much Mike hates private investigators.

'Hang on a minute, Mike.'

'No, you hang on, Kate. Taking an interest in Jaq's case is one thing but acting like you're still a detective is just not on. Your fingerprints will be all over this too.' He points to the plastic bag.

I'm tempted to shout back at him but decide his remorse will be satisfaction enough if I can get him to listen.

'Stop jumping to conclusions and let me explain.'

He glares at me but lets me speak. I take pains to go over the circumstances of my discovery and then wait for his reaction. He appears to be struggling for the right words.

'Sorry about the outburst. Too much work and not enough time or manpower.'

Same old story. It hardly explains such a vehement outburst. He should be used to dealing with the stress.

'I'd be surprised if it's not cocaine and it's a lot just for personal use. It must be worth quite a bit on the streets. You'll have to look into that now, surely.'

He looks as though he's about to erupt again.

'How many times do I have to tell you to back off the drug angle, Kate?'

He finishes his coffee and runs his fingers through his hair.

I ignore his antagonist behaviour.

'Won't you be needing a statement from me?'

He pushes a piece of paper over to me and hands me a pen.

'Just a few lines will do.'

I scribble away for a while, then add my signature and the date and hand it back to him. He puts the paper in the desk drawer with the bag of presumed cocaine. All a bit irregular, but I'm not going to risk his wrath by questioning his actions, I just want to get out of the station.

I walk down to Churchill Square to get a bus back to Chris's house. I can't stop thinking about Mike's behaviour. His outburst was unexpected and excessive and his sweeping the bag of cocaine and my statement into a drawer rather odd.

I find Chris alone in the sitting room, hunched over a post-supper coffee. There are already a few cigarette stubs in the ashtray. I'm starving but ignore my hunger pangs and join her.

'How did it go with Jaq's parents?' she asks.

'It was sad to see them so upset and it's going to get worse.'

I tell her I found in Jaq's bedroom then take a sip of my coffee, waiting for Chris's response.

'Did you say anything to Jaq's parents?'

'No, I just handed it in to Mike for analysis and here's the strange thing. He just stuffed it in a drawer and got me to scribble something down instead of following the normal procedure. He said he'd sort it out later. I didn't like to query it. If I challenge him on anything, he just accuses me of meddling.'

Chris takes a large gulp of brandy.

'Are you a medic or a frustrated detective? No wonder Mike keeps warning you not to get involved. Have you considered just stepping back and letting him get on with his work?'

Chapter Fourteen

Thursday 14 May

I lie awake wondering about Chris's suggestion. It's still plaguing me in the morning. I run through what I've discovered so far and consider whether I have been getting too involved. Perhaps Mike is right to remind me I'm not part of the police investigation and out-of-touch with current *modus operandi*. I've been away from detective work for a long while. But I can't ignore my increasing doubts about Mike and his handling of the investigation. I think of his reluctance to search for Chiara, his initial reassurance about my involvement with Jaq's death and then setting me up for an interrogation, his refusal to consider drugs as a motivation for Jaq's murder, his conversation with the woman at the church, the irregular way he dealt with what I'd found in Jaq's room, his sudden mood changes and his evasiveness about meeting up with the punk girl.

After all, a GP uncovers a pattern of symptoms and comes up with a diagnosis just as a homicide detective uncovers a pattern of events and evidence and comes up with a murderer's identity. It's not so very different. If Mike's trying to undermine my search for answers, I'm going to find out why.

My first move is to hop on a bus at the end of the day. I'm going to take a closer look at what drew Mike to the house in

Regent Street with the punk girl. My assumption that he was getting information on Jaq's case could be misplaced. I get off at North Street and walk across the Pavilion gardens towards the back streets. I plan to knock on the door and see where that leads me but I'm a few yards from the house, when a guy stumbles out. He turns to face the person who's trying to shut the door on him. I can see he's bubbling over with anger, even if I can't hear what he's saying. The door is soon slammed in his face. He continues his ranting as I approach him thinking it may be the most reckless thing I've ever done. He could be a paranoid schizophrenic with a potentially lethal knife in his pocket. He looks at me with loathing.

'What you staring at?'

I ignore the question. 'That was nasty to throw you out on the street. No one should treat you like that.'

He loses his angry expression.

'You some do-gooder. Don't want none of them. Meddlers they are.'

'What *do* you want?'

'You a cop?'

'No.'

'What you think I want?'

He holds out his arms which are covered in needle marks.

'Their shit ain't no good anyways..' He looks back at the house. 'Think you can help with that, eh?'

'Ever tried giving up?'

'You nuts? Them programmes are a load of crap.'

'I....'

He interrupts me. 'You got a fiver?'

I look at him. We both know what that means.

'No, guess not.'

He slopes off down the street, his anger exhausted. There's no need to gain entry to the house now; it's a point of supply for hard drugs. It's a good bet Mike's encounter with the punk girl was to get a supply for personal use. If so, it's no wonder he's reluctant to put forward drugs as a motive for Jaq's murder. Too close to home and it could well explain his recent odd behaviour but I have to find a way of being sure.

There's no one in when I get back to the house so I eat in the kitchen. After a microwaved lasagne which I vow never again to buy, I drown the taste with a very decent Valpolicella then pick up my phone and ring Mike. I invite him out for a meal the next evening.

'I thought some chill-out time would do you good. How about that Chinese restaurant at the bottom of Preston Street?'

'Is this a devious way to get me to talk about Jaq's investigation?'

'No, no. I mean it, just a bit of time out for us both.'

'In that case, I've got a better idea. Just give me a sec and I'll get back to you.'

I'm wondering just what he means but I don't have to wait long for his call.

'I've got a reservation at The Meadow. It's got a Michelin star so you can dress up a bit.'

I look up the restaurant on the internet. It's on Western Road and the photo shows a corner site building, which could once have been a bank. I'm curious at Mike's choice, he's always been known more as a curry or burger type of guy. But whether high-end cuisine or take-away chain food, it doesn't change my plan for the evening.

Chapter Fifteen

Friday 15 May

Mike gives me a peck on the cheek when I arrive outside the restaurant.

'You look stunning, Kate.'

I've dug out my little black lacy designer dress and matching stiletto heels for the occasion, two extravagances that Steve persuaded me into a few years ago, now very rarely worn. I acknowledge Mike's compliment in my usual awkward manner. Mike has changed from his dull grey work suit into chinos and a tasteful crumpled linen jacket that I'm sure is worn with the same frequency as my outfit.

The maître d' settles us into our seats. I slip into mine with what I hope is aplomb while Mike betrays his discomfort at the attention by tripping on a chair leg. He orders an aperitif for us both and we chink glasses.

'Santé.'

'Santé,' Mike replies with a heavy English accent.

I stifle a giggle. 'I thought a French toast appropriate given the setting. Just how did you get a reservation at such short notice? When I checked the website, they warned of a waiting list of weeks.'

Before Mike can reply, he's approached by an elegant slim man, perfect teeth and sleek grey hair and emanating a confidence that only wealth can provide. I watch as they exchange greetings and a few pleasantries which include Mike introducing me. I deduce that he's the owner of the restaurant, which Mike later confirms.

'Good to see you, Mike.' He shakes his hand a second time and gives me a farewell nod. 'Anything you want, just ask.'

Mike gives me an explanation for the familiarity without my asking.

'I busted his daughter for possession of cocaine recently. I did him a favour by just giving her a caution; I thought I'd call in the favour.'

'Hence the last-minute booking.'

And there's more. The waiter arrives with a complimentary bottle of champagne. When I see the label, I park my ethical doubts about the evening and decide to make the most of the occasion. I justify this by recalling what I'm here to achieve.

Mike has relaxed now and after ordering, he takes himself off to the bathroom. He returns with the exaggerated energy and sparkle in his eyes that is consistent with what I suspect to be the cause. He takes a sip of the champagne and sits back in his chair. I comment that his injury is healing well.

'You did a good job there.'

'It looks as if you had quite a professional work over.'

'Is that your opinion as a doctor or as an ex-detective.'

'I'll let you decide.'

'You know you were a good cop. It's a pity you left us. What made you go back to Medicine?'

'Medicine's a bit like detective work except that you don't see everyone as a potential criminal.'

'It's a phase you go through.'

'I think I got stuck in it.'

'So now you see everyone as a patient.'

I laugh. 'Not exactly.'

'And is being a GP as stimulating as being a detective?'

'Pattern recognition, memory work, piecing together a puzzle, coming up with answers, it's the same for both.'

Mike purses his lips as if trying to decide whether he agrees or not.

'Interesting idea,' he says, at last. 'Anyway, how come you've ended up in Hove?'

'I'd had enough of being a full-time partner and I wanted a change of scene. When I split up from Steve, it was the right moment to move somewhere else for a while. I like the flexibility of locum work.'

'That's not really answered the question. Was your friend Jacqueline Grey one of the reasons you came to Hove?'

I laugh. The detective in Mike is never far from the surface.

'She'd got in touch with me after years of not responding to my messages. It was a chance to get back a friendship I thought I'd lost forever. It just so happened a locum job came up here at the right time. Jaq was keen for me to take it and move in with her, so I did.'

'Have you thought of bailing out and going back to London, now that she's gone?'

'I thought we'd agreed not to talk about her?'

Mike holds up his hands in surrender and we talk instead about our mutual experiences of London. By the time the main course arrives, we've started on a bottle of a full-bodied Cabernet Sauvignon wine. I'm still eating my guinea fowl with porcini mushrooms as Mike takes the last forkful of his classic steak *au poivre*.

When we have both finished, we sit back as our plates are cleared and our glasses refreshed with the last of the wine. Mike then leans towards me with an intensity in his eyes that gives the impression he's about to kiss me. I shift my chair back to prevent an inappropriate display of emotion just as a notification tone rings on his mobile. He pulls it out of his jacket pocket and taps out a rapid reply to the message. I can see it's unlike the touchscreen phone I found when he was asleep in my London flat. This one is a slider phone with a separate keyboard. He finishes his message just as the waiter brings the dessert menu. Mike puts his phone on the table and takes the menu. He notices I'm staring at it. He snatches it up and tucks it into the inside pocket of his jacket.

'My work phone,' he says. 'I wish they wouldn't call when I'm off duty.'

Mike avoids looking at me and studies the menu in silence. He chooses a chocolate fondant when the waiter returns for our order. There's a moment's awkward silence and then Mike asks if I like jazz music. He surprises me with his admission that he used to play saxophone in a band. When I confess to being an enthusiast for the music of the Beatles, he raises an eyebrow in surprise.

'My friends say I'm a fanatic. What sort of jazz do you go for?'

He reels off names that I've never heard of with the exception of Dave Brubeck.

'Well, if you offer me a nightcap, you can introduce me to one or two of your favourites.'

'Good idea. We'll skip coffee.'

In the taxi he reaches for my hand and gives it a squeeze. At the flat Mike keeps the lights low and chooses a Miles Davies CD, leaving me to listen to it as he disappears off to the bathroom. When he returns, he has a wide grin on his face and strides across the room as if he could take on the whole world single handed. He comes over to me and draws me close. I can feel his excitement. A first tentative touch of our lips, morphs into a passionate kiss and I close my eyes and give myself up to my feelings. We make love on the sofa, not waiting to properly undress, just like a couple of impatient teenagers. Mike gives the impression of being fifteen rather than approaching fifty.

We move into the bedroom where we undress each other slowly and take time to enjoy the intensity of the moment. Afterwards, I wait until Mike's breathing indicates that he's fallen into a deep sleep. When I'm sure he won't wake, I slide out from under the duvet and feel for my handbag in the dark. I grope around inside it for my mobile and manage to spill the contents of the bag onto the floor in the process. I switch on the phone's torch and creep into the bathroom for a look around. I pick out the first signs, a few tiny specs of white powder against the fashionable dark grey floor tiles. I root around in the bathroom cabinet and find what I was expecting, tucked at the back behind a cannister of shaving foam and a large pack of safety razors. I tip a few grains of the white powder into a plastic specimen bag from my handbag and close the seal. My next task will be to find a way to get it analysed. I tip-toe back to bed and sink into a deep sleep, just before dawn creeps over the skyline.

Chapter Sixteen

Saturday 16 May

A few hours later, I open my eyes to bright sunlight creeping around the edges of the blinds. Mike is still oblivious to the world, deep in a post-coital sleep. I deserve to have the mother of all headaches but have avoided it, no doubt due to the good quality of the wine last night. I stretch out slowly and gently so as not to disturb Mike. He stirs, turns away from me and sleeps on. I slip out of bed, and disentangle my clothes from a heap in the centre of the room. I dress in the ensuite, after a rudimentary wash, thinking about the cocaine in the bathroom cabinet. Mike is still sleeping when I creep back into the bedroom. His touchscreen mobile is on the bedside locker but there's no sign of the slider phone. I kneel on the floor to collect up the contents of my handbag which are scattered among Mike's discarded clothes: a motley collection of pens, pencils, make-up, a packet of tissues, various bits of paper and my purse. I stuff them into my handbag and slip out of the room. He has left his jacket over the back of a dining chair. I go through the pockets. The slider phone is there. It's turned on but is protected by a pin code. I stare at it in frustration then replace the phone and scribble a few words on the back of an old receipt. I'm out of the flat before Mike appears.

I make my way to the esplanade and walk back along the seafront. I'm conscious of how incongruous my clothes must appear but no one pays me the slightest attention. One solitary female in an elegant evening dress on a Saturday morning in Brighton is not worth the flutter of an eyelash or a second look from the morning joggers, early day trippers or strolling couples and families.

The festival's outdoor events are already underway. As I reach the Hove end of the promenade the exuberance of Brighton has spilled over onto Hove Lawns and I make my way past children in fancy dress, small magicians, miniature Jedi warriors, princesses, and witches scurrying about with squeals of delight. The air is warm. It wraps itself around me like a second skin and I feel good. It builds on the memory of my night with Mike. There's no point in denying the sexual chemistry between the two of us but it's not a simple pleasure like enjoying the sun on my skin.

I sit down at a beachside café and order an americano and a croissant to offset the effects of last night's alcohol. I rummage around in my bag for my purse only to realise the key to my car is missing. I must have left it at Mike's. I send him a text straight away. He confirms he's found the key.

Can I collect it sometime today?

I'm just off to London.

Tomorrow then?

OK. Be in touch.

He doesn't give a reason for his trip. I leave the café and cross the road to the beach where I take off my shoes. It's a relief to go bare foot. I have a blister on both big toes from walking in stilettos. I can see one or two morning swimmers and I remember the hot summer day when Jaq and I set out to see who could swim farthest from the shore. She won. She was always more daring than me. I start to pick my way down the shingle slope to the shoreline and it's then that I see her. Her long dark hair falls down over a gypsy-style white blouse and the sea is already soaking her bright red skirt as she wades deeper into the water. She stops and turns to look back towards the promenade. I recognise her at once.

Ahead of her, I know the beach slopes suddenly. She'll be out of her depth soon but she continues to move forward as if she wants the sea to swallow her. I shout out but she can't hear. No one is paying any attention to her. I dash across the shingle, throwing my bag and shoes onto the beach before I plough through the water after her, ignoring the risk to us both.

I have to slow down as the water deepens but I manage to get to her just as the waves reach my shoulders. I grab her from behind. Surprised by the unexpected tackle, she doesn't resist as I drag her back onto the beach. We collapse onto the shingle, both breathing heavily and soaking wet. I heave myself into a sitting position and see a couple of teenage girls standing over us.

'Wow. That was cool.'

They have my shoes and bag in their hands and I try my best to smile as they hand them to me. 'Thanks.'

They slope off along the promenade, giggling as if they've just seen some crazy festival performance.

I turn back to Chiara and coax her to sit up. Her long hair has fallen over her face. I gently smooth it back and whisper her name.

'Sorry if I hurt you, but the water gets deep very quickly here.'

She buries her face in her hands and sobs.

I hold her close to me.

'Don't worry, Chiara. It's going to be all right?'

She pulls away from me.

'How you know my name?'

'I'm a friend of Jaq. I have a photo of you with her outside a school in Milan.'

'You are Doctor Kate, then.'

'That's right.'

'Jaqi is telling me of you; she says to trust you.'

She turns around to look back at the promenade, trembling.

'Why don't you come back to my place, Chiara, and tell me about what's happened to you.'

I help her to stand and we scramble up the beach. She stops for a moment as she reaches the end of the shingle and looks around her.

'What's the matter? Shall we sit down for a while?'

I lead her into one of the shelters. She's still shaking. I chat about Chris's house and where I work to put her at ease.

'A lot of young girls come to see me with their problems. There's a special time for them at the doctor's practice where I work.'

All the time her eyes are darting up and down the promenade as if she's on the look-out for someone.

'Here, have a look at this.'

I pull out a business card from my handbag which has the name and address and details of the clinic and a photo of the premises on the back. Rose insisted I carry a supply with me so I can leave them around the pubs and cafés in Hove. She takes the card then stands up to get a better view of the people passing by. I see her eyes show nothing but fear.

'I must go. It is not safe here.'

I grab her arm but she pulls herself free and sprints off along the promenade. I see two men dodging the crowds and heading in her direction. Both have a muscular build and olive skin and one has a beard. They're a good match for Charlie's description of the guys who came into Jaq's bookshop, looking for Chiara. If they're out to catch her, it won't take them long. I run towards them and fling myself at the shorter of the two. He stumbles and knocks the other guy to the ground. As they scramble to their feet, I dart across the road and lose myself in the crowds. I hope I've given Chiara enough time to get away.

There's no sign of her as I walk bare-foot all the way back to Chris's house. I arrive bedraggled and disheartened. People are already wandering around looking at the exhibits of the *Open House*. Chris is just leaving for a meeting in London.

She gives me a quick top-to-toe examination. I glance down at my Versace dress which has had its last outing.

'What happened?'

'Long story. I'll tell you later.'

I shower and change and I'm munching away on a cupcake in the kitchen about to phone Charlie, when she comes in. She helps herself to a coffee and I ask her if she's seen Chiara.

'Why?'

'I think she's in trouble.'

'And what makes think that?'

Charlie fidgets with the sugar spoon, scooping up grains and then letting them drop back into the bowl. She stops and goes over to the sink with her cup, pouring away the remains of her coffee.

'I saw two men chasing her on Brighton seafront. They looked like those guys you described in the bookshop. She's not contacted you then?'

'Why would she?' Charlie jumps up. 'Gotta go.' She rushes out of the room.

Startled by Charlie's reaction, I follow her and look around downstairs expecting to see her surrounded by her artist friends but I can see no sign of her. I go up to my room and flop onto the bed where I replay my encounter with Chiara. I'm frustrated she's slipped away from me. There's a slim chance that she may turn up at the Young People's Clinic but I'm not hopeful. All I can do is head back to the seafront and look for her.

I reach the promenade and pull out the photo of Chiara and ask passers-by if they've seen her. Most are happy to help but no one recognises her. I make my way along the esplanade to the beachfront café just across from Walsingham Road. I pass beach hut after beach hut, all with pale green roofs but otherwise painted in varying colours of bright yellow, dull red, purple, apricot and various shades of blue. Jaq told me that the café is a meeting place for language students. The roar of the traffic along Kingsway is eclipsed by their chatter as they sit at the tables or mill around on the tarmac or the pebbly beach. Snatches of conversation drift towards me and I recognise the odd foreign word or phrase.

I overhear one group laughing at the oddity of English spelling and the difficulties of our pronunciation. They all seem to speak quite good English so I show them the photo of Chiara outside the school in Italy and ask if they've seen her. They shake their heads so I move on to another group with the same result. I'm about to postpone my search, when a tall, dark haired, swarthy guy comes up to me and asks in a heavy accent,

'Just why you want to know where she be?'

I feel uncomfortable at his tone of voice, not exactly threatening but certainly challenging.

'A close friend of mine has just died and she asked me to look out for her. She sent me a message saying she was in some kind of trouble. I want to help her.'

He takes a swig of his lager and fixes me hard in the eye.

'You not telling me the lies?'

'No. Not at all. I'm very concerned about her, believe me.'

There's a silence filled only by the background chatter around us.

'I see her, you know. She come here and want a drink. She is having no money but looked sad so I buy her one.'

'When was that?'

'About two hours gone by.'

'Was she on her own?'

'I see no one with her.'

I feel my muscles relax in relief.

'Did she stay long?'

'Only for the drink. Then she say she is going.'

'Going where?'

He shakes his head.

Not much help in finding Chiara, but at least I can be hopeful the men haven't caught up with her. I wonder where she was heading. The Day Centre isn't open at weekends and the only other place I can think of is the bookshop. The police cordon must be off by now. I jog along the seafront and turn up the expanse of Grand Avenue and then take a left turn at the crossroads along Church Road. I pass an eclectic mix of restaurants: Italian, Spanish, Lebanese, Thai, Indian, Chinese and French. It reminds me of Balham High Street and how similar Jaq and I were in loving the vibes of city life.

When I reach the bookshop, the police cordon has indeed gone. The shop is in darkness so I press my face up against the window to get a better view. There's no sign of anyone inside just shelves of books waiting for customers. I think of how Jaq might have brought in pastries for her coffee-break, and I wonder if she had an Italian Moka for making an authentic expresso. I can see no piles of unopened mail so I guess that Jaq's parents have already made a start on sorting out the shop. That gives me an idea. I phone them and ask if they need any help the next day. They're delighted with my suggestion.

I spend the rest of the evening slumped on the sofa, half-watching a 1940s film noir while thinking about Mike, his cocaine habit and that second mobile.

Chris returns just after midnight and finds me still on the sofa, in the dark and staring at muted TV images of Sky News.

'Mind if I put on the light?'

She does so before I have time to answer, then gestures to the soundless screen.

'Is that a new hobby?'

'It's like looking at a flickering fire. It helps me think. Must be its hypnotic quality, at least if you don't pay too much attention and notice how stupid people look when they're just mouthing words. How did your meeting go?'

'Good. An academic round-up of the latest developments in forensics. The networking's always useful too.' She puts down her briefcase. 'Can we dispense with the flickering TV now?'

She goes into the kitchen and returns with a bottle of brandy and two glasses. She pours out two generous measures.

'So, what's on your mind.'

'I've discovered Mike has a cocaine habit.'

I pull the specimen I collected out of my bag and hand it to her.

'I came across this in his bathroom when I stayed over.'

She peers at the plastic bag.'

'I guessed there was something going on between you two, but the drugs, no, I'd got no idea.'

She picks up her drink and walks over to the window with her back to me.

'Can you use your contacts to get it analysed?'

Chris turns to look at me and frowns.

She hands back the specimen but I refuse to take it.

'Please try. I'm sure Mike is off the mark in handling the investigation into Jaq's murder. Could be that cocaine is the problem. I think it could be affecting his professional judgement. Remember what I told you before when I handed in what I found at Jaq's parents. He just refuses to see any connection between Jaq's drug habit and her death. But that's not all.'

I tell Chris about my encounter with Chiara.

'Mike's supposed to be conducting an official search for her but I'm doubtful. I just don't think he's on top of Jaq's investigation.'

Chris's face is drawn and she's drinking her brandy more quickly than usual. She reaches for her cigarettes.

'You know Kate, you really must leave things to him.'

Now it's my turn to drink my brandy too quickly. I've always counted on Chris for support.

'I can't do that. I'm not going to stop asking questions until I understand just what's going on.'

Chapter Seventeen

Sunday 17 May

Chris gave me no indication last night why she is supporting Mike's view. It has taken me aback as I've always trusted her judgement. Perhaps I am making too much of Mike's penchant for a line of coke or perhaps my emotional proximity to Jaq's case has made me assess things in a distorted light. I'm not convinced by either explanation. Jaq was protecting Chiara from someone. Until I discover the reason for this, I must trust my own judgement and not be swayed by Mike.

Church Road is quiet as I walk to the bookshop. Infrequent buses pass and the odd car and there are very few people about to disturb a quiet Sunday. I push open the bookshop door, determined to see what I can discover inside. June is busy on the computer. She comes over to greet me.

'Yesterday was the first day we've been allowed in,' she explains. 'There's a lot to sort out. Can you wait a minute? I won't be long.'

I wander around the shop while she busies herself on the computer. I go over to the shelves all neatly stacked with books. I run my fingers along a row of titles, feeling grains of dust cling to my fingertips. Jaq would never have allowed dirt to accumulate like that and it upsets me. Books were precious to her. I turn and look around the shop. It feels lacking in soul without Jaq's presence. John is peering into a cardboard box and summarising the contents on the lids. June comes over to join us. She points to the box.

'This must have arrived just before Jaq......' she's unable to finish the sentence.

Her eyes fill with tears. I look away, finding her usual stoicism much easier to handle. 'She's a bit upset,' John explains. 'One of those detectives came round the other day to have a look at Jaq's room. He went all through her things. Nice enough chap, just the one. Black I think he said his name was. Still, it was most unpleasant for us. I don't know what he was expecting to find.'

Mike must have gone to the house to check out the room. Odd that he went on his own. Not the usual procedure.

'I wonder if it was anything to do with the bookshop?' says June.

She's trying hard not to cry.

'You've got quite a job here,' I say. 'Where shall I start?'

I'm soon busy stocktaking, keeping an eye out for anything that might relate to Chiara. Nothing turns up. John suggests a coffee break and heads towards basement to make it. I offer to do it instead. It's the opportunity I've been waiting for. I step down the creaky stairs and find a cloakroom to the left. I open the door to a large room opposite, where piles of books are scattered all over the stained and faded carpet. A couple of boxes labelled as publishers' returns are pushed up against one of the walls. I wonder if all bookshops are blessed with a similar dark hole where unwanted books are sent to languish.

The sink in the corner is stained and a couple of dirty mugs give off an unpleasant smell from mouldy dregs of coffee. I wash them and take three clean mugs from the shelf above and wait for the kettle to boil.

The basement is in such a state that John and June are happy to accept my offer to clean it out. Dust and grime have accumulated and as I scrub and sweep them away I continue looking for clues about Chiara. I open a large cupboard. The smell of cheap perfume hits me. I run my fingers over the empty shelves and a fine layer of dust coats my fingertips. When I take a closer look, there are tiny specs of white mixed in with the grey and a little pile of white powder in one corner of the top shelf. I'm pretty sure it's cocaine. I've got no way of collecting it so I leave it be. It just reinforces my fears that Jaq was a dealer. I find nothing else, no clues as to where Chiara might have gone or why Jaq was hiding her.

At 4pm I leave for a very late lunch at a beach café near Brighton pier. I haven't heard from Mike and I'm just about to send him a text when a call comes through from him as if by telepathy.

'I've just arrived back in Brighton. Shall I call round with your key?'

'I'm on the seafront at the moment, just finishing a late lunch. Why don't you join me? We could have coffee somewhere.'

Twenty minutes later, he joins me outside a café snuggled into the arches underneath the promenade near the main pier. He hands over the key straight away.

'Pity you rushed off on Saturday morning, we could have prolonged a very good night.'

'What about your London trip?'

'I'd have put off leaving until later in the day. Anyway, there's always tonight.'

'If you think I'm up for a sexual marathon on a Sunday night, you must be kidding. Have you ever been in a GP surgery on a Monday morning?'

'Some other time, then.'

'So, how was London?' I can't see any signs of a mugging this time.

'Just some more discussions with Carole.'

He lowers his eyes as he speaks. I ask about his progress with Chiara. He doesn't answer my question but picks up his spoon and stirs his coffee, avoiding any eye contact.

'You know I saw her yesterday?'

Mike looks up, surprised.

I explain the circumstances.

'Unfortunately, she was scared off by a couple of blokes chasing her so I didn't find out very much.'

'What makes you think they were after her? The seafront is crowded with people.'

Mike focuses on his coffee again. I ignore his put-down.

'You know Jaq was hiding her in the basement of her bookshop.'

'Wherever did you get that idea from?'

'Chiara told me.' I don't want to drag Charlie's name up at this stage.

'And you believed her? Come on, Kate.'

If his intention is to undermine me, it has the opposite effect.

'If you're not interested in why Chiara hiding in Jaq's basement perhaps you should have done a thorough search.'

'What are you getting at?'

'I've just been helping Mr and Mrs Grey clean out Jaq's bookshop and I found traces of cocaine in a cupboard down there. Have you thought that Jaq might have been dealing drugs? That would change things.'

It hurts to hear myself voice my suspicions about Jaq. Mike lifts his head with a dark look in his eyes.

'You're not going to revisit that idea of Jaq being killed because of drugs, are you? How many times do I have to tell you to let it drop?'

The animosity in his voice makes me shudder but I won't be intimidated.

'Too scared your own habit will come to light? Don't think I haven't sussed that out.'

I had intended to keep that to myself. I'm expecting a fierce denial from Mike but he just leans forward and talks in a whisper.

'Keep your voice down.' Mike fidgets with his phone. 'We shouldn't be discussing this at all.'

He's slumped over the table and looks exhausted.

'Well, just answer my question then.'

'Look, there's no point in trying to find Chiara or come up with a motive for murder. We're treating it as a suicide now.'

'You're not serious?'

My head is spinning. Jaq was much too squeamish to stab herself to death. She once fainted when I started talking about anatomy dissection over dinner.

'Her fingerprints are the only ones on the knife.'

'You've never mentioned that before. There must be another explanation.'

Mike sits up straight and makes it very clear what he thinks of that.

His bombshell has pushed me to the limit.

'So, I'm just expected to sit back and see my friend Jaq labelled as so psychologically vulnerable that she took her own life while her murderer goes free? Chris was clear it was homicide.'

'Not so loud.'

'Come on, Mike, answer me.'

'There's nothing more to say.'

I stand up, pushing chairs out of the way. One clatters to the ground and several heads turn to look.

'If you don't want to discuss it any further, then there's no point in my staying. You can pay the bill.'

I storm out of the door. I head back to the house to confront Chris with the news. By the time I arrive, my anger and frustration is at the limit. I need to calm down before talking to her. I seize hold of my car keys, slamming the door before accelerating out of Hove. I take the east-bound slip road to the A27. As soon as I join the dual carriageway, I press down on the gas pedal. My muscles relax with the burst of speed and the tension from my encounter with Mike eases. I hit the speed limit in four seconds and settle for a cautious seventy-five miles an hour. I turn off towards Ditchling, passing through the village and then onto the winding byways of the Sussex countryside. At first, I drive steadily, paying attention to landmarks and signs, and then increase my speed as the roads become more familiar and the traffic disappears. I push the car as much as I can into each twist and turn with a smile of satisfaction as I conquer the empty roads and make them mine. I immerse myself in the power of my car. My first driving instructor told me of the psychological benefits of driving. How right he was.

After half an hour, I slow down on the lookout for a country pub. I pass pretty cottages and grand country properties and fantasise about living at the end of a long driveway, screened from the world by a high hedge. I soon spot an idyllic thatched pub, the perfect place for something to eat. After the exhilaration of the drive, the sound of the wind rustling through tree branches in the pub garden reminds me that life is not all anger and grief. It's a respite but it's short-lived.

By the time I arrive back in Hove, my anger has returned. I bang shut the front door and stomp into the siting room where Chris is on the sofa pouring over some research papers. I don't even say hello before challenging her about Mike's decision.

'What's going on, Chris?'

She looks up as I sit down opposite her.

'What do you mean?'

'I've just spoken to Mike. He says he's treating Jaq's death as suicide.

Chris collects up the research papers and goes out of the room. She returns with some brandy and two glasses. She pours one for herself and takes a large sip.

'He shouldn't be talking about it.'

'Maybe, but I'm an ex-cop and I know how an investigation is run. What's more I was the one who found Jaq and your report clearly indicated Jaq's death was a homicide. Has he said anything to you?'

'Actually, he has discussed it with me and he's got a point.'

I'm shocked by her change of mind. I watch as she picks up the lighted cigarette resting in the ashtray and takes several deep drags on it before stubbing it out.

'So why was your original conclusion so certain it was homicide?

'Several points indicated that Jacqueline Grey's death was homicide. I could find no superficial wounds or hesitation marks as we call them, which are usually present in suicide cases. The trajectory of the wounds was horizontal, more common in murder cases, as was the site of the wounds in the anterior chest area. There was more than one wound and also bruising to certain parts of the body which suggested a struggle. I also understand that she didn't leave a suicide note.'

'So why consider suicide?'

I listen in disbelief as she explains how less than 5% of stabbings are self-inflicted though there are instances in which it's difficult to be certain.'

'It's well documented that a suicidal person will want the knife to have direct contact with skin and will lift up or remove clothing. In Jaq's case there were no stab wounds through clothing.'

'But it was a really hot day and when I found Jaq, she was only wearing a pair of shorts and a bikini top.'

Chris doesn't react but carries on her explanation.

'The usual downward trajectory of the stab wound is not always present in self-inflicted wounds. Also, the precordial area of the anterior chest is used by suicidal people who want to aim specifically at the heart. In addition, the bruises could have been caused by her fall down the stairs.'

'But why stab yourself at the top of the stairs?'

Chris continues, unperturbed. 'There was a mirror at the top of the stairs. People who inflict wounds on themselves often look in a mirror to find the exact spot they wish to target.'

'And what about those so-called hesitation wounds?'

'They're absent in 10 – 40% of cases according to studies I've read. And then there was the fact that only Jaq's fingerprints were found on the knife.'

On hearing her confirm what Mike told me, I help myself to some brandy too and feel it burning as I swallow a large gulp. I don't know what to think. I grasp at any possible explanation.

'What if the killer was wearing gloves?'

'That's up to the investigating team to consider.'

I sit trying to compute what she's told me. Her explanation comes up against my instinctive certainty that Jaq couldn't take her own life.

'I just can't see it. Jaq may have had her problems but I know her well enough to completely rule out suicide, certainly not by stabbing herself. She was too squeamish to take her own life, especially like that. Nothing you've told me persuades me it was suicide.'

I stand up and stare down at Chris.

'What's going on? It's not like you to question your own judgement. You can't seriously think that what Mike's saying is right?'

She lowers her eyes and stares into her brandy glass.

'Mike can be very persuasive at times.'

'So, you're going to agree it's suicide?'

She looks up. Her face is pale.

'Come on, Chris. Please tell me.'

Her hands shake as she reaches for a cigarette.

'Please, Kate. Let's just leave it there.'

She refuses to be pushed for an explanation and goes out of the room while I sit staring at the blank screen of the TV in disbelief, wondering what to do next.

Chapter Eighteen

Monday 18 May

I turn up at work on Monday still shocked by the *volte face* of Mike and Chris on the cause of Jaq's death. To me, it's incomprehensible but I've got no evidence of my own to refute the idea of suicide. My only hope is Chiara. I work though my day's appointments hoping she will turn up at the evening's Young People's Clinic. By the end of the clinic, she hasn't appeared. I sweep up the pile of specimens, wishing I could sweep away my anxiety about Chiara with the same ease.

I go into Reception to put the specimens into the collection box and, with a smile of relief, see Chiara sitting quietly in the waiting area. She must have slipped in at the last minute. She looks nervous and is fiddling with a multi-coloured woven friendship band on her wrist. I go over and sit next to her.

'I'm so glad you've come, Chiara.'

Her face is wet with tears. She makes no effort to wipe them away. I fetch a box of tissues and hand her one while I talk softly to reassure her. I point to her wristband and ask if she made it herself. She nods.

'It's very pretty. Have you made others for your friends?'

'I like to do that. '

'Do you always use the same colours and pattern?'

'Oh no. Each of them be different. None are ever same.'

I can see her body starting to relax.

'Let's go to my room now,' I suggest. 'It's more comfortable and private.'

She follows me and sits down by my desk. I decide to defer the usual procedure of documenting name, date of birth and address until she's more at ease. I move my chair next to hers. I'm about ask about the men chasing her on the promenade but she speaks first.

'I am thinking I may have a baby.'

I suggest a pregnancy test.

'I am not liking the needles.'

'Don't worry, it's not that sort of test.'

I put on some sterile gloves and fetch a plastic container from the cupboard. I hand it to her. She looks puzzled so I explain what I want her to do.

I take her along the corridor to the toilet and wait outside until she comes out. Back in my room, I place a few drops of urine onto the test kit and then peel off my gloves and throw them in the bin. I sit down next to her again and take her hand.

'Can you tell me about it?'

She looks down and says nothing.

'Is there anything else worrying you?'

She looks up at me with sad eyes.

'I am missing Jaq. She was good to me.'

'She looked after you, didn't she?'

She nods.

'I know she was hiding you from someone.'

Chiara nods again, too upset to speak.

'Some men came looking for you, didn't they but Jaq didn't let them find you? Are they the reason you think you might be having a baby?'

I lean forward and place my hands gently over hers. Instead of answering, she points to the pregnancy test. I check my watch and look at the test. The result will be ready now. I confirm that she's not pregnant. I should find out more from her before I judge the result to be definitive but she needs reassurance right now. She is shivering, despite the heat in the room.

'You're very scared, aren't you?'

'Why anyone must kill her?'

'You know Jaq's dead?'

'Charlie tells me.'

'Charlie? Jaq's friend?'

Chiara nods. She starts crying again. I pass her a tissue and fetch a plastic cup of water for her. She takes a few sips and puts the cup down on my desk. I think of a few unpleasant medical procedures I'd like to inflict on Charlie for not telling me she was in contact with Chiara.

'When did you last see Charlie?'

'I promise her not to say.'

She looks up at me with terror in her eyes but I know that's not because of Charlie.

'You're very scared, Chiara. I'd like to help you.'

I wait until she's ready to speak.

'If I say things to you, you must not say my name to anyone.'

'Okay, I promise.'

She looks at me with a glimmer of hope in her eyes.

'Those men who chase me, they are at the Excelseus Language School.'

'Where's that?'

'I think it is in Basin.....'

At that point, the door opens and Rose pops her head round.

'I'll be off then, Kate....oh sorry, I didn't know you had someone with you.'

'Don't worry. Chiara, this is Rose, our clinic nurse.'

It's not her fault, but Rose's interruption has broken the delicate balance of the consultation. Chiara jumps up.

'Don't go, Chiara. You're safe here and I can arrange somewhere where you can be looked after.'

She's already opening the door to my room and seconds later, is rushing across reception and out of the front door. I run after her but she's too quick. She's not in the car park. I go into the street and look up and down but I've already lost sight of her. There's little point in running after her. I stand shaking with frustration at losing her again and worried about what could happen to her. I return to the surgery where I tell Rose I'll lock up. As I'm tidying up my desk I see the note I scribbled as Chiara was telling the name of the school.

Excelseus Language School, Basin ...

My hunch about Chiara coming here to improve her English seems likely but I don't remember coming across any such language school when I did an internet search. And why should she feel threatened by such an establishment? I check for a website only to find my search produces nothing. I tap in as many variations on the school's name as seem credible, in case I've written it down incorrectly. Still nothing. That might explain why it wasn't on my list. I can't trace a phone number either. There's no point in asking for Mike's help after our altercation. At least I have a clue as to the address. I use my phone map to search for a Basin Road, Street or Avenue in Brighton or Hove. There's a Basin Road that leads to Shoreham port. It's too late for a school to be open now but I can go there tomorrow lunch time. I'm tidying my desk, ready to leave and go to pick up the plastic container that Chiara used and throw it to the bin. I have second thoughts. It will have her fingerprints on it. I put on another pair of sterile gloves to empty it and then slide it into a specimen bag which I lock in a drawer. Some instinct tells me it could prove useful.

I rush back to ask Chris for Charlie's address. If Chiara has been in recent contact with Charlie, there's a chance she'll know where she could be now. I've no time to explain the urgency of my request but Chris, for once, holds back on the questions and just scribbles it down. The street is familiar to me, one of the rows of Regency terraces that lead up from the seafront. I find the building, and the flat number and ring the bell. There's no intercom so I wait. After a minute or two I press again and then again until, at last, a tall anorectic girl with an unhealthy, pale face opens the main door a fraction. As she finishes fastening a dirty dressing gown, she asks me in non-too-polite language what I think I'm doing creating a disturbance so late in the evening. I swallow my compulsion to tell her to go to hell as it's only 9.30pm and apologise instead. I spin her a story about needing to contact Charlie urgently as her mother is seriously ill and Charlie's not answering her phone.

'And who the fuck is Charlie?'

'She's a friend, a girl with orange hair. She lives in one of the first-floor flats.'

'Never heard of her. We've only been here a week.'

She's well spoken, quite at odds with her use of language. Her features are aristocratic even if her skeletal body suggests a serious drug addiction.

'Can I come in and knock on her front door?

'Why? You're not the police, are you?'

'No. As I said, I'm a friend.'

'Why should I be bothered? Now piss off and leave me alone.'

I push past her and run up the stairs. She follows me, leaving the main door to swing shut. I knock on Charlie's door and wait for a response. The girl stands watching me with her arms folded. I start knocking again and again.

'Are you thick, or what? Your Charlie isn't in. Now push off.'

I turn to face her and see the flat door opposite is ajar. I point to it.

'Is that your place?'

'None of your business.'

'You must've bumped into her.'

'Are you calling me a liar?'

'No, no... it's just...'

'Scram.'

I walk slowly downstairs and open the main door. I hear the door to the girl's flat close. I let the main door close but stay inside and tiptoe back up the stairs. I stand staring at Charlie's door for a few moments, reluctant just to give up. The silence in the hallway is unsettling and combined with a smell of damp and the peeling wallpaper, it's not a welcoming place to be. I put my ear against Charlie's door and it's then that I hear it. A cough which must be coming from her flat. I hear it again and then a scuffling noise the other side of the door followed by silence. I start banging on the door, repeated heavy blows that make my knuckles sore. When that doesn't produce any result, I start shouting. It's not long until the girl opposite reappears.

'If you don't shut the fuck up, you'll have my man out here and that will be very nasty. Now bog off.'

Behind her along the corridor in her flat I can see a figure moving towards the door. He towers over her skinny frame. Muscular, a southern Mediterranean type and not unattractive, he speaks with a heavy accent.

'You have a problem, cara?'

He kisses her neck and then glares at me over her shoulder, throwing daggers with his eyes in my direction.

'You want me to deal with her?'

I get the message.

'I'm just leaving.'

Out in the street, I start shaking. All I've achieved by my efforts is a sense of foreboding about what lies ahead.

Chapter Nineteen

Tuesday 19 May

I arrive at the surgery earlier than usual. I've not stopped thinking about Chiara since I woke up. I barely notice the practice manager deactivating the alarms and switching on the lights or the roar of the vacuum cleaners as the cleaners go about their business. It's the smell of disinfectant that makes me hurry off to my room. Rose corners me just as I open the door and asks if I've got a moment. She apologises for interrupting my consultation with Chiara. I reassure her but she carries on talking.

'It can be so difficult to get these kids to open up. The things they experience, they don't always want to talk about them. I find it often takes more than one visit and then it all comes out, the bullying, the boyfriend problems, family arguments, contraceptive oversights, pregnancy fears, infections, you name it.' And I could.

Rose carries on. 'Boys can be worse, especially when it comes to drugs or HIV, very reluctant to talk about things. Sometimes it feels like we're just putting a sticking plaster over a gaping wound.'

'That's okay. We all need to have a safety valve at times. I'll let you know if I hear anything about Chiara.'

I log onto my appointments list but it's difficult to concentrate. All I want to do is rush off to the Excelseus Language School. My first patient arrives and I rein in my impatience until my final consultation when I face an overweight, wannabe celebrity who insists on a test for thyroid dysfunction instead of the dietary advice I offer. Neither of us are satisfied when she eventually leaves.

I snatch my handbag from the desk drawer ready to rush off to Basin Road when Andrew barges into my room. He sits down with what appears to be serious intent and takes off his jacket. It has a discrete designer label on the top pocket. He throws a set of clinical notes from the Young Person's Clinic on the desk. They belong to Chiara.

'Rose told me one of the girls ran off in the middle of your last consultation.'

He points to Chiara's notes.

'No surname, address or contact phone number. No way of checking up on her. Not good enough.'

'Look, Andrew, you know very well these clinics don't always run by the book. She was frightened. I had to tread carefully. If my procedural *faux pas* bothers you, I'll report it to Clare.'

'There's no mention of her being frightened.'

I had only written down her request for a pregnancy test and the result.

'She didn't say much before Rose came into the room.'

I resent his questions and I'm unsettled by his aggression.

I'm determined not to share any further information with him about Chiara but he surprises me by getting up, putting on his jacket and leaving without a further word. I go to follow him out of the door when the phone on my desk rings. It's Clare who sounds uncharacteristically edgy. She tells me Andrew has just refused to do his allocated home visits. She asks if I'll do them instead. I resign myself to deferring my visit to the language school until the end of the day.

I work through my afternoon appointments as quickly as is consistent with medical thoroughness, hoping to finish early enough to get to the school before it closes. My plan is soon put in jeopardy as I spend ages sorting out a 45-year-old stressed mother of two truanting teenagers, who has chronic kidney failure and multiple problems both medical and social. It's finally thwarted by my last patient, a thin, elderly lady in her eighties, with immaculate grey hair and a wrinkly smile. She's made her way to the surgery by taxi with a dangerously high blood pressure and an obvious left-sided weakness. It takes time to arrange her admission to the hospital stroke unit and even more to reassure her as we wait for the ambulance to arrive.

It's past normal school opening hours by the time I set off for Basin Road but I decide to take a look anyway. I'm hoping the school will be easy enough to identify as I don't have a street number. I follow the computerised voice on my sat nav, driving along Kingsway and turning left at the traffic lights to Shoreham port and Basin Road. The road runs parallel to the main A259, several feet above it, and goes through a depressing industrial wasteland of dockside businesses, a car wash and wholesale warehouses. I drive slowly along the dreary road. It's an unlikely location for a school. I park the car where the road widens and take a look at the buildings on foot. I can't see one that sports the name of the Excelseus Language School but I work it out by a process of elimination. All the other buildings are well signed.

The school has a large car park, closed off by a large metal gate. I can't see a buzzer to request entry so I peer though the bars. There are only a few vehicles in the marked parking spaces. One is a sleek, black QXK Zupro supercar that stands out from the other small city models and SUVs. I know it has a six-figure price tag and stratospheric running costs. I resist the urge to take a closer look and scan the front of the building for any indication that this is, in fact, The Excelseus School. A logo of intertwined letters E, L and S above the main entrance is confirmation enough. I can't find out anything else. The front door is shut and there are no people coming or going. I assume the school is closed for the day. I'll have to come back another time.

I hope for more luck with Charlie but Chris is on her own at the house. She suggests I join her at a festival event.'

'I have to find Charlie. I must talk to her.'

'I'm about to go to something called *Jardin Flambeau* at St Ann's Wells Gardens. Charlie is involved in organising it, she's bound to be there.'

The gardens are part of a small park and I find they've been turned into a sort of *Son et Lumière.* Various light displays are scattered around the place accompanied by a multitude of sounds such as the sea breaking on the shore or trees rustling in the breeze. One display is resonant of Moses and the burning bush. A pattern of flickering lights gives the impression that one of the bushes is burning and the crackling noise of a fire adds to the effect.

I see Charlie at once, skipping around, delighted by the dancing images and as excited as a child seeing its first Christmas tree. Chris's response to the spectacle is more measured. There's an unmistakeable touch of irony to her praise. For me the fire effects in the trees, enhanced by clouds of smoke that smell of wood burning, arouse macabre thoughts of eternal damnation and suffering. I shiver. Chris immediately notices.

'You can't be cold.'

I point to the fire tree. 'This one's spooky, don't you think?'

'Spooky? In what way?'

My explanation produces a wry smile.

'Don't tell that to Charlie. I don't ever recall her mentioning an intention to portray the everlasting pains of hell.'

As if on cue, Charlie bounds up.

'Fantastic, don't you think?'

'Very impressive,' I comment, without elaborating.

'We wanted to capture the feeling of spirits escaping into an ethereal world, create an idea of the freedoms that we can reach if we set our souls alight.'

Chris gives me a wink as Charlie makes to skip off again. I seize hold of Charlie's arm.

'I know you're busy but could I have a quick word?'

'Not now, Kate,' She shakes off my hand and disappears before I can ask her about Chiara.

Chris pushes a drink into my hand and introduces me to a colleague from work.

'I'm not sure you're going to get very far with Charlie this evening. I should've realised she'd be too preoccupied with all this.' Chris waves her hands in the direction of the nearest display.

'I'll see if I can catch her later.'

Some friends of Chris join us and begin swapping opinions of the event.

'...setting our souls alight? Is that how the artists who conceived the work view it?'

'I've no idea. I see it more as abstract sculpture. Quite mesmerising in a way.'

I leave Chris talking with them and walk off to see if I can spot Charlie. I look at the displays again and think that, yes, perhaps after all, there is something magical about them. I help myself to some more of the glühwein on offer and try to relax into the atmosphere of the place. It's impossible. Instead, I march around searching for Charlie until I find her in the centre of an animated group. I make a couple of futile attempts to speak to her but she doesn't acknowledge me.

It's the second frustration of the evening as I think back to the Excelseus School. My impatience to know more about the school leads me to wonder what Mike knows about it. I want to see if it's on the police radar. After my outburst on Sunday, I have reservations about contacting him. I weigh up the dilemma as I walk down Furze Way, across Church Road and past the Brunswick terraces towards the esplanade. There are plenty of people around, wanting to enjoy the night air. Couples of all types saunter along the promenade and groups of foreign students laugh their way onto the beach where people are setting up barbecues. Solitary walkers with their dogs and the occasional jogger add to the scene. If Jaq had been with me, I would be listening to her create fictional anecdotes about the lives of each and every one of them. She was a tireless commentator, rather in the style of Alan Bennet. I miss her humour.

I turn up Hove Street and pass the open-all-hours store. I'm about to buy the best bottle of red wine they have on offer and finish the evening in its company when I pull out my phone on impulse and ring Mike. He picks up at the first ring and I can hear the sound of traffic in the background. I apologise for my outburst on Sunday.

'Oh hell, Kate, I'm only just arriving back at the flat. I'd rather not go out again.'

There's no trace of animosity in his voice.

'How about a take-away? I can come over to your place.'

'I'm whacked, Kate.'

'I'll not stay long.'

Eventually he gives in and I get a cab. Mike looks tired when I arrive. He drags his feet as we walk along the hall to the sitting room. He's waiting for the pizza to arrive.

'Coffee or something stronger?'

'Coffee will be fine, thanks.'

He goes into the kitchen and crashes around with the crockery. I scan the room for any sign of his slider phone. It's not on view and his jacket isn't on the back of the dining chair where he usually leaves it. I abandon the idea of looking for it and open the doors to the balcony. I step outside and look out across the east side of Brighton over to the downs and the racecourse. The city lights are picking out neon patterns in the half gloom of the evening and the hum of traffic reaches me through the cool night air: a place gearing up for the night, with no thought for its hidden underbelly.

Mike calls out that coffee is ready and I step inside. He comes over and I lean my head on his shoulder in what I hope he sees as a gesture of reconciliation. He puts his arm around me and we end up sitting together on the sofa as he gulps down a beer. I lean forward and take a few sips of my coffee. It smells better than it tastes. I sit back and leave the rest of it untouched. Mike is no barista.

'Are you sure you won't have something stronger?' Mike points to the nearly full cup.

'I guess coffee doesn't really go with pizza. I'll have a lager, then.'

Mike goes off to fetch it and I shift around on the sofa trying to find a position which gives the impression of being relaxed. I take a long swig from the bottle he hands me. He's not bothered with glasses.

'You seem a bit tense,' he says. 'Something on your mind?'

Even tired and stressed Mike's professional acumen doesn't desert him. He knows at once when someone is holding back. I'm cautious. I don't want to write the script for a big bust up, that's not my intention.

I'm just weighing up how to begin when the pizza man buzzes. There's another hiatus while Mike gets plates and cutlery from the kitchen. Mike tucks in as if he hasn't eaten for a week. The pizza smells inviting but when I pick up a piece and start chewing I find it difficult to swallow. I've no appetite. I take small mouthfuls while Mike consumes ninety percent of a supersized pizza Napoli with salami and extra olives. When he's finished, he turns to me.

'Well, what's up?'

I take a deep breath and tell him how Chiara turned up at the Young People's Clinic.

'I know you don't want me chasing round after her as if I'm still on the force, so I thought you should know.'

'Fair enough.'

'She was scared and reluctant to say much.'

He doesn't comment but just takes a swig of his beer as though that's the end of the conversation.

'But she did give me a name and address.'

He slams his beer down on the coffee table and turns to me with an ice-cold look in his eyes.

'Go on.'

Mike sits forward, all his muscles tensed.

'It's the Excelseus Language School in Basin Road. Do you know anything about it? You must have come across it during your search for Chiara.'

I'm far from sure about that for more than one reason. He evades the question.

'There are dozens of language schools springing up all the time round here.'

'It's just that it's in such an odd place for a language school.'

'You're not going to tell me you've been there?'

I hesitate. His voice is commanding and unnerving.

'Answer me Kate.' I can see he's only just holding his anger in check.

'What if I have?'

It's as though I've trodden on a brittle twig and snapped it in two. Mike's rage pours out of him and engulfs us.

'What the hell do you think you're doing?'

'For God's sake, calm down. I only went to take a look from the outside. It was after school hours and all locked up. I didn't speak to anyone.'

Mike is pacing up and down as if he'll explode unless he keeps moving.

'If you don't stop all this snooping around, you'll end up in big trouble and I'm not going to be the one to bail you out.'

I've never seen him so furious and I'm struggling to understand.

'What the hell is going on, Mike?'

'That's none of your business but if you keep poking your nose into police business, I'll have you up for obstructing the course of justice.'

The pompous legal term sounds ridiculous in Mike's Geordie accent and I can't help laughing. It's as if I've waved a matador's cape at a wounded bull. Mike explodes and lunges forward, ready to lash out at me with both arms. I dodge out of his way and run out of the flat, hurtling down the stairs, frightened that he'll come after me.

I run all the way to the train station. A line of green and white taxis is waiting. I open the door of the first in the queue and collapse onto the back seat. I manage the few words it takes to give him Chris's address, then fasten my seat belt and take several deep breaths. The taxi picks its way out of the station, avoiding inattentive drunks and other revellers as they spill out into the road. The lights of Brighton at night flash past but I don't see them. All that passes in front of me are images of my encounter with Mike. The intensity of his anger was disconcerting and a bad omen.

Chapter Twenty

Wednesday 20 May

If the intensity of Mike's rage disturbs me, it has done nothing to deter me. After a night' sleep his accusation that I'm interfering with official police work strikes me as an empty threat. His rage was so intense: personal and irrational.

With a free afternoon ahead of me, I rush through me the list of correspondence and admin tasks that result from my morning surgery, As I drive to the seafront to get a sandwich, I mull over how to approach my visit to the school. I find a space in the King Alfred Centre car park and walk back along Hove Street to the small convenience store. I eat my late lunch of a mozzarella and avocado panini in my car. It's a far cry from the picnics Jaq and I used to have in one or other of the London parks. Wine was *de rigeur,* as she would say, and we would spend the rest of the afternoon sunbathing in a pleasant alcoholic haze. I scrunch up the sandwich wrapper and set off for Basin Road.

There's no sign of life when I reach the Excelseus School: no students spilling out of classes, no one chattering about the day's work, anticipating a good evening ahead. Not at all what I expected. The front gate is shut but it opens as I approach to let a vehicle leave. I slip into the car park. The QXK Zupro is in the same spot as yesterday. I imagine what a drive that would be. It's a moment's distraction as I march up to the front door. Unlike the language schools I've visited before it's locked, so I press the intercom buzzer to request entry. A voice asks for my name and the door clicks open. I step into a reception area, with soft lighting, very unlike the usual LED strip lights of most educational institutions. The reception desk is to my left but a woman steps forward to bar my way. There's no mistaking her. I last saw her talking to Mike. With the exception of a different colour suit, her appearance is otherwise exactly as I remember it from Jaq's memorial service.

As she approaches, I'm overwhelmed by a strong scent of exotic spices. Her manner is far from welcoming and the tone of her greeting chilling. She has a sinister way of scrutinising me which is unsettling. I feel so intimidated that I can understand why Chiara asked me not to mention her name. The woman must recognise me even if she gives no indication of this. My brain is in turmoil from the implications. The pretence I have concocted for turning up feels even more tenuous now.

'I don't seem to have your name on our register of visitors,' she glares at me.

Behind her a sign above the reception desk reads *Excelseus Language School.* I take a deep breath, aware that my heart rate is escalating exponentially.

'I'm sorry to bother you but I'm a local GP who's doing research into how often students at language schools in Hove access our services.'

'Might I ask who put you in touch with us.'

'I'm sure that's not important. I'd just like to get the students to fill out a survey and talk to one or two of them.'

She looks at me with ill-disguised disdain.

'That won't be possible. We are a very exclusive boarding establishment and our students expect the maximum discretion from us. We operate on the basis of a rigorous referral system.'

'Oh, I see.'

'Now, if that's all.'

'I don't suppose you have any written information about your school which would help my research. I couldn't find any details on-line.'

'Our website is being updated and we don't provide hard copy brochures.'

She hustles me out of the door and I hear the lock click behind me. A brisk breeze is swirling around the car park. The air is warm on my face and brings with it a strong smell of the sea. I inhale deeply, glad to be away from the claustrophobic atmosphere inside the building and the woman's nauseous perfume. I turn into the wind. The school is close to the quayside and the car park abuts it. This must be the far end of Shoreham port but no boats or ships are moored alongside the quay. I take a final look back at the Excelseus School. The woman is watching me from the doorway. I abandon the idea of taking a peek at the supercar for clues but make a mental note of the registration number. It could be useful as it's clear to me that the establishment is not a bona fide language school. The thought that Mike could be connected to the place is disconcerting as I doubt it's in any official capacity.

The gate opens automatically as I approach it but doesn't close behind me. I hear a car engine starting up with the characteristic roar of a QXK Zupro. It crawls up alongside me then follows me at a walking pace. My heart is pounding as if I'm running a marathon. I speed up until I'm almost running and turn right at the end of the road in the direction of the esplanade. The car sticks close to me until I reach the pedestrian only seafront. I hear it stop and change gear as it effects a U turn and drives off. It's been a warning.

I jog towards the car park where my Zuperga is waiting. I hug the long row of beach huts, taking comfort from the sight of those enjoying the simple pleasures of a seaside holiday. I dodge round the chairs, tables and windbreaks that spill out of the huts onto the asphalt, glad there are so many people around. In my car, I spend more time looking in the rear-view mirror than concentrating on the road ahead. There's no sign of the black supercar but I'm relieved when I park up and finally close the front door behind me. I find a note on the kitchen table saying Chris will be in until late and please to help myself to some of the cassoulet in the fridge. It's the only good thing about the evening. Chris is a talented cook. Apart from that, I'm faced with the tedium of tackling a 50-page list of requirements in anticipation of a forthcoming external audit of the GP surgery. I break up the monotony with frequent attempts to contact Charlie by text and by phone, with no result.

I drag myself into bed just before midnight just as I hear Chris slam the front door. I think about getting up to see if Charlie is with her but can't face the inevitable nightcap. I close my eyes and fold the duvet around me as a comforter, despite the warm night. I'm soon throwing it off and tossing around as sleep eludes me. I switch on the light and read for a while. When I feel sleep creeping over me, I switch off the light but as soon as the room is dark again, my eyes are open and my thoughts are full of Mike, Chiara and the Excelseus Language School.

In the end I give up the struggle. I get dressed and tip toe down the stairs, opening and closing the front door with as little noise as possible. I've no wish to be confronted by Chris asking me where I'm going in the early hours of the morning. Outside, the air is heavy as if a storm is approaching. The humidity is oppressive. I slip into my car and switch on the aircon as I drive towards the esplanade. I take a right turn along Kingsway followed by a left into Basin Road where I slow down to a walking pace. It's a one-way street so I switch off the car lights and creep along in the darkness until I get to the school. The school gate clangs shut just as I reach it. Ahead of me, I can see another vehicle making its way along the road. Its rear lights become red specks as it reaches the end. It stops and then moves forward to join Kingsway. I switch on my headlights and accelerate towards the junction, arriving in time to see which way it turned. I can just make out that it's a black SUV.

It's easy enough to follow as it drives out of Hove. Even at that late hour there's enough traffic around for my car not to be noticed. When it gets to the roundabout leading to the A27, it takes the turn off to the Devil's Dyke. I circle the roundabout while the SUV disappears along the road then I take the same route but pull over and stop. I'm sure of its destination. I wait five minutes then set off and drive down the country road as if it's a rally track. I brush against hedges, driving at the limit of controlling the car. I only slow down as I approach the Devil's Dyke. I crawl into the small overflow car park which is empty, and switch off the engine and lights. At first, it's as if I'm blind, but then my eyes adjust as the distant glow of the city lights tempers the blackness. I proceed on foot to the main carpark taking care not to make a sound as I walk. The SUV is parked at the far end beyond the pub, half camouflaged against the backdrop of a dense copse of trees. There's no one in sight. I approach and peer inside but there's nothing to see at the front and the back windows are tinted black and obstruct my view. I memorise the number plate and walk towards the Devil's Dyke.

The silence is eerie. At first, I see nothing but blackness tinged with the orange glow from distant city lights. As I approach the grassy bowl that dips down ahead of me, a flare shoots into the sky to my left. At least that's my first impression until I realise that the orange and blue streaks of light are not dying away but increasing in both intensity and magnitude. Without doubt they are the flames of a fire. The risk of a catastrophe so close to woodland is clear but the shivers down my spine are for a very different reason. I can just make out two tall figures in the distance running up the slope away from the fire. They have their backs to me and must be heading for the car park. I sprint towards the fire until I'm close enough to have my worst fears confirmed. The smoke stings my eyes and makes me cough. The smell is nauseating but I ignore it. I tear off my jacket and beat at the flames. They diminish but it's not enough. I use what remains of the jacket to smother the fire as best I can and use my feet to press it against a smouldering mass which is unmistakeably the remains of a body.

Just as I think I've put out the fire, the flames start up again. I'm about to tear off my jeans and use them in a final attempt to quell them, when the storm that had been threatening for hours finally breaks. The lightning is impressive, sheeting across the sky around me and forking into the ground. The thunder-rolls are deafening but it's a relief when torrential rain plummets down soaking through my clothes and extinguishing the flames in front of me. I look down at the hideous remains of charred flesh. I can no longer block out the awful smell. I turn away and vomit onto the grass.

I wipe my mouth on the sleeve of my shirt and then grope in the pocket of my jeans for my mobile only to find it's fallen out. I search the wet ground on my hands and knees, cursing and crying in turn. I crawl back along the way I came, fumbling about for it in the grass until my fingers touch the glass screen, by some miracle still intact. I have mud on my hands but manage to switch on the torch and make the call. Rain mingles with my tears as I sink back onto the grass trying to take in what has happened.

By the time the police appear, the physical signs of shock have taken over. I'm trembling all over, a reaction made worse by the damp clothes clinging to my skin. I'm only too happy to be guided back to a police car and sit with a tin foil blanket wrapped round me, wishing I could have a very large glass of brandy. After twenty minutes of trying to piece together a logical narrative for a young police officer, I'm amazed to find my wish fulfilled when someone leans into the car and hands me a hip flask.

'Not the usual place for a nightcap but you'll never have needed one more than now.'

I take a good swig of the flask and look into the face of my saviour. Chris smiles back at me. My trembling eases off.

'Talk later,' she says. 'Got work to do right now.'

Duly fortified, I provide the officer with a more cogent account of what happened and prepare myself mentally for a long night. By the time I'm sitting in the interview room back at Brighton police station with the inevitable hot mug of tea in front of me, my main concern is whether Mike is part of the investigating team and how to handle that. I know there will be detectives all over the station by now. I remember the first few hours of a murder investigation as hectic. He hasn't made an appearance yet, at least not in front of me. I soon have my answer when the door of the room opens and a familiar face comes to sit across the table from me. It's the detective I first encountered in Jaq's flat, Detective Inspector White. I remember Mike referring to him as Tony.

'We meet again, Dr Green. You certainly choose your moments. Pretty ghastly this one, eh. I'm afraid your friend's busy setting up the incident room so I'll be going over your statement.'

Police station gossip has not only registered my past professional connection with Mike, but also the current familiarity between us. The snide emphasis he puts on the words *your friend* makes me wonder if I have to be prepared for a grilling. Still I'm relieved at not having to face Mike. Tony pulls out a cigarette and offers the packet to me. I take one and he lights it for me. I inhale a few times and start coughing. I stub it out in the tin lid that acts as an ash tray. It's like taking my very first smoke all those years ago. I feel sick and my head is spinning.

'You don't mind if I carry on,' he says with a condescending smile.

He soon changes his attitude but when I write down the registration number of the SUV.

'You've not forgotten your training, then.'

From that point on, he adopts a more sympathetic approach. The only awkward moment comes when I explain why I decided to drive to the Devil's Dyke in the early hours of the morning.

'I couldn't sleep. I'd been pouring over an audit document all evening and I wanted to clear my head. I find driving the best way to do that.'

'A bit extreme at two in the morning?'

'Perhaps.'

We go over again some more of the detail in my statement and then he leans forward, and asks the question I'd been dreading.

'The forensic pathologist thinks the victim could be a girl. Do you have any idea who she might be?'

I can feel the blood draining from my face and yet my body feels hot and prickly. Then my face flushes and the rest of me feels as if I'm in an ice bath. These feelings alternate for several moments as I struggle with the memory of a friendship band on the burned girl's wrist. I tell myself that it would only amount to a piece of circumstantial evidence but I can't forget that Chiara told me no band was ever the same.

'Do you want some water?'

'Please.'

He nods to the female police officer in the room who obliges by fetching me one. I drink a whole cup in one gulp.

'So, you do have an idea who it is?' he prompts.

'Perhaps. It's complicated.'

'Just take your time. I'll organise another cup of tea.'

The female officer disappears briefly.

'Are you sure you don't want to smoke?'

I shake my head. He gets up and wanders around the room until the female officer comes back with the tea. I take a few sips and then explain that I'd noticed a friendship band amongst the charred remains. One arm had been spared the ravages of the fire.

'It looked like one I'd seen on a girl who came to our Young People's Clinic.'

I explain about how Chiara had turned up and appeared to be frightened about something or someone.

'She was very anxious so I tried to put her at ease by talking about the friendship band on her wrist. She explained how each one is unique. I can remember hers exactly but I'd have to see a photo of the one from the Devil's Dyke to be sure it was the same.'

Tony makes a quick call then turns back to me.

'Carry on.'

I tell him about Chiara's abrupt exit from the clinic but I've yet to mention her reference to the Excelseus School, when the door opens and Mike strides into the room with a print of a photo in his hand. He puts it down in front of me and sits next to Tony. I look over to Mike, conscious that Tony will be watching my every reaction.

I take my time examining the photo in detail but the friendship band has been torn away in parts.

'I can't be sure.'

'Fair enough. You haven't mentioned the name of the girl yet. That might help.'

I look at Tony and then over to Mike. His face is devoid of expression.

'It's Chiara.' I spell it out and explain how to pronounce it in Italian. 'That's all I've got. I never found out her surname. It was a difficult consultation and I had to let slip the usual protocols.'

'Was it the first time you'd seen her?'

Tony's question makes me hesitate. He notices at once so I don't deny it.

'In the clinic, yes, but I have seen her around. She was near Brighton pier a few days earlier. There appeared to be two men chasing her along the promenade.'

'Could you describe them.'

I have no trouble with that. I got a good look when I forced them to stop.

'What about the people you saw at the Devil's Dyke?'

'They were too far away for a clear view. All I could see were two shadowy figures. They were most likely men from the way they moved.'

'Can you think of anything else that would help our investigation?'

As Tony puts the question, Mike sits forward in his chair, alert and tense. His eyes are fixed on me as if warning me to take care with my answers. I weigh up how much information I should provide. If I knew for sure the body was Chiara, my decision would be easy and Mike would just have to face any repercussions.

'Would a photo help identify the girl because .....'

Mike immediately interrupts me. 'I'm afraid it won't. The girl's face is too badly burnt.'

She was face down when I found her so that detail is new to me and upsetting.

'I see.' My whole body goes cold as if I've just walked into a freezer.

Mike is now sitting back in his chair looking more relaxed and at ease. I tell them I've nothing more to add. As we leave the room after the interview, he's behind me. I feel his hand give me that slap on the back of his. I don't know how to interpret it in the circumstances. All I know for certain is that I no longer trust him.

Chapter Twenty-One

Thursday 21 May

A constable drives me back to Chris's in my Zuperga. A police car follows us to return him to the station.

'I've always wanted a go with one of these,' he comments, as I thank him for the lift.

I close the front door, seized by the urge for a hot chocolate. I rifle around in the kitchen cupboards for some cocoa and then curl up on the sofa in the sitting room, cupping the mug in my hands and expecting its velvety sweetness to soothe me with reminders of childhood bedtime drinks. It does no such thing and I find the taste sickly and repulsive. All I crave is the comfort of more brandy, even if it is seven in the morning. After all, I don't have to work until the afternoon. But just as I stand up to pour myself a good measure, the front door opens and Chris trudges into the sitting room. Her light grey mac is marked with black smudges and her shoes are as muddy and grass stained as mine.

'Want a drink? I was just going to pour myself a brandy.'

She looks at her watch.

'Best not, I'll have to get back to work soon. I'll make some coffee.'

I follow her into the kitchen where she takes off her mac and puts it in the rubbish bin. As the coffee percolates, its aroma masks the unpleasant smell still lingering on our clothes. Chris takes her coffee long and strong. For once, I take mine as a weak latte, I need to sleep.

We face each other across the kitchen table.

'Thanks for the brandy, by the way. Do you always carry a hip flask when you're on-call?'

She nods then glances down at her shoes.

'I'd better take these off or the whole house will be covered in dirt; what a job.'

She's unusually troubled.

'Well, I couldn't do it, that's for sure and I thought I had a strong stomach.'

She goes upstairs to shower and change. I head to my room with the aim of catching a few hours' sleep before going to the GP surgery in the afternoon. I undress and bundle up what I'd been wearing, stuffing it into a plastic bag, ready, like Chris's mac, for the rubbish bin. I enter the shower, intending to snuggle under the duvet afterwards but come out of it with a very different idea. I grab a dress from the wardrobe and rush around getting ready to go out. I'm in my car and on my way to the GP surgery before Chris has left for work. The reception staff are quick to point out that I don't have a patient list until the afternoon. I throw them a cheery greeting and tell them I'm not staying long but I'll be back later, then I hurry off to my room where I rummage around in my bag for the key to my desk drawers. I unlock the one where I've left the specimen pot and put it in my bag.

Andrew is in reception as I make my way out of the building. I rush past him before he has a chance to ask what I'm doing there. I leave my car behind, preferring to take a cab to Brighton Police Station. I'm wondering who the duty DI is and spend the journey thinking about what I'll do if I bump into Mike. I enter the station just behind a skinny, unkempt young man in handcuffs, his Rastafarian dreadlocks hanging like dirty coils of rope against his pale skin. He's being pushed into the building by two uniformed police officers. One is swinging what must be cache of an illicit substance.

'I got nuffink to say. You get me a legal, eh? I knows me rights.'

The man's outburst does nothing to ease my own tension as I take my place in the inevitable queue. At last I explain the reason for my visit and ask to see the Detective Inspector on duty. There's a phone call to the back offices and I'm invited to take a seat again. This time it's not long before I'm ushered into the interview room and find myself sitting opposite Inspector White.

'Dr Green, again.'

We exchange a professional handshake and I get the specimen out of my bag and hand it to him, explaining how it came to have Chiara's fingerprints on it.

'I handled it with surgical gloves, so my prints won't be on it. I thought it could identify Chiara or eliminate her from your enquiries.'

'Whatever made you keep this? I don't suppose it's normal procedure.'

'Just a hunch it could prove useful. Chiara was frightened. I thought she could be in danger.'

'We'll see what we can get.' He smiles at me. 'Are you sure you're in the right job, Dr Green?'

I smile back, thinking of Mike's past reactions.

'Will you let me know the outcome?'

He promises to send me a text. We complete the necessary paper-work and he accompanies me into the reception area. There's been no sign of Mike and I'm glad.

I arrive for my afternoon session at the GP Practice in good time. A few hours of deep sleep have left me restored and ready for the routine of my work. I'm only too pleased for some sense of normality after the turmoil of the past hours. I spot Rose in the office behind the reception and I join her for a quick chat. She's got an afternoon edition of the local newspaper.

'Have you seen this?' She points to the front page.

'Not yet.'

She passes it to me. The Devil's Dyke murder is headline news. The main report points out the difficulty in identifying the girl because of the paucity of intact human tissue. The detail of a friendship band on the wrist is mentioned without comment. It concludes with a mountain of speculation. Reading it takes me back to the awful sight and smell of the charred body.

'It's horrible, just horrible.' Rose cannot hide her emotion. 'You think you've seen it all, but then something like this happens. Do you think it could have been the girl who ran out of our clinic?'

'Anything's possible, Rose.'

I don't like to mention I was the one who came across the body.

She shakes her head. 'I keep thinking about my interruption. She wouldn't have run off like that if I hadn't barged in.'

'Don't worry, Rose. She could've left at any moment. She was really frightened. Please don't blame yourself.'

Rose gives me a weak smile as if she wants to be convinced but isn't quite sure.

'Perhaps we should say something to Clare. If it is the girl from our clinic, then the press will be all over it.'

She has a point. I can just imagine the headlines.

GP surgery fails murdered girl or *Murdered girl left GP surgery without treatment*

'I'll have a word with Clare later.'

We go off to our respective duties and I put my concerns in parenthesis to concentrate on my patients.

At the end of the afternoon, I tell Clare about Chiara's aborted clinic attendance and let her know that she may turn out to be the girl who was murdered on the Devil's Dyke. When I voice my concerns about the press, she says not to worry for now. I admire her calm approach. On my way out of the premises, I pass by the door of Andrew's consulting room, which is shut tight. I can just hear the characteristic inflection of someone speaking on the phone. He sounds agitated and I stop outside his door to listen but I can't make out what he's saying. I hear him slam down the phone so I hurry off. I don't want him rushing out of his room and accusing me of spying on him. I've got more important things to attend to. An idea of how to discover more about Mike's involvement with the Excelsues school is beginning to take shape.

Chapter Twenty-Two

Friday 22 May

Any probe into Mike's possible underworld dealings is not without risk. As if to warn me of what might lie ahead, a violent storm wakes me in the early hours of the morning. I get out of bed to close the window just as a brilliant expanse of sheet lightning transforms the sky. Less than a second later, a thunderclap follows which places the eye of the storm almost directly overhead. The rain begins to fall in torrents as impressive as the ones that came to my rescue in extinguishing the fire on the Devil's Dyke. At first, I just want to close the curtains and block out the memory but as I lie back and watch, I become mesmerised by what is in front of me. I think of how the forces of nature always end in overwhelming our attempts to control their effects but we fight back nonetheless. It's the same against the man-made evils of the world. The search for justice never stops, however difficult. And that is no less true for me and my search for the truth about Jaq's death.

The storm is abating and I've just got out of bed when Chris knocks and pokes her head round the door. She has dark rings around her eyes.

'Bad night?' I ask.

She nods.

'Was it the storm?'

'No, I've got something on my mind. I've got to dash now but I'll tell you about it later.'

She closes the door and runs down the stairs. I hear the front door close. There's nothing I can do except put my curiosity on hold.

On the way to work, I stop at a Newsagents to buy the local paper. I have time before my first appointment to take a quick look at reports on the Devil's Dyke murder. I come across an interesting article tied in to the case. It talks about the problem of County Lines. Brighton and Hove are main target destinations for an influx of drugs brought in by young "mules" from London. The article suggests this drug traffic could provide a motive for the Devil's Dyke murder and mentions a couple of other unsolved killings of teenagers in Brighton. If Chiara had been recruited as a mule, the Excelseus School would have to be involved and could be implicated in her murder. It makes me wonder if the school could be part of a drug cartel grooming and exploiting youngsters as drug mules from a base in Brighton and Hove. Could that be why Jaq was protecting Chiara? If so, it would have implications for Jaq's death and for Mike's probity as an officer of the law.

I take a second look at the newspaper article. It appears to be well researched and is signed by a Jessica Witching. I'd like to talk to her. I put it off until the end of the day when I'm free of the distractions of work. My computer list of patients shows I will have plenty to keep me focused all day. It's much longer than usual so I phone Reception to ask if there's been a mistake. They explain that Andrew has rung in to say he's unwell, a migraine so he said. There's been no time to reschedule his appointments so they've been distributed between the rest of us. It makes for an intense afternoon. I work at speed but I'm still late in finishing. I'm relieved when I see out my last patient, a retired army colonel with a chronic respiratory illness who bids me a cheery goodbye.

The practice staff are keen to lock up so I make the call to Jessica Witching from my car presuming that journalists don't follow office hours. I'm asked to hold when I get through to the paper and soon afterwards a rather brittle female voice comes on the line. I conjure up a childish picture of a thin old lady with a hooked nose and a broomstick, peering into a cauldron of homeopathic potions.

I introduce myself and explain that I want to talk about her article.

'I'm surprised you contacted me. Most GPs think journalists are trouble-makers.'

I ask her if she knows of any set-up in Brighton and Hove that could be recruiting kids locally as drug mules.

'I've not heard anything but it's possible, I guess. Why?'

'One of the girls attending our Young People's Clinic said she was scared of a place called the Excelseus Language School. I wondered if it could be a cover. Do you know anything about it?'

'I did come across the name when I was investigating the standards of local security firms in the area. I'd had a tip off about guards being open to bribes. One of my contacts told me he'd heard a colleague mention the Excesleus School as a good touch but he couldn't tell me anything else.'

My heart rate accelerates as she continues.

'I rooted around to find out a bit more but no luck. No trace of an address or phone number. I did mention the name to the police but they weren't interested.'

'I've found out it's in Basin Road. I went to check it our but only managed to get as far as reception. The woman on reception made me very suspicious of the place.'

We chat for a while about the implications of what we both know. By the time we're finished, we're on first name terms and Jessica promises to do some snooping around and get back in touch with any results. At last I feel I have an ally.

When I get back, Chris has already opened a bottle of a pinot noir and I accept a glass to show I have no hard feelings after our last chat. I tell her I've been speaking to Jessica Witching about a possible County Lines set up in Brighton and Hove and she surprises me by saying they're friends.

'She's an excellent journalist. She used to work on a London daily but she prefers the lifestyle here.'

'That's good to know, she could prove to be a useful contact.'

I swirl the dark wine around and savour its exceptional bouquet before taking a sip. Then I start laughing as I remember how Steve would do this with any type of wine and how pretentious he looked.

'What's so funny?' Chris asks.

I explain. She doesn't smile but gulps down the rest of wine before lighting a cigarette. She blows the smoke way from me and apologises.

'Sorry but I really need one.'

'You said you had something on your mind this morning. Anything to do with the body on the Devil's Dyke?'

She shakes her head and frowns.

'Not unless Mike pokes his nose into my work again.'

I pick up her cue at once.

'What's he been up to?'

She runs her fingers through her hair and sighs and then explains how she's never been convinced by the idea that Jaq's death was suicide.

'I was surprised to hear Mike say that the only finger prints on the knife were hers. The depth of the stab wounds suggests homicide. Pushing a kitchen knife into someone to that extent and at that particular angle is highly unlikely to be a self-inflicted injury.'

'Did you contact Forensics to check the result? Mistakes happen.'

'I thought about it but Mike was adamant that I make the autopsy findings fit a suicide verdict so I didn't see the point.'

'Why's that?

'I can't risk Mike challenging me in a coroner's court.'

She goes on to tell me she once made serious error in an autopsy report.

'Mike spotted it but kept quiet. The trouble is, he's held it over me ever since and now it's pay-back time.'

I keep several expletives to myself as I think about Mike accusing me of interfering when that's exactly his game. I'm not going to let Chris suffer on his account.

'Can you delay your final report? That would give you time to ask for Forensics to check the results. You could request they do a second test too.'

Chris considers the question.

'I could hold back my final report until the full toxicology results come through. Meanwhile I'll put in a request for Forensics to review their fingerprint analyses but if the lab confirms the prints are Jaq's alone then it's still a problem.'

'Let's see what they say. Mike could be trying to mothball the murder investigation on the basis of your evidence or he could just be trying to muddy the waters.'

'Why would he do that?'

I explain how I suspect Mike is involved in some sort of illegal activity, most likely drug related and that I'm trying to get proof of what he's up to.

'Shouldn't you report your concerns to someone senior in the Sussex force?'

'I can't do that yet. I've got no real evidence. I'd just be laughed at. First, I need to get more information.'

I explain how Chiara gave me a lead to the Excelseus School and how Mike appears to be in some way involved with it.

'It didn't feel at all like a *bona fide* language school when I went to check it out. I mentioned the school to Jessica, and she has suspicions of her own about the place. When I mentioned to Mike that I'd taken a look, he exploded and accused me of obstructing a police investigation. Anyway, Jessica's going to snoop around a bit and see if she comes up with anything that helps me find out exactly what's going on there.'

'Be careful, Kate. You're not a detective now.'

She doesn't need to remind me of that but what I have in mind could never figure in an official enquiry.

Chapter Twenty-Three

Saturday 23 May

The next morning, I go downstairs to find Chris busy moving furniture around. When I ask what she's doing she tells me it's for the party that evening.

'What party?'

'It's an end of festival celebration. Charlie talked me into it. I must've forgotten to tell you.'

'But the festival's got another week to run.'

'I know but Charlie says there are so many parties on the last Saturday and she wanted to make sure all her friends would come to hers.'

I offer to help her. It's hard work as we take care not to scratch the polished wood flooring. Afterwards Chris rewards herself by lighting a cigarette.

'Thanks for that.' She takes a long drag. 'Charlie should have been here to help but I've not seen her since the *Jardin Flambeau.* I hope she hasn't forgotten about tonight.'

I leave Chris to her guilty pleasure and make some coffee. As the Moka bubbles away on the hob, I see a way of putting my plan to access Mike's slider phone into action. I join Chris for an espresso and ask if Mike will be at the party.

'I invited him a while back but I've not heard one way or the other. He did say he'd put it in his diary but it might be better if he stays away.'

If he attends the party that will make my plan all the easier.

I leave Chris to sort out some last-minute catering details and spend time coming up with ideas for the pin code on Mike's phone. I combine that with some research about drug mules. I surf the internet and scan various websites for newspaper reports, academic research papers, opinionated blogs, statistical analyses. None of them gets me any closer to confirming my theory about the Excelseus School. At four o'clock I've had enough and on impulse, I go in search of a hair salon with a free appointment. I come out with my hair cut short just as a high spec silver convertible drives past. I'm surprised to see Andrew behind the wheel. It's not the car he drives to work and it's a model which would be outside the reach of even the best paid GP. He must have some lucrative private medicine contract somewhere and I wonder if that explains his odd absences from the GP surgery. My dislike of him ramps up the log scale. I sweeten the sour feeling over a cappuccino and pastry in a café on Church Road and then try to contact Charlie. She hasn't replied to any of my previous attempts so I just tap in a message saying I'll catch her at the party.

In the event she turns up well before the party begins and shuts herself in the dining room refusing to talk to anyone until she's finished transforming the room. Chris and I concentrate on setting out the food then go off to get ready. I choose a sleeveless red dress with a deep scoop neckline, thinking of my plans for the evening.

The party is in full swing when I go downstairs. The dining room has been turned into a disco that is unmistakeably brand Charlie. Given free rein, she has produced something akin to a surreal Santa's Grotto quite at odds with the music that's thumping out. I stare at a neon silver ball and fairy lights in disbelief and shut the door just as Chris comes down the corridor.

She opens the door opposite onto the lounge. Here all is soft lights and sophisticated jazz music.

'Much better,' I concede.

It's as if the house has acquired a split personality. It rather mirrors their relationship. I wonder just how long the two of them will survive as a couple.

'By the way,' Chris adds, 'your hair looks good. It suits you.'

I wander about to the sounds of animated conversation, looking for Mike. I open the door to the dining room where disco music is pumping out and spot Charlie, dressed in a frenzy of bright purple and yellow, gyrating about on the dance floor. I inveigle my way through the crowd until I'm close enough to grab her by the arm and push her out of the room.

She protests that I'm hurting her.

'Sorry, Charlie. It was the only way to get your attention.'

I push her into Chris's study and close the door. The base thump of the music follows us in but it's quiet enough.

'I just want to know if you've seen Chiara.'

'Not Chiara, again.' She pulls away from me but I rush over and block the doorway.

'Look, you've got to answer me.'

'What is this? I'm here for a party, not an interrogation by you.'

'Please, Charlie. I'm really worried about Chiara.'

Whether it's the pleading note in my voice or the desire to cut short an unpleasant interlude, Charlie stands back with her arms folded and stares at me. I tell her about Chiara's visit to the Young People's Clinic and how she ran out on me.

'She was really frightened. I wondered if she'd contacted you.'

Charlie is trembling but defiant. 'I haven't seen her. Now, can I go?'

I open the door and watch her stomp out of the room and back into the disco. Chris is in the hallway and Charlie pushes past her.

'What's up with Charlie?'

'I asked her if she'd seen Chiara. It didn't go down too well.'

I've yet to spot Mike but we both notice him at the same time. He's in conversation with a woman dressed in jeans and a tee shirt, her long dark hair pulled back in a fashionable plait.

'I see Mike's been highjacked by Jessica,' says Chris.

'They don't look too happy with each other.

'When Jessica puts on her investigator's hat, she can be relentless. I bet Mike's regretting he came.'

We approach the waring couple and they break off their exchange with evident signs of relief. Chris introduces me to Jessica then manoeuvres her away from Mike before she can say more. Mike glares after them.

'I need a drink.'

I follow him over to the temporary bar and he helps himself to an open bottle of wine.

'Is there anywhere to escape all this?'

I point him in the direction of the garden. He makes no objection when I accompany him. We walk down to the end of the lawn where the empty chaise longue is swinging gently as the previous occupants cross paths with us. We sit side by side and Mike plants the bottle on the ground. We sitting sipping wine as we look back at the house glowing like a stage set with the sounds of music and chatter eclipsing the traffic noise along the nearby seafront road. Above us the night sky glows orange from the city lights adding to the theatricality of the setting. Mike turns to look at me as if he's only just appreciated my presence.

'That's some dress. You've had your hair cut too, just like....'

'Don't go there, Mike.'

He's thinking I've gone back to the style I had when I was working with him.

'Well, you look stunning.'

I take a swig of my drink to hide my embarrassment, secretly pleased at the progress I'm making.

'No hard feelings about the other night?' he continues.

'Let's just forget it and move on, eh?'

I give him a kiss on the cheek. I can smell the nauseous perfume of the woman from the Excelseus School. He kisses me back.

'I might have over-reacted a bit when you told me about the Excelseus School.'

He can't know about the specimen pot I handed in or he wouldn't be so prepared to admit that. We settle back on the cushions.

'I take it you've not met that Jessica woman before. I'd stay clear of her if I were you. She can be a bloody nuisance. She's always popping up at the station trying to muscle in on the latest investigation.'

An interesting point which I file away. We carry on drinking until the bottle is half empty. It's time to make a move.

'I'm starving. Shall we get something to eat?' I suggest.

'Where's the buffet?'

'It'll be a bit of a scrum in the kitchen. How about going somewhere quieter? There's a great, little tapas place not far from your flat.'

I grin to myself as Mike phones for a taxi.

The heat-wave weather is threatening to break, with dark storm clouds scudding across the channel towards Hove. I take my mac as a precaution. The restaurant is darkly lit with typical Andalusian décor and Spanish owners who turn out to cook the food as well as serve it with enthusiasm and charm. Mike asks for a table in the small back room which has only two tables, both empty. He downs a glass of a heady rioja as we wait for our order. I hold back in order to stay alert. Mike attacks the tapas as if he hasn't eaten for a week. He piles his plate with helpings of: tortilla, patatas bravas, boquerones, ensalada rusa, gambas and Serrano ham. I take a more modest portion and sip my wine slowly.

'Great place,' I say. 'As good as anywhere in London.'

I talk a bit about my favourite eating places in the capital and then in a calculated move, open up about Steve to steer the conversation into more personal waters. Mike offers nothing much about his relationship with Carole but is unstinting in his anecdotes about his boys, adding that he misses them a lot. By the time we've finished eating, the atmosphere between us is intimate enough to leave unspoken the question as to where we go next.

We walk out of the restaurant and turn towards Mike's place. My plan is galloping along. The rain starts to fall in torrents just as we get near. I leave my mac dripping on a peg in the hallway next to his dry one. In the sitting room, the large sliding glass doors to the balcony are closed against the sudden unseasonal autumn coolness. I miss standing in the warm night air, feeling its warmth on my skin. I look through the balcony doors at the city lights stretching like orange stars towards the horizon. The effect of the view is diminished by the glass barrier.

Mike hangs his wet jacket on the back of a dining chair and then puts on a jazz CD by some unpronounceable artist whose name I promptly forget. He passes me a festival brochure and leaves me to skim through it while he goes to into the kitchen. I don't register much of its content as I'm thinking about what comes next. I'm tempted to start going through his jacket pockets but I know it's not the moment. Mike is soon back brandishing a bottle of a vintage red from the Burgundy region.

'This should be really good,' he says.

'Shouldn't you save it for a dinner party? Let's have a brandy instead.'

Mike fetches a bottle and glasses from the cabinet across the room. He puts them on the coffee table in front of us and we settle down together on the sofa. I pour out the brandy, a small one for me, a large one for him. He takes a long sip of his as I play with my glass. His cheeks are flushed as he raises his glass and gulps back his brandy.

'Aren't you tempted to give it another go with Carole? You said you miss your kids.'

'I'm 100% sure Carole wouldn't want me. And jobwise it could be difficult to get a transfer back to London.'

Mike is on his second large brandy but I'm need a coffee. It could be a long night and I want to keep a clear head. I go into the kitchen while he takes himself off to the bathroom. When he comes back, it's clear he's had a fix. I excuse myself and look for signs in the bathroom. I see a scrunched-up piece of paper with specs of white powder clinging to it when I throw a tissue in the waste bin.

On my return, Mike is on his mobile and looking serious. He's not saying much, just the odd *yes* or *no* as he listens to what's being said. He's drinking my coffee after finishing his own. When the call ends, he slams the mobile down on the table. I notice it's the touch screen phone and not the slider.

'Shit.'

'Something wrong?'

'You're not kidding. I've been called out.'

'I thought you were off duty?'

'I am. I don't drink like this on duty. No, they've found another body in a lay-by on the A23. Completely burnt to a cinder this time but could be another young girl. It's everyone hands-on for now.'

'You're in no state to drive.'

'I've got a police car calling for me.'

He peers out of the sliding balcony doors.

'What a bloody awful night too. It's pouring down. I'll need my raincoat.'

The intercom bell rings.

'That's my lift. Gotta go. Look, you stay on here. It'll be hard to get a taxi with this weather. With a bit of luck, I might get back before too long.'

He rushes into the hallway, leaving his jacket on the back of the dining chair.

After he's gone, I sit for a good ten minutes unable to believe that the hand of fate has been so generous. Then I get up and rummage through the pockets of his jacket. My fingers are soon touching something cold and hard and I pull out the slider phone. I try and crack the pin code with combinations that have already occurred to me but without success. I throw the phone on the sofa in frustration then sit back on the sofa thinking about how Mike might go about choosing a PIN.

He's always had a brilliant memory for figures. He could remember case numbers from years ago and only had to hear a security code once to know it forever. I think about birthdays, house number, car registration number and decide that things like that are too obvious for Mike and too easy for people who know him well. What would be unique to him and difficult for others to access? I think of passport number, national insurance number, bank codes. I've no idea where to find these in his flat but some sixth sense tells me they're not personal enough for Mike. What is it that identifies him? It's obvious in the end. He's a police officer and he's got an individual police identification number. It has to be some combination of that. It'll be on his badge but he'll have taken it with him. There's only one thing to do. Go to bed and wait for him to come back. If he's not returned by morning then I'll have to wait until another day to test out my theory. I get a tissue from the bathroom and wipe the phone clean of my finger prints, then slip it back into his jacket pocket and go to bed.

I sleep in fits and starts until I hear Mike come back just before dawn. I hear the front door slam shut. He comes into the bedroom and switches on the light, only to switch it off immediately he sees my figure curled up under the duvet. I keep my eyes closed and hear him undressing and then tip-toeing across the room to the ensuite. For a few minutes there are sounds of a tap running, the noise of an electric toothbrush and the flush of the toilet, then more soft footsteps across the room and a naked Mike slipping into bed beside me. He reaches across to me and touches my breasts. I turn towards him and he runs his hand down my body. I let his fingers go where they will but he's exhausted and the brief attempt at intimacy soon expires. I'm relieved. I wait until his breathing changes to the rhythm of deep sleep then slide out of bed leaving him to his slumbers.

I crouch on the floor until my eyes become accustomed to the dark then crawl across the room to retrieve my clothes. Mike stirs in his sleep and I almost drop my shoes. I hold my breath and open the door, taking care to press down slowly on the handle. I open the door a bare minimum and squeeze through, then close it again without making a noise. I dress in the sitting room and then go through Mike's raincoat. As expected, I find his badge in an inside pocket and memorise the number. I wipe my fingerprints from the badge. Perhaps I'm overcautious, but I can't be too careful. I sit on the hall floor well away from the bedroom and start playing with random combinations of numbers. It's soon clear that it's fruitless, the possibilities run into millions. I have to decide on a system. With six numbers the permutations are endless. I eliminate the first two numbers which indicate the year of registration and concentrate on the last four which are personal to Mike. I use these in sequence without success. Too easy. I try them backwards. That doesn't work either. Even working with four numbers, the possibilities are huge but I persevere. I tap in the first, the third, then the second and finally the fourth and the home screen pops into view. I'm in.

First of all, I check the call log. None of the numbers has a name attached, just initials. There are only three, all from mobile phones. I enter the numbers and the initials into the notes on my phone and check for texts. There are none. If there were any they've all been deleted. I scroll through the phone looking for any saved documents. There's just one. When I open it, I guess it to be some sort of rota. There's an initial against each of what I take to be times on duty. I move on to checking the favourites list and find one bookmarked website for tracking ship movements. When I open this, it shows all the ships entering Shoreham Port, both commercial and private.

One thing is clear. Even without noticing he used his touch screen phone for the work call earlier, the paucity and nature of the entries on the slider phone confirms that it's not the phone he uses for work. I sit staring at it, wondering how to record what I've seen without leaving a digital trace. I opt for photographing the rota and make a note of the bookmarked website. As a last check, I look at the notes and reminder folders. In the notes, I find a list of dates for May. I take a photo of this too and then quickly scroll through settings and find the number of the phone. I add that to my notes and then make sure I've closed all the apps I've opened. Another careful wipe of the phone and then I wrap it in a tissue ready to replace it in his jacket pocket. I'll have to make sense of what I've discovered later. I put on my mac which is still damp and go back into the sitting room to replace the phone. I'm two steps away from the jacket when Mike stumbles into the room.

He's looking rough. I slip the phone up the sleeve of my mac.

'Couldn't sleep,' he says, rubbing his eyes.

'I thought you were out for the count.'

'Are you off?'

'I didn't want to disturb you. Now you're up, any chance of a coffee?'

'Okay.'

I'm relieved when he goes off the kitchen. I rapidly wipe clean the phone and replace it in his jacket pocket. When Mike brings in a large cafetière of strong black coffee, I'm sitting down, still with my mac on. We finish the coffee in silence, each absorbed in our respective and no doubt very different preoccupations.

Chapter Twenty-Four

Sunday 24 May

I take a taxi back. The early Sunday morning sun is chasing away the dampness of the previous night. The glistening pavements are drying out and the day promises a return to the good weather that has characterised most of May. I stare out of the window at the deserted streets then take another look at what I've found on Mike's phone. From the bookmarked website, he seems to be monitoring ship movements into Shoreham Port. The duty rota is headed SPS 2009. I do an internet search and find any number of firms with those initials. I scroll through the list and until I find SPS listed as a security firm based in Shoreham Port. I bookmark the website and wonder if Jessica came across it during her bribery investigation.

I turn to the phone contacts. One is marked as ELS. That has to be the Excelseus Language School. With its position in Shoreham Port a link to the SPS security firm would make sense. A second contact is marked as I.B. SPS, possibly an employee of the firm. Something else to check with Jessica. The initials CCC are more of a puzzle. What is Mike up to? I put my phone away and look out of window trying to come up with a theory. The taxi makes an abrupt stop at traffic lights so I get a clear view of a figure running to catch a bus on the other side of the road. It's Charlie but I think nothing of it as the bus lurches forward.

The house bears all the hallmarks of the previous night's party. My head is aching so I add two paracetamols to a breakfast of cereal and toast and marmalade, downing a large mug of black coffee so strong that it decimates my taste buds. I've just finished when a bleary-eyed Chris wanders into the kitchen.

'Hangover?' I ask.

'A bit. Have you seen Charlie? She said she was popping out to get some milk ages ago but she's not come back. She's just so unreliable sometime. It drives me mad.'

'I saw her getting on a bus by the Town Hall not so long ago.'

As soon as the words are out, my stomach does a somersault. I remember the bus was heading for the Devil's Dyke and thinking back, I recall seeing two people sprinting after her. I had assumed at the time that they were just trying to catch the bus. Now, as I run over the scene again, I'm convinced they were chasing Charlie. I rush out to my car without stopping to give Chris an explanation. I drive out of Hove and turn off to the Devil's Dyke. I find a parking place straightaway thanks to the departure of a family-packed SUV full of a purgatory of squealing children.

My fears for Charlie intensify when I see the QXK Zupro from the Excelseus School in the car park. I approach it with caution but it's empty. I check out the pub but there's no sign of Charlie. The most likely place for her to go will be the woods where there is plenty of cover. I set off in that direction along the track around the top of the Dyke. Its grassy hollow dips downwards like an ice cream cone. I walk along the path on the north side as it slopes down to the woods, kicking up knobbly pieces of chalk as I go. To my left the police investigation tent is still in place over the spot where I found the girl. There's with a cordon round it and one bored police officer on duty.

I reach the gate to the wood and go through, picking my way down the rubbly path edged by overhanging trees. Small globules of sunlight penetrate the rich abundance of leaves, dappling the way ahead. A strange bird sound pierces the air and makes me stop. I hear it again. This time I can tell it's too odd to be a birdcall. It's coming from the direction of a shelter that someone has built in the wood, probably for a kids' game. When I hear the sound a third time, a premonition makes me approach the shelter to see what's going on. There's no game in progress, and no children playing hide and seek, simply a very frightened Charlie.

'Charlie! What's up? You look terrible.'

Not only is she as white as her sundress but she's shivering, despite the heat of the day, and cowering like a caged animal.

She starts crying so I crouch down beside her and put my arm round her.

'Are you on your own?' she asks.

She isn't satisfied with my first reassurance.

'Are you sure?'

When I give the same answer, she's still unhappy.

'Are you absolutely sure you weren't followed?'

'No, Charlie, I wasn't; I've been very careful.'

I sit on the ground next to her. We stare out of the gap that serves as the entrance to the shelter.

'What's going on?'

It takes a while for her to begin speaking.

'I left Chris this morning to get some milk, but just as I got to the supermarket on Church Road, I noticed this black car following me. It was going very slowly. Then it pulled over and these men got out so I just started running. They came after me but then a bus pulled up so I jumped on it. I didn't even know where it was going.'

'Have you seen them before, these men?'

'I'm sure they're the ones who came looking for Chiara that time in Jaq's shop. They followed the bus in their car.'

'A black QXK Zupro?'

'No idea. I don't know anything about cars. It's like a super special sports car.'

'How come they didn't see you?'

'I managed to hide in the middle of a group of people. They made for the pub so I went with them and then headed straight to the ladies' and climbed out of the back window.'

She sinks her head in her hands.

'This is all because of Chiara.'

She lets out a big sob then carries on with her story. It started the day after Chris's dinner party. Charlie got a phone call at about six in the morning.

'It was Chiara. Jaq must have given her my mobile number despite what I said. Chiara had borrowed someone's phone and was begging to come and stay. She'd been roaming the streets for a week after running away from the bookshop. I couldn't say no.'

There's a tremble in Charlie's voice as she continues.

'That Zupro car turned up one day and parked across the street from my flat. It stayed all morning. I was too scared to go out while it was there. I could see two men in the car just watching the flat. They must've known Chiara was inside.'

'Were they the guys who were chasing you today?'

'I think so. I saw them get out of the car for a smoke but I didn't want to look out of the window too long in case they saw me.'

Charlie twists her hands nervously together, then the tears run down her cheeks again. I draw her closer to me. She's shaking all over. My own heart is beating at a prodigious rate and I'm having to make a conscious effort to appear calm.

'I should never have let her stay,' she sobs. 'Those men wouldn't be after me now.'

I hold her even more tightly. She stops sobbing and wipes her face on her skirt.

'I think we should get the police involved.'

That suggestion only makes matters worse. Charlie's becoming hysterical so I take her by the shoulders and shake her, not too hard, but just enough to calm her down. I can see she's in no state to tell me more.

I place a hand over hers and whisper, 'It's all right, Charlie. Let's get you away from here. You can stay at Chris's for a while.'

'No, no. It won't be safe. Please, don't take me there.'

'Okay, okay.'

I turn to plan C, which I've been hoping to avoid.

'I'll take you to London, then. You can stay in my flat for now while we sort out a plan.'

A shadow of a smile crosses her face as we get to our feet. We manage to avoid the officer stationed at the crime scene and make sure to keep a look out for the men. The QXK Zupro is still in the car park but parked well away from my Zuperga. I bundle Charlie into the passenger seat and drive off. The road opens up without any traffic ahead and I throw the car rally style around the corners, enjoying the experience despite the circumstances. My pleasure is short-lived as we come up behind a cautious driver afraid to go above 35 mph on the narrow, twisting roads.

'Can't you overtake?' urges Charlie.

'Not on this road but we're nearly at the roundabout and then we can get straight onto the A23.'

But not soon enough. In the rear-view mirror I can see the black supercar approaching us. It stays back at a distance but follows us onto the A27. When the A23 slip road to London approaches, I accelerate and drive past it.

'You've missed the exit,' says Charlie.

'I know. We've got company and I don't want them following us to London.'

Charlie turns round to take a look.

'What are you going to do?' She's started shaking again.

'Watch me. I hope you don't get car sick.'

I head towards Ditchling and screech along the B roads making sudden turn offs to less trafficked roads when cars ahead threaten to block my way. I'm soon weaving a course through familiar Sussex back roads. I twist and turn through the country lanes confident of where they're taking me. We're well ahead of our tail but I know it isn't enough. When the driveway of a large country house comes into view, I take my chance and turn in. The house is screened from the road by a high hedge and it's easy to stop the car out of sight of passing traffic. I kill the engine and sit listening for the roar of the supercar. We don't have to wait long before I hear it shoot past.

'Can we go now?' said Charlie.

'Not yet. Be patient.'

'What are you going to say to *her* then?'

Charlie points to a woman making her way down the driveway from the house. I get out of the car and meet her half way. She makes no fuss when I offer an explanation that we're lost and without a sat nav. With the impeccable good manners of a country lady she gives clear directions and I pretend to be taking it all in. As I walk back to the car, I hear the roar of the QXK Zupro coming along the road in the opposite direction. By the time we're passing through Burgess Hill, I'm certain I've shaken it off and I join the A23 for the rest of the trip to London.

Charlie sits in silence as the steady rhythm of our progress along the dual carriageway takes over from our frantic B-road drive. She's so quiet that I turn to see if she's all right. She's staring ahead scarcely blinking, as though she's been turned to stone. Rally style driving isn't for everyone, but perhaps it's just fear that's taken her voice away. I push down on the accelerator only to ease off a moment later. The last thing I need is to be stopped by an unmarked police car.

The familiar outskirts of London are reassuring after the incredible events of the past few days. I'm pleased to reach Balham and usher Charlie into my flat. Then I set about dealing with the practicalities of her stay: access, money, clothes, not to mention her boredom. Pity I can't call on Steve to see if he'll keep an eye on her. She's still jittery so I send her off for a shower and put together a concoction of gin, orange juice and sparkling white wine for her. I push it into her hand when she returns in a towelling dressing gown with her wet hair looking even wilder than usual.

'Here, try this. It's a South London Spritzer.' She accepts my invention at face value and takes a gulp and then another longer one.

'Not bad,' she comments. 'Quite strong is it?'

'It'll do you good.'

I sit opposite her with a mineral water as she lolls on the sofa. She finishes my invented cocktail so I make her another hoping she'll open up about Chiara. She's soon racing through details in a nervous voice about how Chiara came from Italy as a language student but found that things were not as she expected.

'In what way?'

'She wouldn't say but she looked really upset. It must have had something to do with those men.'

Charlie gulps down most of her drink.

'I'd warned her about them. I kept on at her to stay in the flat but when I popped back from the *Open House* the Saturday before last, she'd gone out. She came back shortly afterwards, wet through. I was so keyed up by then, I was a bit short with her. That must have been why she went off again the following Monday.'

That would be the evening she came to the Young People's Clinic.

'I haven't seen her since; I bet those men have got her and now they've after me.'

I go and make Charlie another cocktail. She sits cupping the glass in her hand as tears fall into it.

'It's all too horrible,' she says, between sobs. 'Jaq dying, Chiara missing and now those awful men out to get me. You've got to find her, Kate.'

I tell her I'll do my best, though it could well be too late. I'm reluctant to leave but I need to get back to Hove.

It's nearly midnight when I arrive. I'm surprised to see the light on in the sitting room. I guess Chris has just returned from a call-out but I'm wrong. She comes to the door before I've even got out of the car. She rushes out as I walk across the driveway and I soon realise my mistake in not contacting her about my impromptu London trip.

'Kate. Where on earth have you been?' Her tone hovers between anxious and irritated. 'Are you okay? I've been trying to reach you. You looked frantic when you left this morning.'

I pull out my phone to check the call log. The screen is black.

'Sorry. It's been off all day.'

'Did you catch up with Charlie. I'm assuming that's why you rushed off. I've not been able to get hold of her.'

'I did find Charlie. She's been with me most of the day. I should've contacted you. I'd better explain.'

Chris listens patiently while I tell her what's happened and where Charlie is now.

'I don't suppose you could persuade her to go to the Police with what she knows.'

'No. She became hysterical when I suggested it.'

'Not surprising. She was busted for drug possession once. She told me she never wanted to go near the police again. She hated being questioned about Jaq's death.'

'I feel sorry for her, getting caught up in all this.'

'What a situation. Charlie won't cope very well.'

'Not sure I would in the circumstances.'

'Oh, come on.' Chris is having none of it. 'A GP and an ex-cop, you've got more *sang-froid* than most of us.'

'Well, if I have, I'm going to need every last jot. I've come up with some evidence against Mike. I'm going to pin him down.'

'Just be careful, Kate. I don't want to end up doing an autopsy on you.'

Chapter Twenty-Five

Monday 25 May

I phone to check on Charlie first thing in the morning. She's moans that I've woken her up. I promise to call back later and sit down to look at what I've noted down from Mike's slider phone. First, I concentrate on the CCC entry. There's only one way to clarify what it stands for. I tap in the code to block caller recognition and ring the number. A computerised voice answers.

'This is Central Care Consolidates. Please enter the number of the extension you require.'

There's no option to wait for someone to answer and no way of leaving a message. I cancel the call. The name gives me no idea what business the firm undertakes. I turn to the rota. The initials I.B. appear next to certain dates. I look at the dates and times that I noted on Mike's phone and see that they match up. The next date listed is for tomorrow. I check the shipping website to if see if anything tallies with that. A cargo ship called the *Hyrenia* is detailed as due into Shoreham port just before midnight tomorrow.

I call Jessica to find out more about the security firm. I get her voice mail so I leave a message, asking her to ring back. She doesn't take long and asks if I can join her for coffee at St Ann's

Well Gardens in half an hour as she's due to meet up with some former newspaper colleagues from London.

I've yet to see the gardens in daylight. My image of them is based on the twilight setting of my visit to the *Jardin Flambeau* event. The macabre thoughts of that evening are out-of-place now as I walk along a wide stretch of tarmac, passing tennis courts and a bowling green on my left. The air smells fresh from newly mown grass and I follow the path as far as a grassy area where it meanders off among ancient trees which rustle in the warm breeze. I remember Jaq referring to the gardens as a miniature version of London's Regent's Park. That morning, it's a hub for local families preferring the convenience of a child-friendly café to a beach picnic. The café is so popular that every outside seat is taken, except for one, set a little apart at a table for two. The occupant of the other seat is Jessica Witching. She continues to guard my place while I fetch us both a skinny latte.

'You were lucky to get a seat,' I comment, as I return with our order.

'I'm a regular here. I've only got to let the owner, Julie, know when I'm coming and she makes sure there's space for me.'

I laugh. 'What it is to have connections.'

'You soon find your way around and carve out a scene for yourself here. I used to work on the *Evening Standard* in London but I much prefer living and working in Brighton and Hove. Anyway, enough about me, you said you wanted to talk about the Excelseus school when you phoned.'

'I've come across a security firm online called SPS that operates in Shoreham Port. I was wondering if you had any info on the firm as a result of your bribery enquiry and whether they could be linked to the Excelseus Language School.'

'SPS was one of the suspect firms in my enquiry but I drew a blank when I tried to prove that guards were being bribed to turn a blind eye to irregularities in the port. As far as the Excelseus School goes, it may well have its own security guards but even so, I know that all the buildings in the Shoreham Port Complex must have a contract with SPS.'

'So, if a guard working for SPS took a bribe, it could come from the Excelseus School.'

'Right.'

'Do you know the names of the SPS guards? There was no indication on their website.'

'That's not surprising. They come and go. I'd have to check my notes.'

'They would be a help.'

She agrees to email them to me.

'Did your investigation come up with a reason security why guards were taking bribes?'

'Just rumours that it could be to do with drug trafficking.'

'Using Shoreham Port as a point of entry?'

'Right. I spoke to Mike Black about the idea once but got nowhere.'

That doesn't surprise me.

'What do you think of Mike?'

'He can be a sticky character. He doesn't like me too much. Why?'

'I'd like to see how he reacts if I tell him you've got your eye on the Excelseus School again.'

'You're thinking he might be looking into a criminal link between SPS and the school?'

'Something like that.'

I make no reference to my suspicions about Mike. I don't want Jessica's journalistic antenna pointed at him just yet.

'I don't know if it will help, but go ahead. I'm sure you'll get something out of him You seemed to be getting on well with him at the party.'

'He's a former colleague from when I was training to be a detective.'

'Ex-cop turned medic. Now there's a story I'll get out of you before long.'

I decide against asking about Central Care Consolidates. It could open me up to too many awkward questions before I know just where Mike figures in all of this. I leave her to wait for her friends who are about to arrive and wander off around the park, past the fish pond and on to the well. The plaque above the well tells me it's on the site of an eighteenth-century pump house and was a small but important spa. Until 1935, that is, when the well dried up after the creation of new wells nearby. I go and peer into what I expect to be its empty depths, only to be disconcerted when I see it filled in with concrete. It's like staring at a tombstone. It jerks me back to St Andrew's Church graveyard and Jaq's memorial service. It's a painful memory that sends shudders through me and in an attempt to erase it, I run all the way down to the seafront where I gasp in the taste of the sea as I recover my breath. I use the walk back to Chris's house to put myself in the right frame of mind for contacting Mike.

He answers my call straightaway and from the background hum of voices, I guess he's at the station.

'Are you on duty?'

''Fraid so.'

'Is it that case you were called out to?'

'Yeah. It's still a bit frantic. Hang on.'

I hear him talking to a colleague, though I can't make out the precise conversation. He comes back on the line.

'Look I can't talk now, I gotta go.'

I persuade him to ring back. I lie on the bed but I find the waiting unnerving. I put a CD of forties swing music on my Walkman. I listen to a few tracks but none suits my mood or distracts me from my impatient wait. I pull off the earphones and look around for something else. My eye catches the book that I picked up from Jaq's bedroom in her parent's house. It's entitled, *The Former Mattia Pascal:* a translation of an Italian novel that I read years ago when Jaq was enthusing about it. As I pick it up to read the blurb on the back cover, a slip of paper flutters to the ground. There's not much scribbled on it but I recognise Jaq's handwriting, one of her interminable notes that for once, she forgot to throw away. *18.00 special delivery.* I'd like to think it referred to a consignment of books but I'm betting it refers to cocaine. I'm still staring at the note and thinking about Jaq, when Mike calls.

'I've not got long. Why the urgency?'

'I wanted to warn you about Jessica Witching. She's got a theory about the Devil's Dyke murder. She thinks it could be linked to a drug trafficking syndicate operating out of Shoreham Port. She said she was going to do some snooping around tonight.'

'She's a pain in the arse. She tried that idea about Shoreham Port on me once before and didn't get very far. And as for a link to the Devil's Dyke murder, well, you know journalists, they come up with all sorts of unproven ideas about everything.'

I don't respond to the provocation.

'Hang on.' He utters a few monosyllabic replies to someone next to him then comes back to me. 'Look, I'd just ignore Ms Witching and her ideas. She'll soon run out of steam.'

'She doesn't give up easily, you know that. She mentioned a cargo ship due into port tonight. What if she decides to check it out? If there is something in what she says, she could be in danger.'

'You can tell Jessica Witching from me that if she's got any idea about snooping around the port to forget it. She could be had up for trespassing, danger or no danger.'

He hangs up and I prepare myself for the evening ahead. I change into jeans and a sweater and take pains to avoid Chris who is clattering around in the kitchen when I leave. I go to beachside café-bar across the road and hover around until a bench on the decking area becomes free. I sip my lager and stare out at the horizon. For once, the ebb and flow of the sea are barely a whisper and I can just hear the raucous sounds of Brighton pier drifting towards me. The setting sun is fading as a cargo ship appears on the horizon. The ship is too far away for the name to be visible yet. I order a coffee and by 11.30 pm it's close enough to the shore to see that the name is, *Hyrenia*, just as expected. I start walking towards the western end of the promenade where I turn right and then left into Basin Road. I can see the cargo ship making its way into the port as it dips in and out of my view behind the buildings on my left. The gate to the school is predictably closed when I reach it but there are lights on in the building and the QXK Zupro is in the car park along with a couple of SUVs. The ship docks near the Excelseus School but with the main gate shut, there's of way of accessing the quayside. I walk on to see if there is any other way in. There's very little street lighting and the other buildings are in darkness and with impenetrable security gates and CCTV cameras.

I return to the school, sticking to the shadows, pleased at my decision to wear black. I make my way along the side of the road bounded by a wall of rock with frequent indentations that provide me with cover. I pull back into one as a car draws up at the school gate. I recognise the car as Mike's and the gate opens to allow it in. I wait until the gate is almost closed again, then slip through it just before it clangs shut. I duck down behind one of the SUVs. My breathing is rapid and my heart rate up as I poke my head around the car to see Mike walking towards the school. A sensor floods the car park with light and I dodge back behind the SUV.

I hear the front door of the school close and the light fades out. I scurry towards Mike's car and take a shot of it to include the quayside, and a close-up of his number plate. I cross my fingers that the night-time photo function on my phone is adequate. I get back behind the SUV just as the school door opens again and I hear footsteps approaching. I'm just wondering whether to crawl underneath the SUV when they stop.

'No sign of her.' It's Mike speaking.

'Are you sure your source is reliable?'

The voice is that of the women from the school.

'It's not the first time that wretched journalist has been after evidence of drug smuggling. She's approached me a while back. She'd got it into her head that the Excelseus could be involved. Let me tell you, she didn't get that idea from me.'

'Make sure she forgets all about it or there'll be serious repercussions for us all. We'll set up a patrol. You'd better go.'

The sound of a car door opening and closing is followed by the noise of an engine revving and the clatter of the gate opening. The car park is still brightly lit so I daren't follow his car out of the gate.

The woman is speaking again.

'All clear, boys. Get going. Move this lot pronto.'

'What about the patrol?'

'One of you take the SUV.'

'Better kill the lights before we leave, then.'

I hear the march of footsteps back across the car park to the SUV. I crouch down as low as I can as a man gets in and starts up the engine. The car park lights go out and the gate opens. The SUV crawls forward. I'll soon be exposed. I double over myself and move forward with it, praying I can't be seen in the rear-view mirror. It turns left into Basin Road and as it accelerates away, I run frantically in the opposite direction towards the promenade. I've just reached the end of the road when I hear the roar of a car coming in my direction. I turn and see the SUV heading towards me. My skin prickles and my heart thumps. I run as fast as I can to reach the promenade and make it just before the car. I glance over my shoulder to see the SUV has stopped and a muscular guy is now running after me. He's closing down on me. I look frantically around for a way to escape.

Chapter Twenty-Six

Tuesday 26 May

A group of rowdy windsurfers have set up an impromptu open-air party by the lagoon. I scoot towards them and push myself into the middle of the crowd. I grab a plastic beaker of some cheap wine. No one pays me any attention. They're all far too drunk to notice. I keep looking in the direction of my pursuer as the sweat dries on my forehead and my heart beat returns to normal. I wonder how long I can hang about there and what to do next. The music from a portable sound system has reached a head-splitting decibel level but it proves to be my saviour. A police car screams to a halt on Kingsway and two officers get out and stride over to the lagoon and the party. When I take my eyes off the approaching policemen, I see the guy from the Excelseus school scurrying off towards the SUV which soon screeches away from the scene. I leave the windsurfers to deal with their unwelcome visitors and rush off along the promenade. The moment I cross Kingsway to walk up the street to Chris's, I break into a jog. I turn at intervals to look over my shoulder expecting, at any moment, two burly arms to seize me and bundle me into a car. I'm relieved when I turn the key in the lock and slam the front door behind me, leaving my fears on the doorstep.

I'm woken at 6.30 am by the sound of a text notification. I grope around on the bedside locker for my mobile with my eyes half closed. It's from Tony. It confirms a fingerprint match on the specimen pot. The body of the girl is Chiara. I sit up in bed and stare at the few words that have shattered my slim hope that it wasn't her. A tear drops onto my phone. I lie back on the bed with an overwhelming sense of failure. A mental shake reminds me that this is no time for self-recrimination or self-pity. I send Jessica a text saying I've got some news, reasoning she won't object to the early hour. She phones straight back. When she hears that Chiara has been identified, she doesn't hesitate.

'I'll head down to Brighton station and do some probing. Thanks for the tip.'She promises to keep my name out of it but I'm betting Mike will deduce I'm her source. I don't care. I'm too angry at the thought that Mike could have done more to find Chiara and prevent her murder. She asks if I've had a chance to speak to him.

'I didn't get anything out of him, he just told me to warn you not to go snooping around.'

I take myself off for a brisk walk by the sea to reset my emotions.

I arrive at the surgery in good time and brace myself for the moment I tell Rose the news. When I tell her about Tony's text, she's devastated, there's no other word.

'It's all my fault. If I hadn't barged in she wouldn't have run off and she'd still be alive.'

We go through the whole episode in detail. I finally get her to accept that we couldn't have kept Chiara in the surgery against her will and that, at some point, she was going to leave. Rose seems reassured, though our chat does little to assuage my own feelings of remorse. A phone call from Clare jolts me out of my self-pity. She's been with two detectives in her office who are now on their way to speak to me. I recognise the detective sergeant who interviewed me at the station but the other younger guy with greasy blond hair and a large belly is new to me. The DS gives me a nod of recognition and introduces his companion.

'You must be here about Chiara's murder,' I say.

'You've heard she's been identified, then? We've read your previous statement and just want to a few more details about her.'

'Of course. Morning surgery will begin in about twenty minutes. Will that give us enough time?'

'That should be sufficient, thank you, Dr Green.'

His overweight colleague opens his notebook, pen at the ready. In answer to their questions I describe Chiara's appearance and the blue jeans and tee shirt she was wearing at the clinic. I emphasise the friendship band on her wrist.

'Could you run through her visit for us?'

I tell them exactly what happened. The only information I omit is the name of the Excelseus school. I don't want to put Mike on his guard. I ignore the fact that, on this occasion, I really could be seen as obstructing an investigation.

'Did anyone else see Chiara at the clinic?'

'Rose, the clinic nurse, came into my room while I was with Chiara but she didn't talk to her. Chiara ran off when Rose interrupted our conversation.'

There's nothing more I want to add so I accompany them to the reception area where Andrew is berating one of the receptionists for a problem with his morning list.

'Who's that guy?' asks the detective with the notepad.

'Dr Andrew Gull,' I reply.

'Ah, the other clinic doctor. Short fuse, hasn't he?'

They go over to Andrew and introduce themselves and explain why they are at the surgery.

'Could we have a few words about the Young People's Clinic, Sir.'

'I haven't been on duty at the clinic recently.'

'Just a few routine questions, it won't take long.'

Andrew is quick to answer back.

'I've a surgery starting in five minutes; is it really necessary?'

'If it's inconvenient, Sir, you could come to the station to make a statement.'

'No, no.' Andrew is quick to dispel that idea. 'I'll just ask the receptionists to explain there's a delay in starting my list.'

I return to my room, glad to slip into the familiar routine of work. I throw myself into mundane admin tasks and make unnecessarily detailed notes about problematic test results or those that need chasing up. For a while, it's therapeutic, a distraction from a creeping sense of an approaching crisis. As the morning runs on, though, my own preoccupations threaten my concentration. Jessica has sent me the email I asked for with the list of names on the SPS payroll. There's an Ian Bunger, which matches the initials I.B. on Mike's list.

That news only adds to my stress. It escalates further when I have to sit through Clare's announcement of Chiara's murder following her visit to the Young People's Clinic. There's a murmur of disbelief and shock from everyone except Andrew who sits staring across the room without a shadow of emotion on his face. I want to go over and slap him in the face. As if that were not enough, Andrew barges into my room immediately after the meeting. He doesn't bother to sit down, but just stands glaring at me.

'How did they find out it was Chiara who'd been murdered? There's been nothing in the press.'

'It was only confirmed yesterday, so the press wouldn't know about it.'

'That doesn't answer my question.'

'Why would I know? It's a police matter. Anyway, what's it to you? You didn't show any concern at the doctors' meeting.'

'It's just very odd that you seem to be so adept at stumbling across bodies. First Jacqueline Grey and now this Chiara.'

'What exactly are you insinuating here, that I murdered my closest friend and then someone I was trying to help professionally? Come on.'

He storms out of the room and I sit down, shaking all over.

I'll be in no state to face an afternoon surgery unless I get my emotions under control. I leave the premises, telling the reception staff that I'll be back in time for my first appointment. I've no destination in mind. All that matters is to keep walking until I feel calm. By the time I achieve that, I've arrived at Jaq's bookshop. I see a notice in the window saying *Closed until further notice*, but the lights are on. I catch sight of Jaq's mother moving around inside. She spots me and rushes out as though I'm a long-lost friend.

I don't like to refuse her offer to show me around so I follow her inside. Her husband comes over and shakes my hand.

'We're giving the bookshop a go, at least until the lease is up in six months and then we'll see. June's going to run it for now. Quite a change from her usual voluntary work.'

'I'm sure it's what Jaq would've wanted.'

'Come and see what we've done downstairs.' John ushers me into the basement.

It's been redecorated and refurnished, quite a transformation. The boxes of returns are neatly stacked. A couple of Ikea-style easy chairs add a welcoming touch.

'It really good. It looks much more spacious too.'

'Thank you. We might get rid of the cupboard.' He opens the doors onto empty shelves. 'I don't know why that detective was so interested in it this morning, there's nothing inside. We'd not even got round to cleaning it.'

'Was that the detective who came to your house?'

'That's right. He had a good snoop round down here. In the end we left him to it.'

I notice the shelves have now been wiped clean. Was that down to Mike? I climb back up the stairs and see the time on the wall clock. I say a hasty goodbye and rush back to the GP surgery only to bump into Andrew. He's showing out an elderly patient with a walking frame. He glares at me and points to his watch. I ignore him and go into my room. The late start to my list adds to the stress of the afternoon as I push Andrew's unpleasantness aside. As the succession of patients commences, I'm aware that my senses are heightened. The lights above my desk dazzle my eyes, my stethoscope feels ice-cold to touch and the dregs in my coffee mug have a pungent smell that appears to fill the room. My mouth is dry, despite swallowing a large glass of water and the biscuit I munch mid-surgery makes me feel sick. The sooner I finish the better. By the end of the afternoon, I know I have to ask Clare if I can take the rest of the week off. I'm at risk of making a medical error if I carry on at work like this. She's very understanding.

'You've been amazing at not taking any time off before this, after all that has happened. I've appreciated your covering for Andrew's absences, too.'

I arrive back at Chris's that evening with a combined feeling of frustration and relief. It's good to have a few days clear of work. I can use them to make headway with Mike and the Excelseus School. The fact that Chiara has been identified should motivate me but a feeling of culpability over her death is stalling me. Chris is quick to disabuse me of the idea.

'It's not your fault, Kate. Remember that.'

I give her a rueful smile which she ignores.

'If it helps, you might like to know that I have contacted Forensics. I should know the outcome by the end of the week.'

Chapter Twenty-Seven

Wednesday 27 May

A good night's sleep galvanises me into action. I ring Charlie when I deem it's not too early to wake her and tell her I'm coming to London.

'Aren't you working?' she asks.

'I've got the rest of the week off.'

I screech up the A23 and onto the M23, alert for unmarked police cars as I exceed the speed limit. It makes the urban crawl of the rest of the journey bearable. I call out to Charlie as I open the front door to my flat. There's no reply so I go into the sitting room and then into the kitchen. There's no sign of her. I knock on the door to the spare room. When that produces no response, I go in. I always imagined Charlie as a messy type but the bed is neatly made and the room tidy. In a last effort I try the bathroom. She's not there either. I'm about to panic, imagining that something has happened to her or that she's run off, when I hear the flat door close and footsteps coming up the stairs. I turn around and bump into Charlie walking towards the bathroom with a box of sanitary tampons in her hand.

'Charlie. You had me worried.'

'Just had to pop out for these.'

She goes off to sort herself out while I root around in the kitchen for something to eat. I can find nothing that would turn into an edible meal so we go to the Windmill pub on Clapham Common where Mike was heading just a couple of weeks ago. It used to be a familiar haunt for Steve and me, with its wooden floors and distressed furniture. I remember long Sunday lunches and inebriated walks back to my flat for something more than just a coffee.

Between mouthfuls of a vegetarian chilli dish, I tell Charlie she needs to come back to Hove.

She stops eating and puts down her fork.

'You know I can't go back. I'm not going to the police and those men....'

She grips the edge of the table as her voice rises to panic pitch. I put a hand on her arm

'Don't get hysterical, Charlie. Just listen to me, I've got some bad news.'

She stares at me with a wild look in her eyes. I take a swig of my mineral water then look straight back at her. There's no easy way to say it.

'Chiara's been murdered.'

Any hope that she'll take the news calmly is soon shattered.

'You see, you see. How can I possibly go back? I'll be next.'

She jumps up, pushing her chair back with such force that it topples over and runs out of the pub. I rush after her and find her standing at the edge of the nearby pond. She's shaking and in tears. I put my arm round her but she shrugs it off.

'Why did Jaq have to die? None of this would be happening if she were still alive. She shouldn't have died. She was a lovely person.'

'I know, but the important thing is to think what Jaq would want us to do. Isn't that right?'

'I wish she were still here. I never stopped loving her. I always hoped she would come back to me, even when she went off with that doctor who reminded her of you. At least that's what she said.'

That's something else new to me.

'So, come back with me for her sake. I need your help. I want to prove the police wrong. They think Jaq killed herself.'

Charlie stares at me, her eyes wide open in disbelief.

'I know. It can't be true. Someone killed her and I've always been sure that Chiara was the key to finding out who. Now that Chiara's gone, you're the only one I can turn to. We must figure out just who could have murdered Jaq.'

Charlie lets me take her by the arm and we cross the common to Balham High Road. The old oak trees tower over us, giving us some protection from the intense sun. The High Road is its usual buzzy mix of tempting ethnic restaurants and shops. We walk down the road surrounded by sounds and smells that invite me to stop and enjoy a take away kebab or one of the sweet cannoli from an Italian deli. Jaq would have loved the area but she never came to visit.

We're both hot and sweaty when we arrive at my flat. I make us a green tea and when Charlie seems more settled, I ask her if Chiara had mentioned the Excelseus Language School to her.

'I remember Chiara talking about being in a place in Hove and how she hated it there. She never said what sort of place it was or what it was called. She just told me she was glad she managed to run away and find Jaq's bookshop.'

I tell Charlie about the Excelseus Language School and my suspicions. She looks alarmed when I confirm that thugs from the school were the men on the look out for Chiara.

'Do you think they could have killed her?'

'I don't know, but if they did, they could have killed Jaq too.'

Charlie sips her tea with a frown on her face as I continue.

'If I could get inside the school and see what's happening, I could get the proof I need.'

I explain what I have in mind.

'That's too dangerous. You'll end up dead; we'll both end up dead.'

Charlie's voice has risen to an hysterical pitch so I gesture for her to drink her tea and wait for her to calm down.

'If we're careful everything will be okay. It's the only way to get at the truth about Jaq's death. Wouldn't she have wanted that?'

Charlie doesn't say anything. She just sits staring into her cup as if it will give her the answer.

'So, what do you think, will you come back with me?'

Chapter Twenty-Eight

Thursday 28 May....

We arrive in Hove just as the sky takes on a grey hue from threatening rain clouds. The wind is fierce and I hope it blows away the storm. Chris opens the door as I put my key in the front door lock. She puts a protective arm around Charlie and leads her upstairs. Chris has set up one of her spare rooms so Charlie can have some space of her own.

I leave them to chat and take a gin mix up to my room where I text Jessica to let her know that I'm making progress and will be in touch again soon. I lie on my bed thinking about my plan for the Excelseus School. I want Charlie to distract the woman on reception while I can get hold of her key card and gain access to the rest of the school. It took the whole journey back to Hove to persuade Charlie but she eventually agreed.

Later, I'm rooting around in the kitchen for some ideas for supper when Chris puts her head round the door. She's dressed in a chic grey trouser suit with a recently purchased mac over her shoulders.

'Charlie wants to speak to you. She's in the sitting room. I've got an evening meeting at the hospital. I should be back about ten.'

I make up a spritzer for us both and join Charlie. She's sprawled on the sofa, staring up at the ceiling.

'Chris said you wanted to have a chat.'

Charlie sits up and takes the spritzer. She concentrates on drinking most of it before speaking.

'I've changed my mind. I can't do it. I can't go near that school.'

I take a deep breath and make a big effort not to show my frustration at Charlie's change of heart. I thought everything had been decided.

'What if there were another way of finding out about the school?' says Charlie.

'Have you got an idea, then?'

'It's something that Chiara told me. I'd forgotten all about it until I was talking to Chris just now.'

Charlie picks up her drink and finishes the rest of it in one gulp.

'Chiara told me that Jaq had got her to write about what had happened to her since arriving in Hove. Jaq told her to keep it safe.'

'Any idea where it could be?'

'I remember Chiara saying she'd hidden it somewhere in my flat. She wouldn't say where and I never went looking for it.'

'Could it still be there?'

Chiara had nothing with her when she'd come to the Young People's Clinic so there's a good chance. Charlie considers the question.

'It must be, I guess.'

'Why don't we go and look for it?'

'I don't want to go back there. Not tonight anyway. I've had enough for today.'

'I'll go on my own if you lend me your key.'

She hands it over and goes off to make herself another spritzer. I drive over to her place but have to abandon any idea of a search. The black QXK Zupro is parked opposite the flat. I drive straight past, watching in my rear-view mirror to see if I'm followed. They don't know my car so I should be safe enough. I keep an eye out nonetheless as I take the Shoreham Road westbound towards the Sainsbury's on the edge of town. There's no sign of the supercar tailing me but I circle the supermarket carpark just in case until I find a space and stop the car. After fifteen minutes, I feel confident enough to return to Chris's where I say nothing to Charlie about the experience.

'Any luck?' she asks.

'Sorry.' I shake my head. 'I was thinking you might remember where it is after a night's sleep. We'll go back together tomorrow.'

I sleep badly and I'm on my second cup of coffee by the time Chris comes down for breakfast.

'Is Charlie awake?'

'I don't know. We didn't sleep together last night. She said she wanted to be on her own.'

'I'll go and see,' but as I get up to leave the kitchen, Chris grabs my arm.

'She asked not to be disturbed. She said she wanted a lie-in this morning.'

I'm regretting I gave back her key. I resign myself to a fruitless morning when my mobile rings. It's Clare. She's full of apologies for disturbing me so early, especially after we'd agreed on my leave of absence.

'We're really stuck this morning, Kate. Andrew's called in sick again and we're just overwhelmed with appointments. Would you be able to help out, just until lunchtime?'

It solves the problem of hanging around waiting for Charlie to appear, so I'm happy to agree.

I work my way through a series of routine problems which range across every organ in the human body. Without exception, all my patients are courteous and helpful. I'm grateful for the lack of stress. It's a welcome respite. Back at Chris's, I go straight up to Charlie's room and give a gentle knock on the door. She doesn't reply, so I knock louder. There's still no response so I open the door a chink. I call out but there's no answer so I go in.

The room is in darkness with the curtains drawn. There's no sign of Charlie. I check the ensuite bathroom. She's not there either.

I run downstairs and into the kitchen and then tear around the ground floor like a whirling dervish. The front door bangs so I rush towards it expecting to see Charlie. Instead I bump into Chris who's come to get a bite to eat on her way to an afternoon meeting.

'Do you know where Charlie is? She's not in her room and I've just looked everywhere downstairs.'

'What about my room, feel free to see if she's there.'

I march back upstairs. I check Chris's room, my room and the other bedrooms and then return to Charlie's room. Still no sign of her. I rush back downstairs.

'No luck?'

'Nothing.'

'Aren't you panicking a bit,' she suggests.

'You think?'

I thought Charlie was too scared to risk leaving the house on her own.

'I've got to find her, Chris. I'm going to her flat. I'm pretty sure that's where she'll be.'

My first ring on Charlie's buzzer by the front door of the flats goes unanswered. I wait a moment and then try again several times. When that elicits no response, I repeatedly press the buzzer next to hers and brace myself for the anorectic girl's expletives, I'm not disappointed. This time she opens the door in heavy make-up, with dark eyes and her hair styled like Amy Winehouse.

'What the fuck are you doing?' she says as she opens the front door. 'Oh, it's you again. I should have known.'

She tries to slam the door but I wedge my foot in the gap, wincing with pain from the impact.

'Please, this is really important.'

'Matter of life and death, is it?'

'Actually, yes, it is.'

Whether it's my tone of voice or simply the unexpected response, she relaxes her pressure on the door an instant and I push it towards her so I can squeeze past. I bound up the stairs towards Charlie's flat and start hammering on her door. The girl runs after me and grabs my arm.

'You can just stop all that, there's no point.'

I shake off her hand. 'I'll be the judge of that, if you don't mind.'

'Please yourself but you don't know shit, do you. You'll not get a reply even if you stay all day.'

She turns to go back into her flat.

'What do you mean.' I call after her.

She turns around and stares at me with a cold and triumphant look.

'I know she's not there and I doubt she'll be back anytime soon.'

'How do you know?'

'Perhaps I'll tell you, perhaps I won't. I doubt it would help.'

'Why? What's happened? Look, I wasn't kidding about it being a matter of life and death. If my friend turns up dead in an alley somewhere, I'll make sure the police come round here and ask you a lot of questions. Is that what you want?'

She lets out a deep sigh of resignation.

'Okay. I'd just opened my front door to take out the rubbish when I saw that friend of yours coming in the front door. She didn't have a chance to get any further as these two men came up behind her and bundled her back down the steps. I went straight back inside my flat and looked out of my front window, they were pushing her into a car.'

'What did the men look like?'

'You kidding me? I wasn't going to stand and stare at them.'

'What about the car then? Was it a black supercar?'

'Nothing like and it was white. And you're not the police, so bog off now. And if you come around here and threaten me again, you'll have to answer to my man. You're lucky he's out right now.'

She goes back into her flat, leaving me standing like a statue of ice, frozen with fear for Charlie. Then the adrenaline starts to flow and I rush back to my car, driving back at an inadvisable speed. It's raining by the time I burst through the front door. I'm surprised to see Chris in the sitting room with her laptop.

'I thought you had a meeting.'

'It was cancelled so I'm catching up on some research papers. I don't get interrupted at home. Is something the matter. Didn't you find Charlie?'

'She wasn't at her flat but I know where she is.'

I run into the kitchen and pick out a small sharp kitchen knife from the drawer. I grab my mac from the peg in the hall and open the front door.

Chris calls after me. 'Kate. Where are you going?'

The rain is still falling as I drive frantically towards Basin Road. I park in one of the side roads nearby, just off Kingsway where parking is still free and make the rest of the way on foot. The temperature has plummeted from the near tropical heights of the previous days and I pull my hood tightly over my head and down over my eyes. The rain means there are few people around. I approach the Excelseus School with caution. The gate is closed as usual. I can't just press the buzzer and ask if Charlie is inside the school. In my haste, I've not thought about what to do. Heavy grey clouds give the appearance of night closing in and the rain is becoming heavier. A penetrating chill is making me shiver. I cross the road and take shelter in a place where the rock overhangs, just opposite the gate.

A car is speeding down the road. It slows down as it reaches the school gate and its headlights pick out something glistening on the ground. The car carries on up the road. I go over and bend down to pick up a large shiny earing in the shape of an artist's easel. I recognise it as one of a pair that I last saw adorning Charlie's tiny earlobes. I put it in my pocket and walk back down Basin Road. It's all the proof I need. I go back to the shelter of my car, frightened for Charlie. I'll have to get help to free her and there's only one person I can turn to for that. I pull out my phone and call Mike. I'm about to shatter any pretence that I've stopped interfering.

I can hear the hum of a car engine in the background when he answers.

'Mike, it's Kate. Are you driving?'

'I'm just on my way back to the station.'

'I have to see you. Now. It's urgent.' My voice is cracking despite my best efforts to sound unruffled. 'I need help.'

Perhaps it's the tone of my voice but he latches on to the importance of my call.

'Where are you?'

'I'm parked in Leonard Avenue just off Kingsway near Basin Road.'

'I know it. I'll be there in five minutes.'

Ten minutes later, he arrives. I see him park further up the road. I leave my car and run towards his. I'm shaking by the time I slump down into his passenger seat. Mike says nothing but waits for me to calm down. When I'm able to speak, I keep any hint of panic out of my voice.

'They've got Charlie at the Excelseus School. God knows what they'll do with her.'

'Charlie?'

'You know, orange hair, scatty artist, friend of Jaq's.'

'Right, I remember.'

'I've got to get her out.'

'How do you know she's inside?'

I explain while Mike switches on the windscreen wipers. Outside the rain is hammering against the car.

'You told me you'd left all this snooping behind. Anyway, what makes you think I can help you?'

His voice hits me like an icy blast. It takes all the nerve I have to steady my voice.

'I saw you drive into the school car park on Monday night when the *Hyrenia* docked. I sneaked in after you. I heard you talking about a shipment of drugs.'

'So much for your telling me it was Jessica who was planning to snoop around. What if I told you I was undercover?'

I hesitate for a moment but he's unable to maintain eye contact.

'Look, right now I don't care how you're involved with the school. You can tell me the truth some other time. I just want Charlie out before she comes to any harm, so use your contacts to make sure that happens.'

I'm expecting another outburst from Mike but instead he sits forward and grips the steering wheel so hard his knuckles turn white. He stares out of the window as the rain turns to hail and beats down on the car roof so fiercely that it sounds as if we're being battered by gunfire.

At last he turns and speaks to me.

'Okay. I've got an idea. I've got to get back to the station now. I'll ring you as soon as I can.'

I'd rather we could act at once, but I've no choice. I grab the door handle, preparing to face the onslaught of water outside.

'You better change into something dry. Have a bite to eat too. I'll see you later.'

I open the car door and push hard against the wind to get out. I run all the way down the street to my car. I'm soaked by the time I throw myself into the driver's seat. I watch Mike's car disappear into the distance and then drive off with no idea of what to expect.

Chapter Twenty-Nine

....Thursday 28 May....

Chris is out when I get back to the house. She's left a note to say she's gone to a festival flamenco show at the Komedia in Brighton. I half admire her ability to put Charlie's fate to one side for the sake of an enjoyable evening: a sure sign that their relationship is fading fast. I march upstairs to change out of my wet clothes which are clinging to my skin and making me shiver. I start to think more clearly about rescuing Charlie. The immediate panic I felt has subsided and left me regretting that I rushed to contact Mike. I think about submitting an official missing person's report instead but it's too soon. Charlie's only been missing a couple of hours and I've got no hard evidence that she's being held against her will.

I shower and change and go downstairs to get something to eat. All I can find is a frozen pasta dish to microwave which I bolt down along with a mug of strong coffee. Mike still hasn't called me back and I pace up and down waiting for my phone to ring. After an hour I'm convinced he's forgotten or changed his mind. I pull on my mac and drive back to where I parked earlier. After five minutes trying to find a space, I squeeze into one in a permit free road, and wait for the rain to ease. I've no plan as I was relying on Mike and as the rain hammers down on the roof of the car, I'm regretting my impatience. I'm just about to drive back to the house when Mike calls.

'I'm on my way. I'll be at Chris's in about ten minutes.'

'I'm parked just off Kingsway. It's not far to the school. I'll meet you there.'

The rain has stopped but the wind has such a force that I'm almost knocked to the ground as I get out of the car. It worsens as I cross Kingsway and walk towards Basin Road and the port. The sea has a marked swell and the waves have churned up the water turning it a muddy colour. I put up my hood and bend my head into the gusts. I reach the Excelseus School just as Mike's car draws up. The gate opens and Mikes drives in and parks up. I follow the car and wait until Mike gets out. He approaches me with a smile. I wonder if this is a good sign.

'Come on,' he says. 'Let's sort this out.'

I hear the gate clang shut and follow him to the main entrance door of the school, on the alert for what could happen next. It opens as we approach and I follow Mike inside. He tells me to sit on a plush easy chair in Reception while he has a word with the woman. The strong smell of exotic spices from her perfume, combined with my anxiety, make me want to retch. Their voices are too quiet for me to hear the conversation. When they finish talking, the woman presses a buzzer and Mike comes over to me.

'Just a couple more minutes,' he says.

'What's going on?'

'Wait here; I won't be long.'

He smiles again but this time, I'm sure there's something false about it. The woman uses her digital card to open a solid wooden door which connects Reception with the rest of the building and Mike goes through. She returns to the reception desk and busies herself on a computer. I wander over to take a look but she points back to the chair I've been sitting on with a disapproving look. I'm tempted to challenge her but I don't want to put Charlie's freedom at risk. I sit down and fidget with my phone which I notice has no signal inside the building. I'm relieved when I see Mike returning. He's accompanied by a big, swarthy man with a salt and pepper beard. I recognise him as one of the guys who was chasing Chiara. Charlie is in between them. She's trembling but when she sees me, she rushes over.

'Kate. Thank God. It's been awful. I shouldn't have gone to the flat on my own.'

'It's over now. You can tell me all about it later.'

She takes a step back and turns her head away from me.

'What is it, Charlie?'

'I'm sorry, Kate. I didn't know what else to do. They didn't give me a choice.'

'What do you mean?'

Mike comes over and takes a firm grip on Charlie's arm.

'Time to go.'

I'm about to follow him when I discover it's my turn to be grabbed by the burly man.

'Not you,' he says. 'It's a swap.'

I look over to Mike, more furious at his betrayal than worried about its implications.

'How could you, Mike?'

'Like Charlie, I had no choice.'

The woman uses her card to open the main door and Mike leads Charlie out while I'm left in the grip of the man, wondering what comes next for me. I'm not about to wait and see, so I knee him in the groin. He doubles over at the sudden pain. I grab the card that's hanging around his neck and run over to the door. The woman is swift to come out from behind the reception desk and block my way. I push her to one side, remembering the knife in my pocket but reluctant to use it. There's no time, anyway, as I'm grabbed from behind by the man who snatches back his card. The woman uses hers to open the interconnecting door and he bundles me through into corridor. It's then that I start screaming and struggling. It's instinctive even if I know it's a wasted effort. The man shouts to the woman as he tries to get me under control.

'Get the doctor.'

I see her tap a number on her phone and it's not long before I hear footsteps along the corridor. I'm still in the process of doing what I can to free myself, when I look up and recognise the figure coming towards us. I stop struggling as my mouth falls open in amazement. He comes up close to me, pushing his face so close to mine I turn it away to avoid the smell of menthol on his breath.

'Well, well. Dr Green. Now that is a surprise.'

'Andrew. What the hell are you doing here?'

'I might say the same for you. Right now, you have a choice. Walk nice and slowly with us or would you prefer a shot of ketamine.'

He shows me the syringe in his hand.

'There'll be no need for that,' I reply.

Whatever I'm to do to get myself out of this situation, having even a short acting anaesthetic on board is not going to help.

We walk down the corridor which is carpeted in a hard-wearing institutional grey fabric. I'm reminded of a university hall of residence but there are no students spilling out of their rooms to swap notes or chat about the latest in music, TV or films. The man opens the first door on the right with his card and pushes me into the room. As he leers into my face, I can see that his beard is riddled with dandruff. I vent my frustration by telling him he should use a medicated shampoo and some moisturiser. He pushes me onto the only chair and makes as if to hit me. Andrew turns to him.

'I'd like time on my own with her first.'

There seems to be no problem with this, so the man leaves and Andrew sits opposite me on the single bed that is lined up against one of the walls. He puts the syringe on the bed next to him.

'So....'

He pauses. I say nothing.

'Aren't you going to explain?'

'I could ask the same of you. This is supposed to be a language school.'

'Students get ill, don't they?'

'Don't kid me, Andrew. You're not here as a GP. Just what are you up to?'

'We'll come to that later. First I'd like to know just what you're doing here?'

He raises his eyebrows.

'Trying to find a friend of mine, Charlie, if you're really interested. I was sure she'd be here when I saw one of her earrings on the ground by the front gate and I was right.

'Charlie?'

'She was a friend of, Jacqueline Grey. You must remember *her*. It's not that long since Clare was notifying us of her death.'

'Ah, yes. Jacqueline Grey. Go on.'

'I was worried about what would happen to Charlie but she's okay, they've let her go now. They swapped her for me.'

'Why the concern about her?'

'Perhaps you'd like to tell me.'

'I'm surprised your friend, Jaq, didn't give you some idea. She was quite upset when she found out what's been going on.'

I'm still processing what he's just said, when his next words hit me like a slab of ice.

'Nice girl, very sexy, a good lay too, but she had no idea what she was up against.'

He's smirking.

'You mean you and Jaq were.....' .

'I think *having a relationship* is the polite term. *Screwing each other* is a more accurate description.'

I stand up and hit him across the face. He pushes me back into the chair but doesn't retaliate.

What had Charlie said? Jaq went off with a doctor that reminded her of me. She must have meant because Andrew was a GP. I'm even more horrified by his admission because Jaq was a patient of his. That's absolutely against General Medical Council regulations. When I find a way out of here, I'll get him for that, if nothing else.

I clutch my stomach, trying to hold onto its contents but the effort only makes it worse. I rush over to the washbasin in the corner of the room and vomit up the food I ate before coming to the school.

'Feeling better?'

I don't bother to answer. I'm baffled as to how Jaq could ever go with Andrew. My consternation must show on my face.

'We met at a party. Jaq was pretty drunk and was looking for some coke. I gave her a line or two and we got chatting.'

I sit clenching my fists while I listen to him continue.

'I don't think she was interested in more than a one-off with me, at the party she seemed more into the girls there. But then she told me she needed money for that precious bookshop of hers so I took my chance. I said I might be able to arrange for her to earn some good money. We ended up in bed. Anyway, she agreed to hold some drugs for us and do a spot of dealing from time to time. Our relationship, or whatever you want to call it, was part of the agreement. I told her I'd report her to the police as a drug dealer if she walked away.'

'You bastard.'

He just smiles.

'Aren't you going to hit me again?'

'I'm not going to risk damaging my hand a second time.'

'Anyway, I wanted to let you know that I'll square up your absence from the surgery. You'll have gone back to London. Some family crisis or other.'

My brain is whirling. He's sitting forward as though he's getting ready to stand up and leave. I shift my chair closer to the bed, biding my time.

'You mentioned she held drugs for *us*. Meaning who exactly?'

'All this. The Excelseus Language School or whatever you want to call it.' He waves his arms around. 'You'll find out more when I hand you back to the boys.'

The thought of those thugs is the catalyst I need. I dive forward and seize the syringe and plunge it into the deltoid muscle of his arm. He stares back at me in shock then staggers to his feet. I pray the ketamine works quickly as I dodge out of his grasp. One minute later he's lying unconscious on the bed and I'm ripping the digital door opener from the lanyard around his neck.

I open the door cautiously and peep out. No one around. I creep out into the corridor convinced that my heart beat is loud enough to be heard throughout the building. I stop in front of the door opposite and press my ear against it. I can hear muffled voices. It sounds like girls' chatter but I can't make out what's being said. I want to call out but fear I'll be heard. I try to open the door with the digital card. It doesn't work. I'd assumed Andrew was carrying a universal key. I just hope it opens the doors that will let me escape.

I hold up the digital key to the pad on the interconnecting door to the reception area. When the door clicks open, my body relaxes for a second before I tense myself again. Feeling like a low-life criminal, I grasp the knife in my pocket, hoping I won't have to produce it, but the woman has her back to me and there's no one else around. Sweat trickles down my arm and I can feel the knife becoming slippery in my hand. I'm at the point of hyperventilating from anxiety, so I force myself to slow my breathing to a normal rate. I'll have no chance of escape unless I stay calm. I keep my head turned towards the woman who's talking loudly on the phone now. She still has her back to me so I jog across to the entrance door on tip toe. I hold the card against the digital pad and then rush into the carpark as the door quietly opens.

I take a deep breath. The blast of air to my lungs is exhilarating. I'm glad the light is fading fast, aided by an overcast sky. I run to the main gate but can see no way of using the digital card to effect my exit. I position myself to the side of the building where there are no windows. Shadows are falling from the perimeter wall. It's not far from the gate but, right now, it might as well be a hundred miles away. I examine the wall to see if there's any possibility of scaling it. I'm no rock climber and, in any case, I can see no footholds. If Mike arrived, he'd be able to get the gate to open but what use would that be? He'd only come after me. I wander round to the back of the building looking for some other alternative but find none. I check how long it's been since I stabbed Andrew with the ketamine, aware that its effects last at maximum two hours. If I'm unlucky they could wear off within half an hour which would mean I could be hunted down in about fifteen minute's time. I look over to the parked cars hoping in vain that one will leave the car park so that I can slip out of the gate behind them. I push my hand into my mac pocket and grip the handle of the knife to give me courage. It would be a last resort to have to use it and the idea fills me with horror. A chill wind blows across the quayside and I start to shiver. With the minutes passing all too rapidly, I've run out of ideas and the minutes are passing by all too rapidly.

Chapter Thirty

....Thursday 28 May....

It's hard to hold at bay my growing sense of panic. I hear the sound of a car approaching. It slows down as it reaches the school but then speeds up again and the sound of the engine disappears up the road. It's all I can do to stop myself from crying. But then another car approaches and, as if it senses my distress, it stops in front of the gate which opens to let it through. I wait until it has moved into a central position in the car park then sprint through the gate and set off at a furious adrenaline-fuelled pace along Basin Road and back to my car.

Chris is hunched over a large brandy in the sitting room when I burst through the front door and collapse onto the sofa next to her. The lights are low and her face is in shadow as she turns towards me with an astonished look.

'What on earth's going on, Kate? First Charlie rushes in as though she's seen a ghost and now you.'

I snatch the brandy out of her hand and take a swig, then hand it back.

'Didn't Charlie explain?'

'She went straight up to her room. I was concerned so I followed her. At first she didn't want to talk to me but I got through to her in the end.'

I heave myself up ready to climb the stairs to her room but Chris pulls me back down onto the sofa.

'Charlie's gone. Here, read this.'

She hands me one of the postcards used for advertising the *Open House* event. It features one of Charlie's landscapes and on the blank side a message. It only takes seconds to read.

Kate. Don't hate me but I thought I was dead. Those guys at the school, you came just in time. I'm off to Morocco, got arty contacts there. I'll not be back. They gave me money to promise that. Good luck and take care. Charlie.

I slump back on the sofa, exhausted, hoping that Charlie will stay safe. Chris fetches another glass and pours out a brandy for me. The rich aroma is comforting and I enjoy the feeling of warmth that creeps though me.

'What did Charlie tell you?'

Chris confirms what I suspected that Charlie had been abducted as she arrived at her flat.

'She didn't want to go into details she was just relieved to be out of the place..'

'Why on earth did Charlie rush off to her flat without me? What got into her?'

'All she said to me was that she couldn't wait for you to get back. She'd remembered where Chiara had hidden something important.'

'Did she say where?'

Chris shakes her head. 'So, what happened to you, then?'

'I'll explain later. Right now, I need to get into Charlie's flat. Do you have her key?'

I'm careful to make the minimum amount of noise as I enter the building. I open Charlie's front door onto a tiny hallway which leads to a vast room with a high ceiling. The floorboards are painted white, at least that's the colour on one side of the room. On the other, the floor has been spattered with coloured paint as if Charlie has been trying to decorate it Jackson Pollock style. An easel stands folded against the far wall with a few blank canvases and some half-finished paintings. One or two completed ones have been hung on the wall. A quick look around confirms that this is the extent of Charlie's flat, apart from a tiny kitchen space and an even smaller bathroom. I sit down on the blue sofa bed and look around. A couple of mismatched orange and yellow plastic chairs are tucked under a small Perspex dining table. There is a wooden wardrobe painted bright pink and another cupboard in a functional white melamine with a large wicker basket beside it. I have to smile. It could only be Charlie's room.

I notice a rolled up sleeping bag in a corner and choose that as my starting point, assuming Chiara had been using it. There's nothing hidden inside it. I go back to the sofa bed and look around, paying more attention to the artefacts in the room. The cupboards are too obvious but I go and open them in any case. A cursory rummage through them reveals nothing. I defer a more thorough search until I've exhausted other ideas. I pace around the room then stand and look at the paintings hung on the wall. Charlie has been careful to hang them in a co-ordinated pattern and there's a pleasing geometry to her choice. I notice she has been very precise in how she has displayed each painting, that is except for one. While the others sit snugly against the wall, this particular work stands proud from the surface. I go over to it and lift it down. I find an A4 envelope taped to the back of it. I remove it gently as though it's a bomb and sit down to read it.

My hands are trembling as I pull the sheets of paper out of envelope. They are handwritten and headed by the name *Chiara*. I flick through to the end and find a date with Chiara's signature and Jaq's below it as a witness. I go back to the beginning. The sentences have all the grammatical quirks of Chiara's speech. They add to the poignancy of the story, a story of Chiara's illegal passage from Italy into the UK in the hands of traffickers and what happened to her at the Excelseus school. It's a shocking story and upsetting to think what Jaq was risking in helping her, most likely with fatal consequences. What's more, it will still be happening to other girls.

I replace the painting on the wall and make my exit. As I close Charlie's front door, the girl opposite appears with her 'man'. She glares at me.

'It's you again, I told you....'

I don't let her finish.

'Don't worry, I'm just leaving.'

I rush down the stairs keen to show Chris what Chiara has written. She speed reads it and then asks if I'm going to hand it in to the police.

'I'm not sure if it's enough to prove criminal activity. Chiara's not alive to confirm it as genuine and neither is Jaq, and whatever happened to Charlie at the school, she's off the scene.'

I'm also aware that even if the police are convinced enough to act, then it will take time.

'Didn't you find out anything yourself at the school?'

'Not much. I didn't hang around long enough.'

'So, what did happen to you?'

I give her a brief account and she looks shocked when I recount Mike's duplicity. She's nonplussed at my finding Andrew there.

'What are you going to do, now?'

'Go and see Mike.' Dealing with Andrew's involvement will just have to wait.

'Isn't that risky?'

'There are still girls in the school. I heard voices as I was making my escape. I hope Mike's got nothing to do with people trafficking, but in any case, he's my only chance of getting those girls out fast. I know it's a gamble but I can't wait. If you don't hear from me, you can raise the alarm.'

'And just how long do I wait before doing that?'

I shrug my shoulders and leave her with that dilemma as I go upstairs to shower and change. Half an hour later I'm in a taxi on my way to Mike. The traffic is light along Kingsway but the driver is intent on spinning out the time and crawls along below the speed limit. I curb my usual impatience and stare out of the window and over the darkness of the sea. As we pass the West pier, it rises like some *objet trouvé* from its watery base. I've grown to appreciate its tangled iron web, to see it less as a ruin and more as a sculpture that makes a point about the city and the wider world. The main pier is a solid structure rooted in the amusements and diversions that camouflage the pains and tedium of life. The West pier is its antithesis, the skeleton of a pier standing like a shadow that lurks beneath superficial distractions, an ugly scaffold that illustrates the hidden darkness in life.

I'm still musing on the dichotomy of the two piers when we pull up outside Mike's apartment block. I pay off the driver and watch as the cab disappears into the night to look for its next fare. A tremendous feeling of apprehension grips me as I stand alone on the pavement. I take a deep breath and go up to the door and press the intercom. It's past 1am and no time for normal visiting. I wonder if Mike will ignore the buzzer or even sleep through it. When his voice answers it's clear he hasn't been sleeping and has most probably had one too many brandies. When he hears my name, his astonishment is clear.

'Kate? How the... What are you...? When did ....?'

I put a stop to his mumbling. 'Are you going to let me in?'

The door immediately clicks open and I climb the stairs to his flat. I'm too full of nervous energy to wait for the lift. Mike's at the door when I arrive and invites me in. I expect my sudden appearance to be met with an aggressive challenge but instead, Mike appears preoccupied. I notice that his shoulders are drooping and that he's slouching as he walks down the corridor. He heads straight for the brandy when we enter the sitting room and pours himself a large glass.

'Want one?' He downs his drink in one gulp.

'No thanks. I'll get myself a coffee and I think you should have one too.'

He doesn't object as I go into the kitchen to prepare a strong, black one for us both. When I hand him his coffee, he adds an excessive amount of sugar and then stirs it interminably until I relieve him of his spoon. He takes a sip then rushes out of the room. On his return, he's alert and attentive. I assume he's just had a fix.

'So how did you get away?'

'That doesn't matter.'

'What makes you think I'll not just take you straight back there?'

'Chris knows where I am and what happened earlier.'

He opens his mouth to say something then changes his mind.

'I've got something to show you but first, I want to hear about your involvement with the Excelseus School. It's obviously to do with illegal drugs and don't try telling me again that you're acting undercover. I've had a look at what's on that slider phone of yours so I know you're tracking shipping movements into Shoreham Port and that you have an arrangement with a port security guard, Ian Bunger, at SPS. The only thing I couldn't work out was the significance of the contact CCC, Central Care Consolidates.'

'How did you...?'

'You left your phone behind when you rushed out to that body in the A23 layby.'

'You worked out the pin number then. I bet you think you're such a clever bitch.'

'That's hardly the point.'

'No?' Mike is now pacing the room, an angry flush on his face. 'You just can't stop playing the detective, can you?'

'Don't shout at me; you've not denied anything, have you?'

I'm aware that I've raised my voice too.

'Why don't you admit you're getting a big kick out of all this? Ever since you stumbled on Jaqueline Grey's body you've done nothing but meddle.'

Mike is shaking with anger. I take a deep breath and lower my tone. A blazing row will achieve nothing. He's pacing up and down the room. It does nothing to ease the tension between us.

'Just tell me what else you've got yourself into.'

'Like what?'

'Like trafficking girls through Shoreham Port.'

'What on earth are you talking about?' He looks genuinely puzzled.

I hand him Chiara's account.

'Is this genuine?' he asks, after finishing it.

'Well, I can't prove that, which is why I'm here and not at the police station but I recognise Jaq's signature so I'm sure it is.'

I can see he's disconcerted by what he's just read.

'All I know about are the cocaine shipments. I agreed to make sure there was no interference from port security when they were due in; I didn't know this was going on.'

'What about that woman from the school? You told me she was a failed lead to Chiara. You must have had some idea of what she was up to or was that just a blatant lie?'

'I had no idea she was exploiting young girls. I just wanted to get you off my back. I couldn't risk you finding out about my connection to the school and the drug smuggling.'

'Oh, Mike, why?'

'Money, a personal supply of cocaine. You've no idea what things were like for me just then but you've gotta believe, I knew nothing about this other stuff. I don't know what to say, Kate.'

'If I were the Investigating Officer into Chiara's murder, I'd be saying this provides a motive for killing her. You don't let a trafficked young girl run loose with what she knows. What's more I'd also be thinking it could be relevant to the way Jaq died.'

'Why aren't you at the station, then, telling them that?'

He drums his fingers on the table. I can't tell if he's worried or angry.

'I've told you, I've no proof but I'm sure I heard girls' voices from one of the rooms that I passed on my way out. My priority right now is to get those girls away from the school.'

'You can't do that on your own.'

'Which is why I'm here. The school will soon have discovered I got away and they'll think I've gone straight to the police. They know I've not got much I can accuse them of, but they won't want to take any chances. They'll make sure to move the girls straightaway. It's vital to act now and I can't do that without your help.'

'You've got to be kidding. This isn't a Hollywood movie.'

'I know that but there's no alternative.'

Mike goes over to the balcony doors. He stands for several minutes staring out across the Brighton night sky.

'What are you planning to do?' he says, turning around to face me.

'First, take me back to the school, that way they'll think you're still in with them.'

'What then?'

I pull out the digital key card that helped me out of the school and explain my plan.

Mike sits down with his face in his hands then gets up and pours himself another brandy.

'I don't know, Kate. I really don't.'

He's trembling.

'What is it, Mike? Is something else going on?'

He fetches an official envelope from his jacket and tells me to read what's inside. It's a letter warning him of an investigation into suspected misconduct. There are no details. I hand it back. It explains Mike's untypical demeanour when I arrived.

'....if they've any idea about my involvement with the Excelseus School that means big trouble, even more if they think I had any idea about the people trafficking.'

He takes a slug of brandy.

'If I agree to go ahead with your plan, everything about me will come out and that'll be the end of the road for Chief Inspector Black.'

'So, you'd rather protect your job than save those helpless girls and bring down a heinous network of human trafficking?'

He looks up at me. His eyes are red, with a lost look I've never seen in them before. I know what his police career means to him, I guess even more now with his separation from Carole and the boys. I feel a flush of sympathy for him but it doesn't last.

I take the brandy glass out of his hand.

'And self-pity won't help, either.'

'What do you know about self-pity? You're not the one whose career is on the brink.'

He goes over to the window. I follow him and we both stare out at the blackness beyond. I resist the temptation to argue with him and stand by his side as the minutes pass in a strained silence.

'Okay,' he says at last. 'but if your idea works out, just keep it to yourself that I'm involved with the school. Leave me to deal with the police investigation.'

It's nearly 3am when we set off. I insist on stopping off at Chris's house and posting Chiara's account through the letterbox with a note for her to keep it safe. We drive in silence until we turn into Basin Road.

As we approach the Excelseus car park, I'm surprised that the gate is open. We drive in to find the woman from reception talking to the driver of a large white van that's parked near the entrance. Girls are being bundled into the van. The woman breaks off when she sees Mike get out of his car. It's clear my plan is not going to work. Mike leads me over to the van. I can't believe he's betraying me again.

'I think you mislaid this young lady.'

'You've timed your arrival to perfection. She can join the others in the back.'

She bangs on the door of the van and a tall man jumps out of the seat next to the driver, muscles tensed at the ready.

'Here's another one for you,' she says.

I recognise the man I attacked and he instinctively drops his hands in front of his groin. The woman is now frisking me with expert hands and has soon recovered both the small kitchen knife and my mobile phone. She hands them to Mike.

'Get rid of these.'

He takes them and then moves in closer to the burly guy who is now manhandling me towards the back door of the van. He opens it, ready to push me in.

'Hang on a sec.' Mike addresses the guy and moves towards me. He raises his hand and I feel the sting of a slap across my cheek.

'That's for all the trouble you've caused.'

I'm too shocked to react but then he leans towards and I feel him slip my phone into my pocket.

He stands back and focuses on the number plate of the van. I have just enough time to do the same and memorise it before I feel a shove that propels me into the back of the van and into the company of several frightened young girls.

The van drives off and some of the girls start to sob. The near total blackness in the back of the van suggests a lack of visual communication with the driver's compartment. If there's a sliding partition, then it's closed at the moment. I manage to ascertain from one of the girls that we're on our way to London then I pull out the phone. When the screen lights up, I put my fingers to my lips to stop the girls asking questions then tap out a message to Mike.

Kidnap in progress. Abducted with girls from Excelseus School. On way to London white van reg no --------

That should square things with Mike's colleagues. All I can do now is wait.

We've been travelling for half an hour at a speed consistent with a dual carriage way or motorway when I hear the police sirens. The van increases its speed but it's no match for the fast police vehicles chasing it down. When the van finally comes to a halt and the back doors are forced open by the police, I can see we've almost reached the Pease Pottage turn off on the A23 and a road block has been set up. I'm impressed at how quickly Mike has set things in motion. I step out of the van and take refuge on the hard shoulder then look around to see where he is. The girls are tumbling out of the back of the vehicle but the two men are refusing to budge. I can see Mike approaching the vehicle on foot from behind. He's almost reached it when the van starts up and reverses into Mike's path. Mike collapses to the ground like a rag doll. The van attempts to move forward but a police car has already raced to block its path. As I run towards Mike, I see knives flashing in the car headlights as the two men attempt to flee along the slip road. When I next look up, officers in riot gear are manhandling them into a police car.

Mike is moaning on the ground and clutching his ribs. A stream of colourful expletives testifies to the extent of his pain but I'm relieved he's conscious and not in immediate danger. I check his carotid pulse and breathing just in case, and look for external signs of bleeding. Seeing none, all I can do is wait for the ambulance and hope there's no internal trauma. I lean over him so I don't have to raise my voice.

'Thanks for the prompt response, Mike. Well played.'

He tries to lift his head to speak but gives up and pulls me closer to him so I can hear what he's saying.

'Well played you too. Now get the fucking ambulance. I'm in agony here.'

Right on cue, I can see blue flashing lights racing towards us and Mike is soon on his way to the Royal Sussex County Hospital in Brighton. My destination is another visit to Brighton Station, this time in the company of six bewildered and apprehensive young girls. I lean back in the seat of the squad car and feel a gradual relaxing of the muscular tension that has been such a feature of the past few hours. The Sussex countryside flashes past, hidden by a moonless night. I let the rhythmic sounds of the tyres on the road lull me. I'm not looking forward to the tedium and unpleasantness of another police interview.

Chapter Thirty-One

....Thursday 28 May

I'm met with a pleasant surprise on arrival at the station. Whether because of my past history with the force or because of my recent involvement with Chiara's murder, I'm allowed to make a brief statement with an agreement to return the next day to provide a full explanation of my involvement. Perhaps the investigating team is just glad to have one less person to deal with. I don't envy them the task of teasing out the truth from the six girls who file in ahead of me. They may have some grasp of English but I foresee a search for appropriate translators and the need for a considerable amount of interviewer patience.

A taxi takes me to the hospital. I want to check on Mike. I phone Chris as the driver weaves his way through the back streets. I'm just in time to stop her reporting my absence. I tell her I'm safe and unharmed and en route to see Mike in hospital.

'Why? What's happened?'

I give her an outline of the night's events.

'Is he going to be all right?'

'I'll know more when I visit him.'

'Keep me up to speed, will you? I'm leaving for a conference in London today. I'll be away all weekend but I'll see if I can visit him before I go.'

'Any news from the Forensics lab.'

'Not yet.'

'And what about the *Open House*?'

'I've cancelled it. It's the final weekend and with Charlie gone, there didn't seem much point. Must dash now; you can tell me everything when I get back.'

I arrive at the Royal Sussex County Hospital and follow the signs to the Emergency Department. The sound of my footsteps echoes around me as I plunge into the strange world of a hospital at night: deserted passageways stretching endlessly ahead of me, rectangular tubes stripped of their daytime bustle, solitary spaces with bright lights and a strong smell of disinfectant. I walk along remembering my days as a junior doctor on night shift when my feet pounded just such corridors, like a lone traveller in a time capsule. But this time I'm not making my way to a patient with chest pain, or breathlessness or an overdose; I'm in a very different present, as a visitor.

As a serving police office, Mike has already been found a place in a side room on the Admissions Ward. He is half-sitting, half-lying in bed with the usual paraphernalia of a hospital ward around him. A nurse is taking his observations. He spots me straight away and acknowledges my presence with a weak smile. I wait until the nurse has finished before approaching him. His hair is dishevelled and his forehead bruised. His usually swarthy skin is pale and his eyes dull. I take a quick peek at the monitor screen: blood pressure, pulse and oxygen levels all normal, nothing worrying there.

'What's the verdict, Mike?' Strange how I opt for a legal rather than a medical word.

'Fractured ribs. Nothing else except a lot of bruising.' He indicates his arms and legs.

'You look like you need a good rest.'

'In here? Fat chance. Even in this room I can't get away from buzzers and bells going off all the time, to say nothing of those blessed hourly checks. It's like being tortured.'

I take the point. It wasn't something I had to think about as a hospital doctor. I had other priorities: an accurate diagnosis and appropriate treatment, I paid no heed to the hours a patient would spend in a bed, on a busy ward with little chance of proper rest. I experience a totally useless sense of retrospective guilt.

Mike brings me back to the present by asking if my face hurts.

'I wasn't expecting that. Luckily, there's no mark. Are the girls okay?'

'They'll have been taken to some refuge or other.'

'Poor kids. I just hope they go easy on them. They're the victims here, not to mention Chiara of course, any progress on that?'

'I've not heard anything. They're still holding the guys they arrested, trying to get them to talk. They're waiting on a DNA test. It just stinks, all this business with school.'

'So how did you get so tied up with the Excelseus?'

'It started way back when I was still in London.'

Work pressures, a marriage falling apart led him to take refuge in cocaine to keep himself afloat. A first line at a friend's dinner party and he was hooked. Then the debts began to mount up and the arguments with Carole increase in number and intensity.

I don't interrupt as Mike continues with the detail of how he slid effortlessly into that group of public servants who are prepared to ensure a ready supply of journalistic scoops as long as the money keeps coming. He regularly passed tit-bits of supposedly confidential police information to a close circle of less scrupulous members of the press. It supported his addiction until rumours about him began to circulate inside his department.

'Things were getting out-of-hand so I decided the best thing was to move away. I applied for a transfer to Brighton. I really thought I could make a go of things here, get clean, pay off my debts, start again.'

'But it didn't work out.'

'Far from it. I couldn't stop my cocaine habit and I'd lost my source of extracurricular income. Anyway, by then journalists' hand-outs were not going to clear my debts. I had to get my hands on a big sum of money and quickly. Drug syndicates don't act with velvet gloves if you don't pay up.'

'I'm guessing that was why you were beaten up in London.'

'I was supposed to go to the Windmill Pub on Clapham Common for a meet arranged by the school with their chief syndicate rep in London. Of course, I never got into the pub. Turned out I was duffed up just to make sure I toed the line with the school. If it had been anything more serious, I'd not have got off so lightly.'

'You still haven't explained how you got involved with the Excelseus School.'

Mike stares ahead without speaking, as if he's struggling to talk about it. I wait patiently until he finds the words he needs or the willingness to express them.

'I was helping out with an investigation into the school as a distribution hub for illegal drugs.'

He goes on to describe how he saw the chance of getting enough money to clear his drug debts by making sure the investigation went nowhere.

'The school is tied to the London syndicate I owed money to, so we came to an agreement.'

'But that wasn't the end of it.'

'No. They got their claws into me.'

They wanted him to liaise with one of the port security guards who was in their pay and make sure he was on duty the day drug consignments arrived at the port.

'It was blackmail but I agreed as it meant I could get a regular supply of cocaine.'

'Couldn't they have liaised with the guard themselves?'

'They're too clever to have any direct contacts like that.'

'You know if you'd busted the school for drug smuggling during that investigation, you would've stopped the exploitation of a lot of young girls.'

Mike looks down at the crumpled hospital blanket over his legs.

'I was desperate, Kate. I didn't know about the trafficking set-up. That doesn't excuse what I did but I couldn't see any other way out. I'm not proud of myself but the drug syndicate in London was threatening my family if I didn't pay my cocaine debts. I couldn't risk that.'

'You could have got help for your addiction.'

But he was too deep with the school by then. The London syndicate and the Excelseus School turned out to be a part of a larger organisation, Central Care Consolidates.

'CCC is a powerful organisation, probably has mafia links somewhere along the line. I had no way out.'

No wonder I got nowhere when I rang their number. I'm not sure how to react. With anger, sympathy, condemnation?

'That's a lot to digest, Mike.'

He nods and sinks down into the bed. I leave him to struggle with his conscience while I struggle with the implications of his confession and what I should do about them.

Chapter Thirty-Two

Friday 29 May

I sleep late but wake in plenty of time for my appointment at Brighton Police Station. When I look at my phone, I see that Jessica has left me repeated text messages. I put off replying and go downstairs to make breakfast. There are still flyers for the Open House dotted about the place and Charlie's paintings hanging on the walls. Some have *sold* labels on them and I wonder if she's already received payment for them. I wander about looking at them and pick out one of the Seven Sisters that I'd like to have. It would remind me of Jaq

I go on foot to the police station as the weather has come back to its former glory. Summer is bursting out again with the sunlight projecting sharp images against a clear blue sky. The walk gives me time to think about what to say in the interview if I'm to avoid compromising Mike. I buy the local paper on the way and sit on a bench facing the sea to read it. The story of the girls' rescue from the van is front page news. I'm pleased to see there's no mention of my name. There's no reference to the Excelseus School either. I would have expected a police raid by now on the basis of the girls' testimonies. I'm about to continue on towards the police station, when my phone rings. It's Jessica. I apologise for ignoring her texts but explain that it's been a difficult couple of days. She wants to know if I can give her any insider info on the abduction of the girls. She's not happy when I stall her yet again, telling her I've got to make a statement to the police first.

She tries to push me but I hold my ground and she capitulates. As I head along the esplanade in the direction of the West Pier, the sounds of people's conversations vie with the steady hum of the constant traffic. Beach huts are being opened and windbreaks unfurled as families get ready for the day ahead. People are settling down on folding chairs in front of their huts and the odd barbecue is underway despite the flouting of regulations restricting them to the evening. I smell the sizzling sausages and burgers as bicycles speed past me, ignoring the dedicated track on Kingsway. I dodge the roller blades and kids' scooters and I find myself smiling despite everything. It's a good place to be and I'll miss it when I leave. That admission takes me by surprise.

As I enter the police station, I'm struck by how much the reception area reminds me of a hospital emergency department. Fractious conversations, anxious faces, complaints about the long waiting time and a constant assault on the front desk. The interview room I'm shown into is now all too familiar to me, as is DI Tony White and the pony-tailed DC from my first interview following Jaq's death. They sit down opposite me and Tony opens the proceedings with the usual formalities.

'Okay. So, let's go over how you came to be in that van with those girls.'

I hand him the envelope with Chiara's account.

'I think you should read this before I answer.'

He takes the sheets of paper out of the envelope and goes through them.

'Why didn't you bring this in for us to action?'

'And would you have, without further evidence?'

Tony smiles, confirming what I thought. I give him a brief and factual account of my abduction, leaving out any mention of Mike's involvement.

'Didn't it occur to you that you were taking a big risk?'

'But it got results, didn't it?'

He raises his eyebrows.

'Let's talk about the message you sent to Chief Inspector Black.'

'I couldn't risk a phone call to the emergency services. It would have been overheard. It seemed the best thing to do in the circumstances.'

'You were lucky they didn't take your phone off you. Rather an oversight, don't you think?'

'They were in a hurry to be off. It was a mistake on their part.'

'Good call to have included the registration number of the van.'

He smiles and picks up Chiara's account.

'So, how did you get hold of this?'

'It was hidden in the house of a friend who used to work in Jaq's book shop.'

I go over the details of what led to the discovery and he asks for Charlie's particulars. I've never known Charlie's surname but I give him her Hove address, explaining that she's gone abroad for the foreseeable future and I've no idea where. He speed-reads the A4 sheets and jots down a few notes.

'So, Chiara writes that she was trafficked by boat into the UK along with other girls and ended up at the Excelseus Language School.'

'The school is in Shoreham Port,' I add.

He pauses. 'We'll check out the security set-up there.'

He returns to his notes and continues his summary.

'Chiara then describes how she was forced into prostitution at the school. It sounds like it was a sort of brothel using girls trafficked through the port.'

It's uncomfortable hearing him summarise Chiara's poignant account with such dispassion, but he's just doing his job.

'No doubt we'll get confirmation of what's been going on at the school when we get more out of the girls.'

He continues scanning the pages and then frowns.

'Do you know who this Jacqui is that Chiara refers to?'

'Jacqueline Grey. The girl ....

'....whose body you found. So she was connected in some way with the Excelseus School.'

He shows me the paragraph where Chiara talks of seeing Jaq there. I explain that Jaq supplied the school with books which would have helped with their cover as a bona fide teaching institution. I say nothing about Jaq's drug dealing.

'What I don't understand is how the men from the school suspected that Ms Grey might be protecting Chiara after she ran away.'

I explain that Chiara had been forced to hand over a photo of Jaq that she always carried with her, adding that Jaq's bookshop would be an obvious place to look when Chiara ran off.

'It was a risky thing for Jaq to hide Chiara. It put her in danger as much as Chiara,' I add.

'Are you implying that the school could be involved in murdering both Chiara and Ms Grey?'

'I certainly wouldn't rule it out.'

'So, you don't believe that Ms Grey took her own life?'

'No and I think if you look into it again, you'll find that most unlikely.'

He makes a note of what I've said.

'The final autopsy report on Ms Grey is due Monday morning. I'll take another look her case notes in the light of what we now know about the Excelseus School and see what needs to be done.'

I'm relieved Mike's in no position to argue against that decision. For the first time, I see a chink of hope. I just hope Chris comes up with something positive from Forensics. A few more routine questions follow about the abduction of the girls and when I have nothing further to add, he formally concludes the recording and pushes back his chair.

'Send Mike my best when you see him.' He winks at me.

I wonder what his colleague makes of this familiarity or indeed of the whole interview, during which she's not said a word. She goes out, leaving us to exchange a professional handshake before being accompanied back to reception.

I'm curious to see Mike's reaction when I tell him Jaq's case is to be reassessed. Meantime I want to find out what Andrew knows about last night's events and whether he got caught up in them. I phone the surgery to see if he's at work and I'm not surprised to hear he's called in sick. I wonder why I didn't mention him during my interview. Was it a misplaced desire to confront him myself or an oversight? In either case, it's an omission I now regret.

Undecided about what to do about Andrew, I pay Mike a second visit. He's now on the Emergency ward in another side room. His face has a bit more colour and he's sitting up in bed. I pass on DI White's good wishes and hand Mike a bunch of grapes.

'I thought only old ladies got these.' He helps himself to a handful, stuffing them in his mouth before putting them on the bedside cabinet.

'You don't seem to mind.'

'Anything but hospital food, it's crap.' He doesn't bother to lower his voice. The bad language is unusual for him when off-duty. 'Can't wait to get out of here. I'm to be reviewed by the consultant on Monday. The sooner the better.'

I sit down next to the bed. Mike is anxious to know how my interview went.

'Don't worry, I kept your name out of it.'

I run through what I said and his face relaxes into a smile of relief.

'DI White interviewed me. He's agreed to reassess Jaq's case in the light of Chiara's account. The final autopsy report is due in on Monday too.'

Mike doesn't look bothered. He shrugs then leans over and moans as he grabs a handful of grapes. He clutches his ribs and then sits back with a grimace of pain on his face.

'He'll not find much to get his teeth into there.'

I say nothing while I think about whether to mention Chris's change of heart. Mike misconstrues my silence.

'Look, I know you're still upset about what happened to your friend. I'm sorry she died like that too. I liked her but the evidence is what it is.'

'What did you say?'

'The evidence is .....'

'Not that bit.'

I get up and push my face up close to his. 'You knew her, didn't you?'

Mike turns and presses the buzzer for help.

'I need the bottle. I've got to pee.'

'Oh no you don't.' I reach over and cancel the call

'You mean to say you knew Jaq and you never told me?'

Mike is trying to retrieve the buzzer which I've dropped on the floor.

'Just answer me, Mike.'

He gives up his attempt to get hold of the buzzer and faces me. 'Yes, I knew her.'

I take a long deep breath.

'How come?'

He hesitates and then sees that, trapped in a hospital bed, he's got no choice but to go on.

'I used to get my drugs from her.'

'You saw her regularly, then?' I hiss.

'On and off.'

'And you never told me.'

I think back, trying to recall all those conversations about Jaq, all those times when Mike knew things about her that he hadn't mentioned.

'Why didn't you tell me you knew her?'

He looks straight at me. 'It was hardly the moment when I bumped into you in the station after her death.'

'And later?'

'Would it really have helped? You were very upset by the fact that she had a drug habit, let alone being a dealer.'

'If I thought you were just trying to spare my feelings, I might not be so upset but that's not it, is it?'

He shifts about in the bed until the pain makes him stop.

'Does it help if I tell you Jaq wasn't happy with the situation she'd got into? She kept saying that she wanted out of the drugs scene.'

He lowers his eyes.

'The truth is, Kate I was scared to tell you Jaq was supplying my drugs from the Excelseus school. You were finding out all sorts of things about the school. I felt threatened. Think about it?'

'But I'd got no idea at that stage that you had a drug habit or were involved with the Excelseus Language School.'

'I had to protect myself.'

'And did protecting yourself include starting our affair? Must've been a good way to keep an eye on what I was doing.'

'You know I find you very attractive, Kate. I'd have found it hard to resist you anyway.'

I stare at him in disbelief at his cheek.

'Anyway, you can't deny you've not been straight with me yourself,' he continues, 'pretending to get back together with me to sneak a look at my phone.'

'I'm not going to deny that, but I don't have on my conscience the fact that I blocked an investigation into the Excelseus school which would not only have uncovered its drug smuggling and distribution network but also put an end to the trafficking and exploitation of girls.'

'You don't have to go through that again.'

'What's worse is that two young people might not have died and Jaq might still be alive, too.'

Mike looks crushed. He slides down the bed and turns away from me. I leave him with one final thought.

'I'll take responsibility for my actions but you'll have to face up to yours.'

I storm off to the seafront, all thoughts of Andrew forgotten. I walk along the esplanade, an unfamiliar stretch for me that borders the Kemp Town area to the east of the main pier. Its bohemian ambience does nothing to lift my mood and by the time I reach the grandeur of the seafront buildings nothing registers with me except my anger. I cross the road to the beach which is crowded, unsurprising on a hot Sunday afternoon. The pier is bursting with people and the funfair at its tip is pumping out music loud enough to be heard above the traffic noise. I head towards Hove where I pass families with happy smiling faces, couples laughing, groups of young people joshing and teasing each other. Behind these facades of happiness perhaps they're nursing thoughts as dark as mine. Who knows? I wonder how I look to them. Perhaps I look happy too. Perhaps there's no trace in my expression of my disillusion with Mike or my dejection at being no further forward in getting to the truth about Jaq's death.

Chapter Thirty-Three

Saturday 30 May....

I wake late the next morning with a headache so severe that I imagine I have a subarachnoid brain haemorrhage. Then I remember the vast quantity of alcohol I consumed last evening and stagger into the en-suite to get some paracetamol. Mike's revelations are crashing around my head which is still thumping when I finish a breakfast of scrambled eggs. I take a mug of coffee into the sitting room and collapse onto the sofa. I plonk the mug down on the coffee table, pushing to one side an empty bottle of wine and glass still half full of brandy. The local paper that I bought yesterday on my way back from the hospital falls onto the floor. I haven't read it yet so I pick it up and look at the front page. There's a report about a raid on the Excelseus School. Reference is made to the school as a cover for illegal activities, without going into detail. The article confirms that people have been taken into custody and are helping the police with their enquiries. There's no mention of Andrew and the usual platitudes tell me nothing specific. It says that a further police statement will be issued in due course. I finish my coffee which gives me enough energy to set about clearing up last night's mess, even if drum rolls continue to reverberate in my head. They make it impossible to think clearly Andrew's involvement with the Excelseus School or my duty as a doctor to report

Andrew to the General Medical Council for unprofessional behaviour with Jaq.

I head towards the seafront for some much-needed fresh air. The sun appears in fits and starts as wisps of cloud scud across it. The gentle breeze that propels them is warm. Already my headache is easing as I pick my way across the pebbly beach. People are staked out for a day and disconnected phrases and half-finished comments drift towards me: inconsequential opinions on diets, the weather, fashion, music, restaurants, holidays, cars. I pick my way down to the shoreline. The tide is far out and I can walk along the beach without the usual hindrance of the groynes that dip down into the water at high tide. I take off my sandals and sink my toes into the damp sand leaving imprints that disappear as soon as I lift my foot.

I walked on this beach with Jaq when we were students, so long ago now. We were invincible then, nothing was going to stop us making a success of our lives. Failure was not a part of our world. I wonder if she cut herself off from me because she saw herself falling short of our ideal. It must have cost her a lot to reach out to me these last few weeks. Now I'm the one to feel a failure. That will linger until I know the truth about her death. I'm counting on DI White keeping his word about taking a fresh look at Jaq's investigation and on Chris confirming homicide in her autopsy report.

I return to the house frustrated that there's nothing more I can do. My mood is not improved by finding that my car has a flat tyre. On a Saturday, the chances of finding a mechanic who'll answer a call out are slim. I get out the car jack and spend the next hour in sweated labour replacing the damaged tyre with the space-saving one in the boot.

After a quick shower, I take off to get a new tyre fitted. The short drive gives me a good feeling. My car is a solid constant that is always under my control. Unlike my efforts to find out what happened to Jaq which has been like trying to catch hold of a cloud. I leave the mechanics to sort out the tyre and avoid the boredom of a wait by walking to the surgery to pick up any personal mail from London. I'd forgotten to check it when I went in to work on Thursday.

There are a few envelopes on my desk and I sort through them expecting only the usual business correspondence. But I'm wrong. One envelope carries a series of redirection stamps testifying to a circuitous journey thanks to the vagaries of the postal service. My heart misses several beats as I recognise the handwriting. I pick up the envelope and look at the original postmark dated a couple of days after my meeting with Jaq in London, and just three days before I left London for Hove. I hold the envelope as if it's a precious jewel and open it with care. I have to use two hands to hold the letter inside as I'm trembling so much.

Hove, 28 April 2009

Hi Kate,

Hope you find everything ok in the flat when you arrive. Bed is made up ready. Looking forward to catching up when I get back. Meantime, if you could pop into my bookshop as soon as you can, you'll meet a girl called Chiara who's got something for you to read. It'll give you some idea of what's been happening here. I didn't say anything when we met in London as it's all rather complicated. Just keep an eye out for her, she's in real trouble. I've got a lot to tell you when I see you. I can't trust email or messaging at the moment. I've got myself mixed up in something bad. I'll need your help in sorting it all out. You're such a friend I know I can count on you. All the best with the new job. Not that you need it, star that you are. I'm so glad you'll be there when I get back.

See you soon,

Love Jaq xx

I read the note several times. It's as if she's whispering in my ear. I can just imagine her scribbling away, with her eyes dancing along the page. Reading the last words she ever wrote to me makes her feel alive again. I look up and imagine her laughing at me and then the thought that I'll never see her again crashes over me like a tsunami. I start sobbing, the tears I've been holding back until now. I wonder what would have happened if Jaq's letter hadn't been delayed. What if I'd received it before arriving in Hove as she'd intended, if I'd been able to read what Chiara had written, if ....

I'm in a daze on the way back and I arrive just as Chris turns up in a taxi. She pays the driver and strides over to me as I fumble with my front door key.

'I thought you weren't due back till tomorrow,' I say.

'The conference was a bore so I left early. How's Mike? I didn't get a chance to see him before I left.' She looks at me with a concerned expression.

'What's the matter, Kate? You're shaking all over.'

She ushers me into the house and makes us both a cup of black chai tea. We sit opposite each other at the kitchen table. Chris goes to light a cigarette, then puts it back in the packet and hands it to me.

'Get rid of these, will you.' She throws me a half empty cigarette packet and then shows me her nicotine patch.

'I must say you look better now,' she continues. 'You seemed pretty shaken up before.'

'I've just received a letter Jaq sent to me. She wrote it a few days before she died. It's taken this long to arrive. It was quite a shock to read it. I wish it had arrived earlier. I would have been able to confront Mike.'

'What's the news about him?'

I get Chris up to speed on Mike's progress and then tell her how DI White is going to take another look at Jaq's case in the light of Chiara's report.

'He told me your final autopsy report is due tomorrow. Have you heard back from Forensics about the fingerprints?'

'I got the results just before I left for London on Friday. I should've contacted you. I'd already decided not to give in to Mike and just take the consequences. One mistake is quite enough and the first I made wasn't intentional. I was just swamped with work and cut corners so that a murderer got off.'

'So, what did Forensics have to say?'

Chris puts down her cup.

'It seems there was a previous analysis that found two fingerprints detailed enough to get a result. One was Jacqueline Grey's. They didn't get a match for the other when they ran it through the police data base. Then Mike pressed them to do a second analysis three days later. This time they found that both fingerprints matched your friend's.'

'That's odd ... unless.....'

I compute the information in a nanosecond and I can see from Chris's expression that she's come to the same conclusion.

'Are you thinking what I'm thinking?' she says.

'Mike tampered with the evidence.'

I'm shocked and furious at the implications.

'I should've checked the results before now,' Chris adds.

'Well, if he has tampered with evidence, you'll have nothing to worry about from him. He's already had a letter saying he's under review for misconduct. When his involvement with the Excelseus School comes out, he'll be facing a charge of corruption.'

My brain is whirring as I process at warp speed the implications of what Mike has done. My voice is hoarse and angry when I next speak.

'He must be protecting someone and I'm sure as hell going to find out who.'

I rush out of the house and drive straight to the hospital. I drive round and round the car park, cursing out loud until I find a space. On entering the hospital, the corridors are thronged with visitors making for the wards. Most head straight for the lifts, sure of their destination. Some look disorientated or lost and stare at the direction signs with expressions of distress or impatience. I hurry off along familiar corridors to confront Mike.

He's sitting in a chair next to the bed, reading the sports' pages of a Sunday newspaper. I grab a plastic chair from a pile outside the door and set the chair down in front of him. He looks up from the paper.

'I wasn't expecting you to come after yesterday but now you're here, I've got some news you might like to hear.'

'Which is?'

I'm struggling to contain the fury of my emotions but hold them in check for a little longer in order to hear what Mike has to say.

'They've charged those two guys from the Excelseus School with Chiara's murder.'

Feelings of relief, anger and immense sadness produce an odd mix of emotions which I have no intention of sharing with Mike.

Mike looks nonplussed when I don't react.

'I thought you'd be pleased. The rapid DNA testing on the guy with the beard came up trumps on a sample of his dandruff. You must have noticed it?'

He pauses for my comment which is not forthcoming.

'Anyway,' he continues, 'they found enough on Chiara's body to get a reasonable match. The other guy was quick to see what was what and pointed the finger at his sidekick, not only for Chiara's murder but also the other girl we found in the layby on the A23. The two of them all but came to blows after that. We'll sort out later if they both played an active part in the killing.'

'And Jaq. What about her?'

The bitterness in my voice is unmistakeable but Mike is either incapable of hearing it or happy to ignore it.

'They denied having anything to do with killing her. The more the pressure, the more they were adamant they had nothing to do with her death. I told you he'd not get very far with proving she was murdered.'

'That's not surprising is it? You've been tampering with the evidence to make Jaq's death look like a suicide.'

Mike's usual ruddy complexion changes in an instant to the colour of his bed sheets. He grabs the plastic cup by his bed and fills it with water which he swigs down in one gulp. As his colour comes back to his cheeks, he challenges me.

'Don't be ridiculous.'

'I'm not being ridiculous. This is far too serious. Chris has checked with forensics. There were two different fingerprints when they first looked. It was only after you asked them to repeat the analysis that they found both to be Jaq's fingerprints. What do have to say to that?'

He doesn't reply but just stares ahead at the wall opposite.

'Come on, Mike. Tell me what the hell you've been up to. Did the Excelseus School ask you to cover up Jaq's murder and fake it as suicide?'

'Keep your voice down; the door's open.'

'I'm practically whispering. It's your conscience that's screaming out loud.'

He sits forward and puts his face in his hands. When he looks up again, I can see his eyes are bloodshot.

'Okay, you're right, I falsified the evidence. It wasn't easy either. I had to go to the mortuary and make sure I was left on my own with her body. After that, it didn't take long to wipe the knife clean and get a fresh set of her prints on the knife.'

'Oh, Mike. What have you done?'

'I know, it looks awful but they were threatening to kidnap my kids and you know how that would have ended.'

Instead, Mike is facing the prospect of his career and his life crumbling about him. I'm trying hard not to pass judgement, trying hard to understand what it must be like to see your family's lives in jeopardy. But it could all have been avoided if he'd stayed away from cocaine.

'So, who were you protecting?'

'I don't know.'

'Oh, come on, that won't do.'

'It's true. For once I'm telling you the truth. I've no idea. It must be someone worth protecting. Some big shot in the organisation. I'm only a minnow in their pool.'

I stare him in the face and see a defeated man who's been trying to cling on to his identity as a cop and protect his kids from his own stupidity. I shouldn't feel sorry for him, but for a moment, I do.

'So why not do one decent thing and help get Jaq's killer behind bars. Can you not think of anyone who might know who it could be?'

'Madame would know, for sure.'

'Madame?'

'That's what she liked to be called, the woman in the Excelseus reception but she'll be long gone by now. She was close to the big shots.'

'How about Andrew, then?'

'Who's he?'

'You never bumped into a tall, slim, blond guy, expensive clothes, Rolex watch, superior manner?'

'Nope.'

I tell Mike about Andrew being a GP colleague and about my experiences with him at the Excelseus School.

'You never mentioned this before.'

'Too much else going on, Mike.'

Mike is fiddling with his call button.

'What's the matter? Do you need a nurse?'

'No, it's just that there's something I'd forgotten about. I told you those guys who've been charged with Chiara's murder refused point blank to admit killing Jaq, however hard they were pushed. Well, they just kept on saying we should talk to the doctor.'

I stare at Mike. For a brief instance, it's as if time is frozen. From his expression I can see that we both have the same thought.

'You mean they were trying to say that .....' I can't finish the sentence.

I can hardly take in the idea. Andrew is annoying, supercilious, arrogant and corrupt, but a murderer? It seems incredible. My plan to get him hauled before the General Medical Council for unprofessional conduct with Jaq recedes far into the background. He's a murderer but the unsubstantiated hearsay of two criminals is not going to be enough to prove it.

'If I could get hold of something that proves he's connected to the Excelseus School, then he could be brought in for questioning.'

I'm desperately thinking about what that can be, when it hits me. I snatch up my handbag from the floor and ratchet around in it until I find the Lanyard I took from Andrew to escape from the school. The key card has his name and photo on it. I show it to Mike.

'It's not enough to prove he killed Jaq.'

'But it's a start. It proves he's connected to the school. That must enough for him to be brought in for questioning.'

'And if he can't be traced?'

I jump up and push my chair out of the way.

'Where are you going?'

'To the GP surgery.'

Chapter Thirty-Four

....Saturday 30 May

I avoid Kingsway and drive via the Seven Dials road junction and Cromwell Road towards Hove and the GP surgery. The traffic is much less than on the seafront and there are no speed cameras. I screech into the practice car park, currently empty, unlike during GP opening hours. The LED lights in the reception area make me blink as I switch them on. I deactivate the alarm system and make sure to secure the front door behind me. My footsteps are the only sound in the eerie silence as I make my way along the corridor to Andrew's room, thankful that the consulting rooms all have the same keycode.

The venetian blinds are closed but some light seeps through the slats onto the main road. It's not something that concerns me. There'll be no one around to notice this late on a Saturday. A quick glance round the room shows the usual GP paraphernalia, an examination couch, a plastic model of the spine, wall charts about asthma, smoking, heart disease and a copy of the British Medical Journal on top of his desk. Nothing of use to me in my search for evidence. But then what did I expect? No cop would ever have been so impulsive. I flush at the thought that I would once have been reprimanded for such behaviour. I should not have been so hasty but I'm here now so I might as well carry on.

I sit down at Andrew's desk and try the drawers in turn. The top one contains a few pens and pencils, some business cards from various drug reps and a prescription pad, for the odd times the computer system goes down. The middle drawer is a repository for various printouts of research papers and medical guidelines. The bottom drawer is locked. I remember Andrew's comment about locking away anything of value. I rattle the drawer handle to see if it will open nevertheless. To no effect. I've got nothing on me that could force the lock and there's nothing obvious to hand.

I turn my attention to the cupboard under the sink across the other side of the room near the examination couch. I root around among boxes of latex gloves, anti-bacterial wipes, various specimen pots and cleaning materials but find nothing that would help me force a lock and nothing incriminating.

All that remains is a computer search. It's unlikely I'll find any evidence that could convict Andrew but I should be able to access his personal details. I use my password to log on. A few clicks of the mouse and I'm into the system. I open the pages outlining appointments, admin details, lists of protocols and then take a quick look at his recent research log. There's nothing untoward. I have no problem opening the page with his personal details. It includes his qualifications, training posts, employment history and General Medical Council registration number. There are no indications of any past complaints or suspensions. His private address is there and forgetting my previous thought about hasty decisions, I scribble it down ready to rush off and confront him. I do at least have the foresight to call Mike on my mobile to give him the address. He answers straight away.

'Kate. Where are you?' The anxiety in his voice surprises me.

'At the surgery. I'm in Andrew's room. I didn't find anything of use but one of his desk drawers is locked and I can't find a way of forcing it. At least I've got Andrew's address. Can you jot it down, I.........'

I break off as I hear footsteps in the corridor. I hide my phone under the journal on the desk just as a figure appears in the doorway. Andrew marches into the room. He's carrying a briefcase.

'Well, well, what a surprise. Our little medical detective. And just what are you doing in my room?'

He comes over and puts down the briefcase. He leans across my right shoulder peering down at the computer screen. He brushes against my cheek as he does so and I pull away from him in disgust. He glances down at the notepad and then tears off the top sheet with his address on it and stuffs it in his pocket.

'That wouldn't do you much good, anyway. I'm not going back there. You can log off now.'

I stand up. 'You do it. I'm leaving.'

I'm thinking I might get as far as the phone in reception to call the police.

'I don't think so.'

'How are you going to stop me? Use the ketamine trick again?'

'No need.'

He produces a retractable knife and flicks it open.

'And I'll use it if you don't sit down.'

I do what he wants. He takes out a key and unlocks the desk drawer and takes out a vacuum pack of what I assume to be a substantial amount of cocaine. It would have a huge street value.

'I don't have to ask what that is, do I?'

'None of your business. Let's just say it's my insurance policy.'

He picks up the briefcase and puts the pack inside.

'Insurance against what? A charge of people trafficking or murder. I know you killed Jaq.'

'You've no proof of that.'

'Why, Andrew? Just tell me why. I thought you and Jaq were lovers.'

'It was her fault, getting mixed up with that stupid girl, Chiara.'

'How dare you talk about her like that. She was smuggled into the country and tricked into prostitution at the Excelseus School.'

'So, you know about that. Well, if you prefer to think it was Jaq who was stupid, fair enough.'

I raise my hand to hit him but he drops the briefcase and grabs my arm.

'We'll have none of that.'

He holds the knife up close to me and pushes me back down onto the chair.

'So, what did you do to Jaq?'

'Do you really want to know?'

'Yes, I do.'

He tells me. I never let my eyes shift away from his but I give nothing away of my emotional turmoil as I listen, impassive, to what he has to say.

Jaq rang him one day to say she was pulling out of their arrangement. He was furious.

'I went to her flat to put her right. When I asked why she wouldn't carry on dealing, she said she was disgusted with me. She'd found out from Chiara what was going on at the school. I'll skip the details as you seem to know all about them.'

Andrew's face creases with anger as he recounts the huge argument that followed. They were in the kitchen where Jaq had been chopping up some vegetables to put in the freezer. She told him to get out and picked up a large kitchen knife and waived it at him as a threat, pushing him through the kitchen door and onto the landing at the top of the stairs.

'She said she was going to the police with what she knew. I just saw red. She was going to put our whole network at risk. Millions of pounds and my life on the scrapheap. She still had the knife in her hand but she tripped and it fell on the floor. I got to it before she did and that was it.'

I glance at the desk, wondering if Mike is still listening in to the call.

'This network, would it be called Central Care Consolidates?'

'How do you know that?'

I ignore the question.

'Just where do you fit into the network?'

'I helped set up the trafficking business. It was also my job to monitor the girls when they arrived, make sure they had no medical issues that would cause problems.'

'No wonder you gave me the third degree when Chiara turned up at the Young People's Clinic and there was no way of tracing her.'

I go to hit him again despite the threat of the knife but it's a futile attempt as he grabs my arm again. In the process he dislodges the journal on his desk and sees my phone with the line still open.

'What the...?'

He cancels the call and puts the phone in his pocket. He slaps me hard across the cheek. A second blow makes my head spin. Then he grabs hold of me and hustles me out of the door, his briefcase under his arm and the knife in his free hand. He manhandles me into the car park and stops dead. Two uniformed police officers are getting out of a patrol car. He drops the knife as they rush to block his path.

'Good evening, Sir.'

'What the hell...'

'We've been notified by someone at the hospital of a dangerous situation at this GP surgery. Can I ask what you're doing here, Sir?'

'My colleague and I have been discussing medical matters.'

'And you are?'

'Dr Andrew Gull and you've no right to stop a citizen going about their business.'

One of the officers picks up the knife.

'And just what business would that be?'

I suggest they look in his briefcase.

'If you wouldn't mind, Sir.' One of the officers holds out his hand.

Andrew stands very still and puts a hand in his pocket. The unlocking lights of his car flash as he presses the digital release. He thrusts the briefcase into the chest of the officer and bolts towards his car. The second officer rushes after him and grabs him just before he reaches the driving seat. In one dextrous move, he handcuffs him and manoeuvres him over to the patrol car where the other officer is opening the brief case. He holds up the pack of cocaine.

'Anything you wish to say?'

Andrew glares back at him. 'Not without a solicitor.'

He pushes Andrew into the back seat of the patrol car.

Chris is still up when I return from Brighton police station just before midnight. I find her in the sitting room with a half empty bottle of wine, engrossed in a pile of papers on the coffee table. She waves to me to join her.

'How did you get on with Mike?'

'He's really got himself into a mess, but that's not the half of it.'

Chapter Thirty-Five

Sunday 31 May

The wind is whipping up the waves and a grey overcast sky and chill sea breeze accompany my drive along the seafront the next morning on my way to talk to Clare about Andrew. Two uniformed officers are just leaving the GP surgery as I arrive. I explain to Clare how I came to be involved with the case against Andrew. She's shocked to think that someone with the propensity for violence and the exploitation of vulnerable girls has been at work in the GP practice. She puts her feelings to one side to focus on practical matters.

'I'll need another locum asap and then there'll be the matter of appointing a full-time GP. Would you consider it? You've fitted in well and our patients seem extremely pleased with you.'

With Jaq gone, I can think of no good reason to defer a return to London after my locum contract ends but I tell her I'll think about it.

As we go our separate ways, I think about calling Jessica. I defer it once again. I want to know how Mike's situation is evolving before contacting her. I'm bracing myself for another hospital visit, when I discover there's no point. Mike is waiting in his car outside Chris's house.

He opens the car window. 'Chris said you wouldn't be long so I thought I'd wait for you here.'

'You've been discharged, then.'

'Not exactly. I couldn't wait for the consultant's decision tomorrow I signed myself out first thing. I wanted to get to the station to see what the score is before Monday morning.'

'Are you okay?'

'Feeling knackered right now.'

I open the passenger door of his car and get in. 'I fancy an ice cream.'

He drives to the King Alfred Centre car park and winces as he manoeuvres himself out of the car.

'I'd no idea broken ribs were so bloody painful.'

'Did they give you anything?'

'Some sticky stuff to put on. Any good?'

'They'll be anaesthetic patches. Very good short term. I bet you were given some anti-inflammatories too.'

'Sounds like the tablets I got.'

We walk the short distance to the ice cream kiosk on the seafront with Mike clutching his side. I order a large chocolate cone and Mike choses a tiramisù flavour. We find a bench on the esplanade and sit, like two holiday-makers with nothing better to do, eating our ice creams and taking in the view. The sea breeze is a little warmer now as we stare out at a grey sea merging on the horizon with an even greyer sky.

'Have you heard anything about Andrew?' I ask.

'They're holding him on possession of cocaine and a lethal weapon for now, though they're saying his legal team looks sharp enough to find some loophole.'

He's bound to have a top defence barrister especially if Central Care Consolidates have mafia connections. They can't afford a conviction, though I can see them dealing with Andrew in their own way later. Not something I'll feel sorry about but the organisation will still be free to carry on its evil trade and justice won't have been done.

'What about the murder charge? They've got that first fingerprint analysis. He won't be able to wriggle out of that.'

'No news yet.'

'And what about you. Mike?'

He astonishes me by suggesting he could plead poor judgement because of his cocaine habit.

'I'd offer to commit to a rehab programme, of course.'

'Well you need rehab for sure but tampering with evidence and accepting bribes, do you really think poor judgement will get you off the hook?'

'I could say I was acting undercover on my own initiative to get info on the illegal drug trade at the school.'

'What about that big bribe from the Excelseus School?'

'You're the only one outside the school who knows about that. That's one of the reasons I wanted to see you. Would you report me for that if I keep quiet about it?'

'I've already told you what I think about your calling off the first investigation into the school, but I haven't thought about reporting you. That's not going to bring back Chiara or Jaq. And do you really think you'll get away with tampering with evidence?'

'I could just deny that. It would be difficult to prove unless I confess.'

I'm taken aback by Mike's lack of scruples.

'You don't honestly believe what you're suggesting will work?'

'It might, if I resign.'

There's a bitter edge to his voice. It's something I never thought I'd hear Mike say. His detective work is fundamental to his identity; it's who he is.

'It's my only hope of avoiding repercussions, now. If I'm no longer in the police force, I can't be suspended and I'll avoid any disciplinary action.'

I'm not too sure about that or about his chances of avoiding prosecution but I say nothing. From his expression, Mike also has his doubts. Whatever happens, he loses the career that's become his life.

'I also thought about what it would do to Carole and the kids if I didn't resign. A protracted period of suspension with an accusation of corruption hanging over me! Even if it all turned out in my favour and I just got shunted into some backwater post, some of the dirt would stick. It would be terrible for them either way.'

'Aren't you getting a divorce?'

He lands another surprise by telling me that his wife has suggested giving his marriage a second chance.

'I could become a private Dick.'

If it's meant as a joke, he isn't laughing.

'You're not serious?'

'Who knows? It's not Hollywood Bogart stuff these days. It's all computers and IT now.'

I just can't see it: Mike confined to a desk, immersed in data. Neither of us says a word as he drives me back, each immersed in our different thoughts. We both get out of the car.

'I guess this is goodbye, then.' He opens his arms for an embrace.

'Best not, eh?'

He drops his arms. I plant a quick kiss on his cheek.

'Let me know what happens with Andrew, and Mike, ... get yourself sorted.'

I go into the house without turning back. Chris is in the sitting room engrossed in a pile of papers on the coffee table. She acknowledges my arrival with a wave of the hand, and offers to put the kettle on. We take our cups into the sitting and settle back on the sofa, sipping tea like genteel ladies from times gone by. Chris is keen to get news about Mike.

'He took his own discharge from hospital this morning and went straight to Brighton Police Station. He's decided to resign.'

'Well, well, that'll be two of us then.'

I've just taken a mouthful of tea and have difficulty in not spitting it across the room. Instead I make some sort of vague choking noise and put down the cup.

'You're kidding?'

'Not at all. I'm not handing in my notice straight away. I'll wait until I've got another job lined up. I've just been applying for one. I want to get an academic position. I've been doing field work for long enough. It's time to move on.'

'Why now? I thought you loved forensic work. I'd no idea you were hatching an alternative plan.'

'I only decided about a week ago though I've been thinking about it for a while. Dealing with Chiara's case gave me the push I needed. Anyway, there's this post in London. I should stand a good chance.'

I can't hide my surprise.

'So, just as I get an offer to stay on in Hove, you'll be moving to London.'

I tell her about Clare's offer but with Jaq gone, I'm not sure I've any reason to stay on in Hove.

'Are you going to continue as a GP? No change of course?'

I wonder what Steve would say if I decided to go back to police work. He'd be incapable of understanding any such move. He had enough of a problem with the change in direction of my medical career. Then I imagine Mike's reaction and I laugh.

'If I went back to detective work, I'd have to get over seeing everyone as a potential criminal.'

'I wonder,' Chris says, with that annoying enigmatic expression she adopts when she's sure she knows better than me, just like her time as my anatomy demonstrator. She changes the subject.

'Jessica's coming to dinner, by the way. She gave me quite a blasting about you not contacting her.'

She turns up at seven thirty and Chris presses a large gin and tonic into her hand. I apologise for not contacting her.

'Once I tell you what's been going on, you'll understand.'

'Shall we have a crime-free dinner first?' Chris suggests. 'We can watch the local evening news afterwards to see if there's been any developments and then take it from there.'

Chris soon has us savouring a superior Bourgogne wine and admiring her fine dining skills. By the time we've finished off a cheese soufflé, sole meuniere and a delicious tarte tatin, it's time for the late-night regional news. The Excelseus School police raid proves to be the opening item. A reporter is standing outside the gate to the school.

Following yesterday's raid on the so-called Excelseus Language School in Basin Road, Hove, we can now confirm that the principal of the establishment is among those taken into custody for questioning in connection with the smuggling of drugs into Shoreham Port.

A photo of the woman known as Madame flashes onto the screen and I silently cheer.

Consignments of cocaine have been confirmed as illegally entering Shoreham Port where the school is thought to form part of a distribution network. Two men working for the Excelseus School have also been charged with the recent murder of two young girls whose bodies were found on the Devil's Dyke and in a layby on the London bound A23 dual carriageway. One unconfirmed report suggests that these girls had been trafficked into the UK by the same network for the purposes of prostitution organised by the Excelseus School. A police statement will be issued tomorrow morning.

The reporter then goes on to discuss the emotional trauma of trafficking victims before moving on to victims of the current credit crunch and banker's misdemeanours.

Jessica turns to me.

'The drug smuggling comes as no surprise but trafficking girls as prostitutes Shoreham Port, that's incredible. How did you get to know about that?'

'It's quite a story.'

I use Charlie's abduction as the starting point and give an edited version of swappping her incarceration for mine. I make no mention of Mike's involvement - a misplaced sense of loyalty or just prudence. I'm not sure. When it cmes to my escape I also keep Andrew's name out of it.

'There's a lot more but I'd rather you take a look at something.'

I tell her I'll be right back and fetch my photocopy of Chiara's account. After reading it, Jessica puts it down with a frown on her face.

'Terrible. I still get taken aback by the evil in some people despite my years of reporting some pretty gruesome stories.'

'It's strictly off-the-record for now. The police have the original as part of their evidence.'

'I'll find the right moment to make use of it. Don't worry.'

She's curious to know how I came across Chiara's account and it becomes the focus of our discussions for the rest of the evening.

As Jessica is leaving, I receive a text notification. It's from Mike. I read it on the way up to my room.

Fingerprint on knife matches Andrew's.

I send a reply to the text then shut my bedroom door on a welcome silence. I lie on the bed thinking about Jaq. Now that it's all over, I wish I could talk to her, ask her what she thinks about what's happened. Perhaps she would say the world is too evil to hope for change but that we have to try nevertheless, just as she did with her efforts to help Chiara. How we do it is a personal choice. There are the campaigners, the social workers, the police and even us medics, to name just a few who battle in different ways against the injustices of human existence. I wonder which I really belong to. Perhaps Jaq would have told me.

I go over and open the window. The curtains billow out as a warm breeze caresses my cheeks. I close my eyes and see myself with Jaq in our university days, sitting in her room crushed in among her fellow students, passing round a bottle of wine, while I listen to them deep in passionate discussions about the meaning of existence, the roles we adopt and whether they define who we are. It was a world of words far from my medical studies but it comes back to me now as I try to make sense of her death. I lie back on the bed while faint traffic sounds drift through the open window like soothing white noise. As the seconds merge into minutes and then hours, I see that there is no making sense of her death. All that remains is the memory of a friendship and a future that must be carved out from what's left.

Epilogue

My name is Chiara Lautari. I have 16 years. This is my story.

I come from a camp near to Milan. It is in Italy. My people are Romany. They make houses for the camp out of many things, cardboard, wood bits, some bricks, stone bits, anything they can find. It is a dirty place. When there is rain there is mud everywhere. When it is cold it is hard to be warm. In the camp there are many of us. We do not have papers of identity. A proper job for us is impossible. We work at all things, fruit picking, building work, selling flowers. The jobs are never long. Often we go to beg. I went to school. I learn English there. I am the only one to do that. Other of our children do not stay at school. They say there is no point. My father said to ignore them. He said that school was my only chance. In Italy no one likes us. They say we do bad things like stealing and killing people. I say this is not true. My people do not steal or kill. The police are not believing us. They came for my father. He had not done wrong. They took him away and I have not seen him in a long time. He told me to stay in school and not give up.

An English lady came to our school once. She was telling of England and her bookshop in a place called Hove. We had a photo with her. She was very pretty and I liked her. Her name was Jacqi. I dream to go one day to her bookshop. I tell Jacqi about the camp then. She is sad.

One day Mamma was outside my school. She said our camp was a fire. Our house it was burned. We went and we watched the flames. No one came to stop the fire. There were no fire engines, no policemen, no ambulances. Soon there was no camp. That night a man came to us and said he had us a place to live. We went with him to a house and into the basement. It was a large room. Mattresses were on the floor. The man wanted me to do work like the other girls there. My mother said no. She said I was clever, speaking English. Next night, the man came back with other man. He spoke me in English. He said in England there was a good work. My mother said I had no papers. He said not to worry.

The man said the work was in the English language school. The man put us in a big lorry. It was cold and no comfort. We had no food. Only little water. We were five girls. We got out after long time and it was night. I hear the sea. They took us to large metal box on a ship and locked us in. We were five girls. We went across the sea to a port. The school was there. It is named the Excelseus Language School.

We each had a room with a proper bed. It was very comfortable. Next morning, we did cleaning early in the school. Then they locked us in our room. They brought us food. In the evening we had other work. I went to another room. The room had a big bed and a soft floor. A man was in the room. He told me to take all my clothes off and lie on the bed. He took all his clothes off also and then he did things that made me hurt. I was proud not to cry. After, there were other men. I hear some girls cry. We did our two jobs every day. In the morning the cleaning and at night with men. Sundays we go outside for little to get fresh air.

A Sunday morning, I see Jacqi. She is at the school. A man gives to her a parcel. Another day a van is there too to take us to London. I see the back door is not closed good. I jump out at the end of road when van go slow. I run and run and the van went. I hid. Then I go and am looking for Jacqi and her bookshop. I walk a lot and I find it. I tell Jacqi of the school. I stay in the bookshop down the stairs. Jacqi says to go to the police but I am scared. One day two men come to the shop. I hear them talk to Jacqi. They are very angry. They are from the Excelseus school. They look for me. They have my photo with Jacqi outside my school at Milan. Jacqi is clever and she send them away. She says me not to worry. Now she takes care of me. She says she will get them in prison. She goes to Italy soon. I worry without her. I hope the men not come again. I think if they are finding me they kill me then they kill Jacqi too.

26 April 2009

Acknowledgments

To Peter for his patience and his love

Afterword

What if Jaq's death is judged to be a strange accident but Kate has her doubts? What will Kate do? Find out in *Tomorrow Today* - coming soon.

Christine Mustchin is a prize-winning short story writer and author of the thriller *From Nemesis Island*. She wrote a doctoral thesis on Samuel Beckett's prose trilogy before studying Medicine and becoming a GP.

She lived for many years in London before relocating to Cumbria. Lately she has lived in Hove and is currently based in Aldwick, West Sussex. She likes to spend time with her husband at their converted barn on the shores of Lake Como in Italy.

Lightning Source UK Ltd.
Milton Keynes UK
UKHW012156060422
401190UK00001B/72